SEEING RED

A Pedagogy
of Parallax

SEEING RED

A Pedagogy of Parallax

An Epistolary Bildungsroman
on Artful Scholarly Inquiry

Pauline Sameshima

CAMBRIA
PRESS

YOUNGSTOWN, NEW YORK

Requests for permission should be directed to permissions@cambriapress. com, or mailed to Permissions, Cambria Press, PO Box 350, Youngstown, New York 14174-0350.

Library of Congress Cataloging-in-Publication Data

Sameshima, Pauline.
    Seeing red : a pedagogy of parallax an epistolary bildungsroman on artful scholarly inquiry / Pauline Sameshima.
        p. cm.
    Includes bibliographical references and index.
    ISBN 978-1-934043-52-3 (alk. paper: hardcover) ISBN 978-1-934043-64-6 (pbk.)
1. Critical pedagogy. 2. Self-knowledge, Theory of. 3. Epistolary fiction. I. Title.

    LC196.S26 2007
    370.11'5--dc22

2007005391

For Michael

TABLE OF CONTENTS

ILLUSTRATIONS

Original works © Pauline Sameshima

PROLOGUE

Seeing Red: A Pedagogy of Parallax is a scholarly work written in the form of an epistolary *bildungsroman*—a didactic novel of personal developmental journeying. It shares the possibilities of how artful research informs processes of scholarly inquiry and honours the reader's multi-perspective as integral to the research project's transformative potential. *Parallax* is the apparent change of location of an object against a background due to a change in observer position or perspective shift. The concept of parallax encourages researchers and teachers to acknowledge and value the power of their own and their readers' and students' shifting subjectivities and situatedness which directly influence the constructs of perception, interpretation, and learning. This work makes three claims:

- that the sharing of stories encourages reflexive inquiries in ethical self-consciousness, enlarges paradigms of the "normative," and develops pedagogical practices of liberation and acceptance of diversity;
- that form determines possibilities for content and function thus the use of an alternate format can significantly open new spaces for inquiry; and,
- that transformational learning may be significantly deepened

in pedagogical practice through the intentional development of *embodied aesthetic wholeness* and of eros in the dynamic space between teacher and learner. Embodied aesthetic wholeness attends to teaching and learning holistically through the body with consideration to: increasing receptivity and openness to learning; fostering skills of relationality; modeling wholeness-in-process in explicit reflexive texts; layering multiple strategies of inquiry, research experiences, and presentation; and acknowledging ecological and intuitive resonances.

FOREWORD
CONVERSATIONS

Dr. Carl Leggo
Professor of Language and Literacy Education
University of British Columbia

Poetry of Love & Love of Poetry

In *Seeing Red* Pauline Sameshima exemplifies what Paulo Freire calls "aesthetic curiosity" (p. 95) and "epistemological curiosity" (p. 97). She writes about love, romance, desire, passion, eros, and hope—the familiar dynamics that animate the tangled relationships lived every day by teachers and learners in and out of classrooms. Pauline holds fast to the exhilaration and the danger of love, as well as the integral necessity of acknowledging love in all our relationships. Her convictions resonate with bell hooks who claims that "to open our hearts more fully to love's power and grace we must dare to acknowledge how little we know of love in both theory and practice" (xxix). hooks is concerned that because we have been "taught to believe that the mind, not the heart, is the seat of learning, many of us believe that to speak of love with any emotional intensity means we will be perceived as weak and irrational" (xxvii). Like hooks, Pauline questions love with a scholar's vigorous rigor, and she lives love with a poet's steadfast commitment to the vitality and veracity of language, and she dreams love with an artist's inimitable imagination.

Seeing Red is a love story, a story of desire and intrigue and mystery, a story of teaching and learning, a story that sears the heart with a seer's prophetic vision. With unsettling insight, Pauline understands how research in the social sciences must begin with stories that help readers revisit and revision their understanding of the fabric of daily lives. In the novel *Straight Man* by Richard Russo, the narrator is William Henry Devereaux, Jr., chair of the English department at West Central Pennsylvania University. Devereaux observes: "Despite having endured endless faculty meetings, I can't remember the last time anyone changed his (or her!) mind as a result of reasoned discourse. Anyone who observed us would conclude the purpose of all academic discussion was to provide the grounds for becoming further entrenched in our original positions" (p. 201). Pauline is a wise scholar, and she engages in "reasoned discourse" with stiletto sharp precision, but her wisdom extends to an appreciation of the limits of "reasoned discourse," and so she acknowledges how other ways of knowing— artistic, poetic, narrative, autobiographical, artographic, creative, emotional, imaginative—are also integral to scholarly adventures of researching and living.

In my scholarly and creative journeys with Pauline, I have learned to live with more courage, more conviction, more constancy. I have been a language teacher all my adult life. And for most of my adult life I have also been a poet. I claim that I live in language, and that language lives in me. I am awash in language, espoused and exposed in language. While others are busy running the country, and selling real estate, and diagnosing illness, and constructing the latest popular culture fad, and making millions in wheeling and dealing, I teach and write poetry. I am a promoter, proponent, prophet, and pedagogue of language. But for all my daily and life-long devotion to language, I must still make a confession. I live in fear. All the time. I am afraid of upsetting others. I am afraid of offending others. I am afraid of insults and criticism and rejection. Above all, I am afraid of truth. I am a language educator, and still I am afraid of speaking and writing truth. I tell lies all the time. I am a language educator and I am afraid of language, afraid of the uncontrollable, untameable, wild energy of language. I need to attend to Betsy Warland's wisdom:

> i believe writing we value is writing which springs from necessity. the necessity to speak the unspoken, the taboo of our lives. if we do not, we BETRAY: 'trans-, over + dare, to give' ourselves over, turn ourselves in, become agents of our own absence. (1990 p. 30).

Pauline teaches me to be less frightened of the "boo" in "taboo," to "speak the unspoken," to know that research and education are always about seeking truth (especially in fiction) in order to avoid betraying ourselves. In *Seeing Red* Pauline teaches me about love, in love, how to love. So, my preface is a love note to her, offered with eager gratefulness.

References:

Freire, P. (1977). *Pedagogy of the heart.* (D. Macedo & A. Oliveira, Trans.). New York: Continuum.

hooks, b. (2000). *All about love: New visions.* New York: William Morrow.

Russo, R. (1997). *Straight man.* New York: Random House.

Warland, B. (1990). *Proper deafinitions: Collected theorograms.* Vancouver: Press Gang.

Dr. Anthony Clarke
Associate Professor of Curriculum Studies
University of British Columbia

Teacher Red

The importance of *Seeing Red* for teacher education is that it challenges teachers to think differently about their interactions with the world. Teachers' interactions are represented and mediated by the pedagogical stances they adopt. Such stances are ever-present and constantly changing, sometimes imperceptibly and at other times dramatically. *Seeing Red* takes the reader beyond boundaries typically acknowledged within education. It invites one to think differently, more expansively, about how one is complicit in the world of teaching and learning. As such, the story is deliberately provocative. *Seeing Red* causes a quick intake of breath akin to plunging into the cold waters of an ocean on a hot summer's day. The undercurrents of the story swirl about and buffet the reader as the story unfolds. Julia's letters summon participation. Her perspectives have the potential to inform, alter, and change one's view of teaching and learning and the pedagogical stance that one adopts in educational contexts. *Seeing Red* defines a new way of thinking about scholarship. It presents "the possibilities and potential of artful research" (p. 283). It is, simply, a/r/tographic in every sense of the word: artist, researcher, and teacher.

Scholarly projects like *Seeing Red* require courage, stamina, and imagination. As such, *Seeing Red* is exemplary and groundbreaking. The rigor with which *Seeing Red* was formulated, undertaken, and presented is not readily obvious when first read. However, the attention to detail, the judicious choices made, and the strong narrative thread become evident when one considers the impact that the project has on one's sensibilities. The beauty of *Seeing Red* is its ability to invite conversation (and argument) as much as it is to provide an alternative way of thinking about educational scholarship.

....

Dr. J. Gary Knowles
Professor of Creative Inquiry and Adult Learning
Ontario Institute for Studies in Education
of the University of Toronto

Finding Voice, Finding Form

How did Pauline come to find the heart of this work – the story of Julia and her academic supervisor – amid the routines of working in schools and with young children? How did she find her way through the labyrinth of places called classrooms and schools and universities where conformity rules the day, day after day? How did she come to this work amid the busyness of family and work? How did she learn not to conform to the pressures of traditional inquiry and the templates of scholarship?

As a man living in the world of the academy the concept of form is important in my life. My interests in form permeate my thinking about the natural world, the atmosphere, the built environment, the places I dwell, the clothes I wear, that which I choose to read. I have some sense as to how I came to think this way. Working in architecture taught me an enduring principle (passé in some circles), simple in its articulation, powerful in its influence. Form follows function. I know this in my heart.

But how did Pauline come to break out of the mold? What is the source for her vision about the possibilities of how scholarship may be presented, read, and felt? And read and re-read? *Seeing Red*? How did she come to find form in the epistolary novel? What is the source of her authority? (I do not mean authority as in expert but, rather, her authorial voice.) These are just some of the questions that floated in my consciousness when I first picked up *Seeing Red* – A Pedagogy of Parallax – and turned its pages. These pages revealed the power and simplicity of letters written and sent (and unsent) to tell an untold story with conviction and creativity. The heart of the matter is the emotional strings that letters create.

Seeing Red reminds me of the many ways that form plays out in creative scholarship informed by the arts and envisioned by artists. Pauline uses letters to provide a structure to the work. Yet they are also the genre or medium of the piece. The letters give the work a certain appearance and there is comfort in their irregular regularity. I (and I imagine most readers) know and experience letters, even if they be more of the electronic kind than I prefer. I have a sense of what to expect of them yet they are bound to provide surprising twists and turns. As such they possess a certain aesthetic but, as I say that, I am also reminded of their potency as method. Exchanges between persons in relation have a rhythm and a cadence and a structure and vocabulary that aids in making sense of the relational world they represent. The letters were, I imagine, at first only a possibility for revealing her scholarship; but the letters unfolded as Pauline explored the relational heart of *Seeing Red*.

Dr. Rita L. Irwin
Professor of Art Education and Curriculum Studies
Associate Dean of Teacher Education
University of British Columbia

Embrace the Freedom to Create

I had the privilege of teaching Pauline in her first PhD curriculum course. At that time, Pauline was an exceptional classroom teacher. Now she is an exceptional scholar who has brought the aesthetics of her work into the very lifeblood of her writing and discourse. She has been transformed and her dissertation is a testament to the depth and range of her change. Her dissertation is an exemplar of currere as complicit curriculum conversation. It is pedagogy of parallax because it exemplifies conversations for understanding through multiple layers of perception. This perception underscores an embodied aesthetic wholeness – an a/r/tographic way of being in the world that penetrates our senses and reaches into our depths and causes us to question our own perceptions. As readers we are changed. Pauline, as an a/r/tographer, was inspired by her art forms and her pedagogy, as she pursued her inquiry and gave full attention toward her heart, mind, body, and spirit. As a result, she examined difficult concepts in sensitive, compassionate yet demanding ways.

It seems an epistolary foreword should echo the value of the characters and relationships in the epistolary novel. And so I invite you to be equally involved in the creation of this text. Pauline Sameshima writes an epistolary bildungsroman, a didactic novel of personal journeying through artful scholarly inquiry. Parallax is a play on perspective, shifting perceptions and interpretations. If you enter into this experience with an open mind, an imaginative spirit, and a reflexive gaze, you too will enter into a space of personal artful yet scholarly inquiry. Embrace the aesthetics of this incredible text and you may be transported to, or transformed by, new ideas and identities. Several years ago I wrote an article with several students of mine. It was a couple of years before the word a/r/tography would be coined but the concept was very much developed. In that group of women I found myself exploring this concept: 'as I create I am created' (Irwin et. al. 2001). To me this is another example of the pedagogy of parallax. As we perform, paint, write music or poetry or fiction, we are conveying complex ideas and often these ideas are the complex parts of ourselves we are coming to understand as we are creating. In the doing, in the creating, we are becoming. We are transforming ourselves. In reading this volume, I urge you to embrace the freedom to create and re-create this text – to share in the creation of this text. You may come to understand, or create, another side of yourself. It will be a joyful and profound experience.

References:

Irwin, R. L., Stephenson, W., Robertson, H., & Reynolds, J. K. (2001). Passionate creativity, compassionate community. *Canadian Review of Art Education, 28*(2), 15-34.

PREFACE

Living in the Amber:
Conversations between Red and Greene

I am sitting with Maxine Greene, in my dream.

She sits at a small round metal table. The air is damp and grey but I do not feel the chill even though my hair keeps blowing across my cheek, irritatingly sticking to my lipstick, reminding me of my unsettledness even in joy. The cobblestone street makes the flimsy table wobble when she decisively taps her cigarette in a staccato movement on the glass ashtray centered on the table. We are smoking with gloved fingers, legs crossed, crimson lipstick stained on our filters, perfectly natural in another era, a different context. I see the smoke but cannot smell it and wonder if the haze in front of her eyes is just my own breath blurring my vision. I imagine her eyes are green but this is my fiction. We're sipping something thick and almost syrupy but it bites my throat with an echoing the way her words are electrifying my synapses—strangely fast, yet smooth and warm, gliding knowingness and recognition into my capillaries and spreading through my emptiness. I feel myself in the limen, teetering on the edge, uncomfortable in the brink but filled with desire to stay. I feel in love, engulfed in the anticipated moment of realization, in the love of desire to learn, knowing the space before me is all open.

Greene (2006) writes in a prologue titled "From Jagged Landscapes to Possibility":

> the crucial demand of our time is to attend, to pay heed. . . . To speak of dialogue is to suggest multiple relationships, multiple perspectives. There must be a connectedness among persons, each with a sense of agency, each with a project. And there must be a capacity to imagine, to think of things as if they could be otherwise. . . . Thoughtfulness, imagination, encounters with the arts and sciences from the grounds of lived life: this is the beginning and the opening to what might be. . . . There must be an ability to anticipate and accept incompleteness. Even when a controversy appears to be resolved, gaps and spaces remain, and the need for open questions. And where there is a space, a gap, there is the possibility of new choices, renewed reflection.

This is my curriculum. This is my hope, that my work can render points along an unseen path; to chart the roads of the unsaid; to begin to map a rhizomatic research; to speak the iterations for those without words; to broaden the margins; to search for alternate forms which open spaces; and to share an agency that slowly iterates what is, pervading, in a stable diffusion with strength in integrity, a hope that holds love and sees joy in all the truths we live.

I use techniques and thought processes of symbolic interaction as Norman Denzin (2002, p. 255) describes:

> The process of writing was a process of self-construction and then reconstruction. This process was based on ongoing

conversations with myself and with memories from my past. These memories were reconstructed through an interior dialogue [and] a meaningful reality was created out of this interpretive process.

Carl Leggo (2002, p. 2) describes his living as:

> desire, insatiable desire
> to know, to quest/ion, to seek.
> So, I explore ways of writing
> that expose lies like vermilion threads
> tangled in the illusion of a linear composition

To introduce the work I share a few of the questions which guided its development:

How does personal identity influence pedagogy?

- How do misconceptions of rootedness, sense-of-place, and constructs of belonging frame teacher identity in unhealthy ascetic motivations which promote precarious pedagogical perspectives and punitive standardization?

How are body, love, and desire connected to public conceptions of learning and teaching?

- How can a new embodied aesthetic of personal and plural "wholeness" merge culturally constructed unconscious and dichotomous ways of thinking about pedagogy which inherently separate, define, and prevent holistic learning and teaching?
- What influence does the student/teacher relationship have on student learning? What is the edge of love? Where is the limen of learning?

How does form influence and shape thinking?

- How does Julia separate her learning (private) from her living
  (public)? If the researcher believes that the ultimate goal of
  research is to articulate and improve the current contexts of
  learning, how can the researcher both honour private learning
  and remain responsible to the public audience in the presentation
  of research?
- How does the external frame set around particular notions
  of thinking and representation affect the possibilities of the
  content and its interpretation?

I am disrupted by language

invaded by dreams

punctured by love

bleeding for the silenced

scribbling down

the moment

all to construct

now

Pauline Sameshima

2007

ACKNOWLEDGEMENTS

gratitude, thankfulness,
appreciation, pleasure, and joy
I am indebted

to more than I can mention here

some do not know their influence
nor perhaps do I yet recognize their guidance

these I know

my husband Michael is patient, kind, a shape shifter filling
the cracks of my living and materializing dreams in the miasma
my children Madison and Cameo make me know love as lips and skin
my mother Dorothy is creative, energized, and loves beyond limits
my father Kee is innovative, handy, generous, and loves to a fault
my mother-in-law Margaret loves and nourishes my family with time
my mentor Carl knows no edge of love, filled with poetic mystery
my mentor Tony lets no stone rest, loves with attention to the moment
my mentor Rita lovingly paints the stars in the night sky to guide me
my mentor Gary prunes, feeds, and waters, tending with love
my peers love in laughter, warmth, and sojourning
the journey of learning
this life, this book

is love

Our strategy should be not only to confront empire but to lay siege to it. To deprive it of oxygen. To shame it. To mock it. With our art, our music, our literature, our stubbornness, our joy, our brilliance, our sheer relentlessness—and our ability to tell our own stories. Stories that are different from the ones we're being brainwashed to believe. The corporate revolution will collapse if we refuse to buy what they are selling—their ideas, their version of history, their wars, their weapons, their notion of inevitability.

Arundhati Roy, 2003, p. 103

THE
CRITICAL
PERSONAL
NARRATIVE

Critical personal narratives are counternarratives, testimonies, autoethnographies, performance text, stories, and accounts that disrupt and disturb discourse by exposing the complexities and contradictions that exist under official history (Mutua & Swadener, 2004). The critical personal narrative is a central genre of contemporary decolonizing writing. As a creative analytic practice, it is used to criticize "prevailing structures and relationships of power and inequity in a relational context" (p. 16). . . . The utopian counternarrative offers hope, showing others how to engage in actions that decolonize, heal, and transform. . . . The critical democratic storytelling imagination is pedagogical. As a form of instruction, it helps persons think critically, historically, and sociologically. It exposes the pedagogies of oppression that produce injustice (see Freire, 2001, p. 54). It contributes to a reflective ethical self-consciousness. It gives people a language and a set of pedagogical practices that turn oppression into freedom, despair into hope, hatred into love, doubt into trust.

Norman Denzin, 2005, pp. 946-948

SEEING RED

A Pedagogy
of Parallax

EDITOR'S
NOTE

i must search
i must write
must express all
construct myself understanding

Julia disappeared in May 2005. My obsession to share the collected letters and recovered documents of Julia Quan's unfinished dissertation has consumed me for a number of years. My body hears her calling me, to look deeper and more closely through the layers in her letters which I believe explain what happened to her.

Let me enlighten. In 2010, in the third year of my PhD program in the Department of Curriculum Studies at the University of British Columbia, as a research assistant for the celebrated Dr. Cliff Conrad, I was asked to gather data on recent North American and international PhD dissertations which incorporated innovative forms of qualitative research. UBC was and is a progressive leader in promoting and celebrating alternative ways of knowing and representing learning. This is how I stumbled onto a number of publications and conference proceedings written by Julia Quan on her in-progress epistolary novel dissertation—a first for that style. I was intrigued by her work, her mind, and her mystery.

Julia was last seen in May 2005 at the First International Congress of Qualitative Inquiry in Urbana, Illinois. In 2010 I tentatively approached Luke, Julia's husband, with the proposal of going through Julia's incomplete dissertation with the hopes of editing and possibly creating a collected works of sorts. I gratefully acknowledge all the assistance Luke gave me in putting this collection together. I was struck by his notion that through me Julia was being brought back to life.

Most intriguing of the data collected were the two discs which were password protected. I am continually surprised at how the inaccessible and visually "absent" can be so inviting. One was a Maxell brand disc labeled "Seasons," the same brand as all the other discs, and the other was a Sony brand disc labeled "Julia." I was only able to access the files on the Maxell disc. The password was simply "empress." I understood Julia's fascination with pretty, iconoclastic, romantic words so I started with fairytale vocabulary. The disc contained five folders: Spring, Summer, Late Summer, Fall, and Winter. These files contained letters to Red dated March 2004 to March 2005.

By comparing a couple of the letters against letters which were published, I realized that this version was definitely an early rough draft. The letters were shocking and raw in their devoted attention to theorizing teaching in the classroom, remembered stories, love and desire, art-making, and the pedagogical significance of her in-love experience with Red, one of her dissertation committee advisors. The work did not look like fiction, yet there were instances where Julia referred to the reader suggesting that very

early on she knew she was going to publish the letters. The
compilations simply looked like emails in chronological order.
The dates were sporadic so I'm not sure if emails on missing dates
were deleted or if there were no correspondence on those days. I
doubt the latter considering Julia's prolific style. I was surprised
to find sometimes 10 emails to Red on a single day! Her collection
reminded me of Anne Carson's discussion of the Greek myth of
Stesichoros. Carson said "the history of text is like a long caress."
It appeared:

> that Stesichoros had composed a substantial narrative poem
> then ripped it to pieces and buried the pieces in a box with
> some song lyrics and lecture notes and scraps of meat. The
> fragment numbers tell you roughly how the pieces fell out
> of the box. You can of course keep shaking the box. (1998,
> pp. 6-7)

Thus, I share these fragments with you in the hopes that you can
divine a story that makes sense to you. Or perhaps this whole
exercise of publishing these letters is an example of my notion of
what curriculum means. Here is one of my favourite images:

> Understanding   curriculum   as   deconstructed   text
> acknowledges knowledge as preeminently historical. Here,
> however, history is not understood as only ideologically
> constructed, rather as a series of narratives superimposed
> upon each other, interlaced among each other, layers of
> story merged and separated like colors in a Jackson Pollock
> painting. . . . To understand curriculum as deconstructed (and
> deconstructing) text is to tell stories that never end, stories in
> which the listener, the "narratee," may become a character
> or indeed the narrator, in which all structure is provisional,
> momentary, a collection of twinkling stars in a firmament of
> flux. (Pinar, Reynolds, Slattery & Taubman, 1995, p. 449)

I was not able to track down any of the three advisors on Julia's committee. Winnie Crates retired in 2005 to a remote island off the coast of Australia. Will McCarthy was on extended sabbatical, and Jared Zeno had moved to Tulane University in Florida before Hurricane Katrina. I realized that the files I had were not the actual dissertation because the letters were unformatted and according to the timeline set out in her dissertation proposal, her first full draft was due soon after she returned from the Illinois Conference. I have left the letters in the same chronological order but for practical purposes, could not print all the letters. I also tried to clarify some points Julia had left in draft form. Last, a few of the letters have been significantly revised for style and content for this publication. The letters theorize conceptions of the teacher/student relationship, identity, love, desire, belonging, feminist perspectives, canonized myth, and the power of presentation and form to shape learning, understanding, and constitutive cultural knowledge.

This text you are reading, *Seeing Red*, is thus Julia's selected and edited letters and her dissertation proposal which was intentionally written as the Epilogue. I name this a postmodern fictional memoir because it is not even clear to me what is based on experience, what is invented in Julia's original text, or exactly what I have inferred in my inclusions and deletions. Perhaps I just don't want the text in the letters to sit still. In some strange way, I feel that I will come to understand her mystery if I keep the words in the letters moving—articulating her and carrying on her story. Pinar explains this movement through deconstruction for the sake of construction. Pinar says, "Autobiography takes this task [of deconstruction] seriously, as it is the task of self formation, deformation, learning, and unlearning" (1988, p. 27). He explains that:

one way to keep moving is to understand that the stories

we tell, however provisional, always exclude other stories, which may also be true. . . . We are not the stories we tell as much as we are the modes of relation to others our stories imply, modes of relation implied by what we delete as much as what we include. (p. 28)

Pinar goes on to say that in seeking to find the included and excluded we may be able, as Nietzsche said, "to experience the history of humanity as a whole as [our own] history" (Pinar et al., 1995, p. 494).

Although many question how autobiographic Julia's letters are and how ethical it is for me to publish this work, Luke gives full consent for the publication. Luke knew that Julia was writing an epistolary love story for her dissertation. He is adamant that Julia's love for him was always true, that the letters were all fictionally constructed, and that the work was a testament to Julia's imaginative writing and deep urge to present innovative research in accessible forms. He said Julia would have been proud to know her work reached beyond academic borders-that was her goal.

This collection is not only Julia's story of Red, of love, of desire, but of belief that "theory does not express, translate, or serve to apply practice: it is practice" (Hwu, 1993, p. 198). Through contemporary autobiography, poetry, and a/r/tographic practice (see Irwin, 2004) layered with arts-informed inquiry (see Cole & Knowles, 2001b), Julia uses relational entanglements between her living and scholarly studies to inform pedagogical practice. Her letters themselves are the intended "teacher," interactively (by way of ambiguity and openness to interpretation) walking the reader through a year of learning in love through the passage of curriculum itself (see Daignault, 1988).

Through her letters, Julia reveals the inner life of an artist, researcher, and teacher in her movement through thought in her passage of becoming. Through writing, Julia carries herself through the joy and danger Neilsen (1998) speaks about, reinventing herself toward new identities.

I admit, I am obsessed with Julia, who she was, is, and who I want her to become, as if she will suddenly materialize when I come to really understand what her letters are trying to convey. The love theme is strongly connected to the idea of Amelia Jones' process of *reversibility* whereby:

> The relation to the self, the relation to the world, the relation to the other, all are constituted through a reversibility of seeing and being seen, perceiving and being perceived, and this entails a reciprocity and contingency for the subject(s) in the world. (1998, p. 41)

Julia writes of her love for Red while concurrently being loved by others. She lives in a space of feeling "going out" and simultaneously acknowledging the "coming in" of others' feelings. When she is disappointed in Red, she takes on the disappointment she simultaneously causes for those who love her, intensifying and exaggerating her disappointment in Red and thus creating a distorted view of Red. Key characters entangled in her letters include her husband-Luke; daughters-Jade and Savannah; dissertation committee advisors-Winifred Crates, Will McCarthy, and Jared Zeno; Red's partner-Clare; and a beginning teacher-Chris.

I am obsessed with this "recursive process translating thought to language, building the knowing on the known" (Neilsen, 1998, p. 40). This search "to engage in the deliberate structure of the web of meaning" (Vygotsky, 1962, p. 100) has consumed me. I have learned much already from the way Julia renders her work. I see her texts unfolding, carrying me along in their wake. Maybe this is the plan—that in my search of her, I find myself. Perhaps together we can fabricate our own truths.

Georgia Lang
April 15, 2015

This then is my story. I have reread it. It has bits of marrow sticking to it, and blood, and beautiful bright-green flies. At this or that twist of it I feel my slippery self eluding me, gliding into deeper and darker waters than I care to probe. I have camouflaged what I could so as not to hurt people. And I have toyed with many pseudonyms for myself before I hit on a particularly apt one.

Vladimir Nabokov, 1955, p. 280

Epilobium coloratum

Wood
Hun (active awareness)

east wind blows
aquamarine spring
dawn arousal hollers

1
East
Wind
Blows

Love, she had determined, was the necessary
catalyst to reach the creative edges of the self.

Rosemary Sullivan on Elizabeth Smart, 1992, p. 2

Three letters—to provide a flavour and the option of continuing.

May 31

Red, you were in my dreams last night. You were in a hot tub and I was in a bath nearby. I was relaxing in the bubbles, not watching you, but knowing where you were. When I called, you didn't answer and I worried. I got out of the tub not caring about exposing myself which is unusual because there was an unfamiliar woman in the hot tub with you. She didn't notice what was happening. I got into the water with you and when I called you again, you still did not respond. I pulled you up to me from your reclining position and held you in my arms. Your heart was beating strong and fast and I could hear your breath. Your eyes were closed and you wouldn't answer me. I held you close to me, felt my lips on your forehead, your breath on my heart and when I pulled away to look at you again, you were the same, still, but your eyes were smiling at me, the way you melt me. I think I looked at you for a long time and tried to remember you all and you kissed me. Not deep, but lightly and outside, but for a long time, until I felt the foreverness, and I closed my eyes and forgot about my body.

You feel responsibility for me because you are older. I feel responsibility for you because you're older. Is that love?

....

June 18
UNSENT

I spray the white trail of mousse directly along the top of her hair. Using the orange fine-toothed comb, I work the mousse into each strand along the hairline as I gently rake through, over and over along the top, scalp visible in the lines of the teeth. I pull her long hair quickly and effortlessly into two ponytails secured with the red baubles she's chosen. A perfectly straight part down the middle separates each side. Jade is drawing in her Etch-a-Sketch as we stand in my bathroom. Doing hair is a comforting and loving ritual I cherish with the girls. I deftly braid both sides, secure the ends and say, "There!" She looks up and smiles at herself in the mirror, thanks me in a voice that makes the missing start and runs out to get her coat and shoes. I look at the Etch-a-Sketch on the counter. I am surprised. Two salacious snakes flank a lopsided heart in the center. Detailed patterns mirror each other like a mysterious Rorschach print. It's a complex piece for a six-year old. The image makes me proud—the sophistication and symmetry, and yet I am troubled by the darkness of the snakes and the heart. Maybe Jade sees my life in the mirror. Can she read me without words? Does her rendering show understanding of her unarticulated, unconscious body knowledge of my lopsided heart, snakes slithering guilt through my blood?

At the door, Jade tells me her new favourite word is "symmetry." She asks if I like the picture she drew in the bathroom. She asks if I like the way she can do her "S" backwards so the picture looks like it can fold into itself, hiding in complication. At school, she made butterfly prints by painting on paper and folding the paper in half. Oh, so they are not snakes, only "S's" with eyes. I don't know how to think. If I folded my heart in half, the two sides would not fit; one is the real, the other is the dream—evil snakes anyway you turn the page. I'm losing it. My mind is unraveling, yarn tangled in a mess of writhing worms, continuously crawling away as I try to organize the reknitting that is taking place beyond my control by the very wool that covers my eyes.

I remember this feeling even when I was a child; this fear of passivity, uncontrol and perhaps surrender. As a child, I had a reoccurring dream of being in a bare, dark room with a polished cement floor. I stood near the wall and watched the drain in the center. I was small, alone, standing very still as I watched my life spirit swirl, white feathers in the air, toward the drain while at the same time afraid of what was coming up through the drain. I never thought about leaving the room even though I could see the open door. What will I subject myself to in order to learn, know, understand? Do I satiate mind at the expense of body? Hegel, in *The Phenomenology of Spirit (1807)*, asks us to consider:

> how a struggle between two distinct consciousnesses, let us say a violent "life-or-death" struggle, would lead to one consciousness surrendering and submitting to the

other out of fear of death. . . . This consciousness is given acknowledgement of its freedom through the submission and dependence of the other, which turns out paradoxically to be a deficient recognition in that the dominant one fails to see a reflection of itself in the subservient one. (*Internet Encyclopedia of Philosophy*, 2006, ¶4)

I'm taken to the high pitched taunting rhymes of my childhood. "Chinese, Japanese, money please!" I turn my head toward the sound of irritation and in slow motion hear a small rock whiz by my ear narrowly missing my cheekbone. Up above the 8-foot grey concrete wall that completely surrounds our South African home leers a White boy's face, head poking over the top. His shoulders rear up as his arm cocks back for his second pitch at me. I run for the fig tree fully aware of the squelching soft figs bursting under my bare feet. I drink the sweet intoxicating smell, ripe as I lean my cheek against the rough trunk, my heart in my mouth. I peer through the leafy branches. He is laughing, a strange scary laugh, a laugh that makes me feel so helpless. His head disappears. I know he is reloading. Should I make a dash for the house or hold out?

He is unrelenting. His rocks and stones hit the leaves and branches. Cowering behind the tree, I lift my elbow over my head to protect myself from falling fruit. Then I see my aunt wild with rage. She picks up a fair size rock and drills it squarely at the boy's forehead. He falls backward with a thud not even registering what has occurred.

I rack my brain to try to recall how I felt in that moment. Was I happy he was hit or sad he was hurt? It had never occurred to me to throw a rock back. I am shocked at the violence in my youth. Why didn't I just run into the house? What does this memory tell me? Is my will my demise? Will I continue to subject myself to the negative, not run away, see it out to the end? Where is the end? Can I make myself draw the line when I'm too afraid to? Can I sever my own limb to release myself like the Canadian hiker who saved himself after being trapped for seven days, his hand pinched under a fallen boulder? No, I am not strong. I do not know how to write new stories by myself. How do I love when I am already in love?

Have you read "Grasshopper," a poem by Jeanne Murray Walker (2004)? She writes about the grasshopper courageously biting off his broken leg so the new leg can replace it. You can read it at: http://www.versedaily.org/grasshopper.shtml. Here's my response to that poem.

GRASSHOPPER'S DEAF SKIN CANNOT LOVE EVERYONE HAPPILY EVER AFTER

I do not fall I cannot fall I must not fall
like you do, open smiles twinkling eyes open vulnerability
easily and down the nape, bristling skin

I hold tight, resist and wrestle an accident wrecked
roll this confusion around in my hands
try to still the bifurcated self at neck
but the faceless juggler will not need my cries
finger white grips and callous hands holding
holding to prevent the balls from hatching

I hear the bodies calling fluid raw heat
my own and the other
screeching with delirium
strong wrapped wings

force the agitating heart
from resonating
squeezing tight till the blood
drips through the membranous pores

I won't bite my leg when it's perfectly healthy
don't think I'm a hypocrite a tease a thick skinned whore
how do I stop new legs from growing
from singing unsolicited songs
for making me love more than one

In this life I cannot be yours too
sink into love, drown and be reborn in your heart
sing the silent harmonies that still the roar of the real
till the grass sways tall
grown around our blanket on the grass
and we are hidden
matted grass our only trace
no, my loving you will start whispers and spite
of the ugly, the grotesque
an unaccepted multi-legged grasshopper
with legs that will run me around in circles
off the grid of the fairytale path of always
only one

deep in a trench set out for me
graves are already dug for the loves I bite off
and leave behind
body thick with scars
until my skin can rest
deaf in the silence of the first story I chose
deaf to the longing lament in the choral sky

of grasshoppers sawing songs
crying out the curse for all the broken to hear

I know we are what we have become. Through experience, we
create our understandings of life and who we are, what we stand
for and what our conceptions of the world are. Our experiences
create who we are. Carl Leggo says, "My past is always included
in the present, implicated, inextricably present with the present"
(2004, p. 22). This is so true. Our ecological, cultural, ethical,
gendered, and embodied positionings are embedded within the
theories we embrace consciously and unconsciously as researchers,
learners and educators, and these beliefs inform our relationships,
teaching, and ways of being. Yes, I know this but how can I get
out? You're helping me, aren't you?

....

March 25
UNSENT

I will go back and read all the letters I've written. Gather them up
like firewood and watch the flames to try to understand how I can
love with so much pain.

2
Aquamarine
Spring

*Love that Red, the name, I think, of a lipstick color. Love that red
of my own lips, dressed not in metaphors of berries or flowers,
but in a blast of color that speaks belief in a vibrant voice . . . I
line and color my mouth to exert the autoerotic faculty of speech.*

Joanna Frueh, 1996, p. 7

I just want you to be. Be with me. Be in the moment.
Red, May 30, 2004, personal communication

March 26

Good morning, Professor! I hope you are well. Today is the vernal
equinox, the beginning of astronomical spring in the Northern
Hemisphere. You're beginning fall. Our rhythms will be different.
My Grandma says New Year's resolutions don't work in Canada
because January is not a birthing time. She tells me to set my goals
for the year in early spring. As a child, Grandma warned me not to
fall in love with anyone who came from far away (I think she was

talking about ethnicity). She said the distance to travel back was too far to cover in one life-time. I didn't understand. She said only the greatest love could fly that expanse. Maybe she was talking about distance in terms of time, geography, seasons, and culture. She was a mail-order bride full of stories I couldn't understand and it wasn't just a language barrier.

....

March 29

I'm beginning to associate the negative with "sabbatical." Why did you have to plan on going so far away!

By the way, your last email made me smile. Now I know I'm not just a mouse following my Pied Piper! Also, why would you want to spend more time talking to me in a semi-intoxicated state? Is the unguarded me easier and smoother around the edges? Do you feel you can have your way with me when I've had a few drinks? Ha, ha! Maybe being in that state is being in the inbetween, only half lucid, free.

I'm touched by the deepness of reading work written by people I know. I just spent all morning reading your work online. Thank you. You are an amazing wordsmith. I'm so intrigued. I imagine watching you create a paper—mapping you in some way so that I could see the art unfolding like watching an artist paint something into being. Reading you online is almost voyeuristic, an unpeeling of surprises. I consciously feel myself readjusting my conception of you the more I read. At the same time, I'm conscious that it is text and I realize that it has been manipulated. Your written work is a great record of your feelings about the world, an unsaid autobiography of influences and observations, and an explicit visual of how you render—a gift that holds the past of you in it.

I like the sense of freedom and openness, perhaps a languidity about your writing, unusual for academic writing.

Reading a conventional theoretical text is so different even if the writer shares perspectives and opinions. The rush of information coming from the page does not allow the reader to go "upstream" into the writer's head. The intention of your writing is so much inviting, so much like you, a meandering voyage of discovery. You like being alone, don't you?

Last night I dreamt of bodies as landscapes of learning, that bodies were texts. I've hardly dreamt since the PhD started. I know you think it's good to dream. You've said to allow myself the luxury to remember. How?

It's pouring here. I love the rain—cleansing. The rain refreshes the smells and life of the earth. What's the weather like there? I'm going to lie on some grass soon, when it dries. Miss you.

What do you mean you're thinking of all that's in front of me? Are you being fresh?

....

April 1

Thank you, regarding the front of me (metaphorically, literally, and physically). Wow, that's forward of you, Professor!

I like the suggestions you've sent regarding my proposal. I'll try to answer your questions below:
1. What's is my rationale? *To interrupt discourse, demonstrate connections.*
2. Why it is important? *To build better communication practices, raise accessibility issues.*

3. What potential insights might be gained? *That teacher identity is critical to successful teaching; connectedness spills over life into the classroom, into teaching and learning.*
4. How might I influence theory and practice? *My work can be used in teacher education programs; telling stories will enlarge the notion of "normative."*

Is that too simplistic—to think I can actually make a difference?

My very large extended family had a get-together last night. There were about 130 people at the restaurant. It was good to see all my cousins. There was too much to eat as usual. Since the PhD program started I know I'm different. I feel like an island, untouchable, a bit alone, can't explain. At the end of the evening, I was standing on the sidewalk waiting for Luke and the girls who went back into the restaurant. It was dark and there were still people milling about. I distinctly felt out of place as if I was standing *on* the sidewalk. Yes, I was on the sidewalk but I felt unnatural as if my heels were really high and I wasn't touching very much of the concrete. I think our disconnections are always related to groundings to the earth in some way.

You're so silly. First, I think of you too, and how can you say being attended to by me feels like heaven? What on earth are you talking about? I'm only writing! Attending would be much more than that.

....

April 2

Tired of me yet? This is my way of working. I really want to produce a work that people can understand. Lorri Neilsen says the esoteric language public intellectuals use creates a gap between lived experience and understanding. She says the "discourse most valued by the academy distances us all. . . . Women [she has] worked with—whether they are students or colleagues—most often prefer to write in a genre . . . that is closest to the heart" (2002, p. 7).

So I would like to create a heartful work that is accessible but I also want critique from the edges. I'm seeking the responses from those who can see in the outlying bands, on the fringes— those who can see the specifics with an informed eye. I've been thinking about a woman who did a short dance to represent her understanding at a conference. Ray Goodfriend says, "There's just so much about dance you can't absorb until you participate in it. Otherwise you just sit there and it either goes right by you or you become overwhelmed by it" (2002. p. 33). Yes, we always need something to attach newness to, a reference. We need to articulate our processes more. I noticed that after the performance there was a noticeably long silence—the kind that always follows something evocative but feels urgent. I used to be discouraged when I presented something in an artful way and no one said anything. Of course, there might be bubbly compliments but I always want a deeper response (though I'm not sure what that is). I like the advice Will gave me. He said that most of the time, people are overwhelmed and intimidated; they're not sure what to say and I shouldn't worry because the arts leave an impression—the realization or revelations are not so easily translated into words. So he says I may have more response at a later date or I may have none, but should know that my work has influenced and changed a path for many in that small moment of performance time. I appreciate this.

And about being disrespectful: I am only disrespectful because I can be! I just hope my directness builds a solid trusting relationship! Jane Gallop says the "crude and schematic is usually all too apt"

(1995, p. 80). I would agree. Sometimes we wrap our words so tightly we can't see the gifts in them—same with our research.

....

April 4

I feel like I'm on a roll of revelation or something lately. I was thinking about visualizing and imaging the possible and I even have a story to go with it! As part of the Chinese Dance Syllabus exam this year, I have to do all kinds of unnatural contortions and get marked! I love stretching my body to its limits. There's this one move that I'm really proud to have worked toward this year. I'm at the barre and I swing my leg back and lift my hand up and look back trying to connect my foot with my hand above my head. I always felt that there was no way I could get my back to bend enough, but it was really in the rotation of the hip socket. All I did one day was look at myself in the mirror as I was doing it and suddenly my back was slightly turned and my hip was open. A minor adjustment or angle makes such a difference in life. It all has to do with how we see.

Yes, thanks Red, I'll "be whatever I want to be." That's an interesting closing.

....

April 5

What do you mean you've missed my words? You expect too much! I wrote to you three times yesterday! Is writing morning, noon, and night not enough?

I have an interesting relationship with Will. I could tell you about him but we've never experienced anything together outside of the academic world. I asked him if he wanted to present at a conference with me. I could do the presentation by myself but I like the conversational aspect of two voices in presentation as if it's a performance. He said he's happy to present and I believe his sincerity. He said he's already going to be at the conference and presenting with others. Do I always have to ask? Why do I expect so much? He says we're friends but if we were, he would ask me things about myself or share the personal. Come to think of it, you don't ask or share anything without me asking first either. Are you both in your roles? Then again, what is the definition of a friend? Are you foremost my advisor, mentor, or friend? I can't be a friend to Will because he is a guide and cannot be next to me if he is guiding me. He hurts me a lot and he doesn't know. You'll say I'm being too sensitive. The sad fact is that when I'm writing to you I'm away from the harshness of the real world. Does that mean that what we have is not the "real world"?

Someone in the peer cohort asked if you were enjoying your sabbatical. He said I was so fortunate to have you as an advisor. Little does he know how picky I am and that I'm still surveying the goods!

....

April 9

Thanks so much for the books you sent. It's a good feeling—getting academic books as gifts. In another life I would have thought it heartless and yet now there's something strangely romantic about getting books to help me with my work. Thank you. You are very kind.

I must go work now, or am I working? What am I preparing myself for, Red?

April 11

I got the perfect jobs for September! I'll have a part-time position in the elementary classroom and a part-time position in teacher education. All's meant to be, right?

....

April 12

How should I conceive of love, if not belonging? Can I belong without subservience? There is also a sense of confinement even in marriage. I mean, every time we build community within, the walls become stronger to contain, thus excluding. Are you saying that all I do (education, dance, and art-making) bear witness to the inability of Luke to completely satisfy me? I take offence. Despite my actions with you, I am happily married. I suppose that sounds incongruent too.

I'll tell you what belonging without confinement is called: a two-week stand! Ha, ha! Maybe that's the freedom I have with you. I do have some sense of belonging in that I'm under your wing but I'm not expecting you to take care of me. At the conference, on the grass, I felt owned, loved—by earth and you. That day was a pivotal moment. There's something here about environment and place.

....

April 13
UNSENT

hear a motorcycle accelerating a long way off
the fake watery sound of traffic somewhere
feel the late night air
wish you

Thank you for being here with me Red. I come to you to breathe, to escape. I think I'm falling in love or are you saving me or am I feeling my belonging or am I losing control?

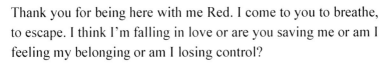

April 14

Do you like cherry tomatoes—so perfectly round, tight, surprising inside. I went to the beach today. I sat on a log—wet grass, open, remote. The clouds were grey, but beautiful and defined. Rained a bit. A black crow landed on some dry branches—I looked away and it was gone. The fleeting nature of nature is so glorious.

You used those dreaded three words of endearment! Since you didn't frame those words with the silly "You're so open" or "I mean it in the most wholesome kind of way" (whatever that means), I'm taking them to heart! But you always do find a need to diminish what you mean by them or are you trying to explain which love you're talking about so I understand your commitment to your words? Or are you worried about people reading my email? You know what this means, don't you? Serious obligations until I'm a Dr.! Then it's really over!

wishing you wholesome
call me tonight

April 15

Luke says I'm too open and emotional and these things are misinterpreted including my interest in listening to people's stories. You feel my openness and you are affected. I think I'm in love with you (Disclaimer: I can't get enough mind-stirring from you). I also have some connection with your body (Disclaimer: your well being). You make me feel strong and beautiful in a clean way (Catholic thoughts?). Do not let my disclaimers diminish my words.

I'll be away from email for tomorrow—going away for a few days. Smooth white skies. Good to get away to the trees. I will miss you.

It would be uncouth of you as a professor to tell me that you miss me, wouldn't it?

Why do I think of this?

only 3 words

3
Dawn Arousal
Hollers

*The passages contained in this brief chapter are but fragments
of memory, bits of a life, snippets of meaning-making, qualities
from the heart of pedagogy.*

J. Gary Knowles, 2001, p. 95

April 19

I've started dreaming and remembering my dreams. I'm learning,
even from my dreams! What does that mean? Is the conscious and
unconscious separate and each trying to control?

I am more and more conscious of the limitations of our
communications. Even the phone has restrictions. You need time
to let words settle, to sink into the cracks that are you—I can hear
it in your silences when I'm with you. I think we can communicate
with each other in ways I have not experienced before. It's a
sense of interweaving that is constantly happening in the silences
we have, when we are immersed in the wonder of just being in

presence and being in the world. The comfort in silence is a good indicator for me of understanding and connectivity. Our current working relationship of implied meanings or maybe my conjured up misreadings of your lyrical words always provide a fantasy of reality. Our email connection also encourages a playing with words, sometimes using metaphor/imagery/multiple meaning—yes, you are extending me beyond my articulated perception. I'm inclined to think this is better—I have space/time to work alone, concoct meanings you didn't intend and now it's too late to admit that our brief tryst is meaningless! You're right, our rhythms are actually very different. Plus, there most likely would be issues of balance in spirit, mind and body between us.

I finished a granite and tile mosaic today. It's called "Licorice Dreams."

Licorice Dreams, 2006, granite, marble and tile. 51" x 35"

I was thinking of you. Licorice looks so quiet but it is so surprising to the tongue. The piece goes with Margaret Atwood's poem

"Variations on the Word Sleep" (1987). I like the part about wishing I could enter you as sleep slides its smooth dark wave over my head, washing me in. I imagine walking with you in the poem, lost in the words, in a forest of blue green leaves. I dream about Atwood's words—wishing that I could inhabit you like air, as unnoticed and as completely necessary. Please read the poem online at http://www.poets.org/viewmedia.php/prmMID/16221.

I'm really tired and fading fast. I want to fade with you but am unable to do anything but imagine the imaginable as soothing and comforting. You know, I loved talking to you on the phone when lying down today. Thank you.

I've been thinking about all this writing I'm doing. I could start a book of memoirs! How about a novel on the professor/student relationship as curriculum discourse or something like that? It would be a voyeuristic peak into the crazy mind of a ranting lunatic and her beautiful, submissive teacher!

………………….......……………………………………………

April 21

I wish others could get the imagery I get from you. I feel so much pleasure, and encouragement from your thoughts and endearments. You really do build me. I feel a warmth that spreads through me, a filling and yet emptiness that never fills. It's not just your words (text) going into my head through my eyes, but the images you create that swallow me into you. I'm also talking about perhaps the strength and wonder of learning and realizing that I'm learning and being guided by someone who loves me as well. This is important, isn't it? This explains why some great teachers have loved their students as parents or guardians or as those with very vested interests. I really do think significant, transformational learning is influenced by a strong, even loving, teacher/learner relationship. This also explains why home-educated children do so well (Knowles, 1989, 1991).

Three words. Think in Chinese. The words are not dependent on each other and are balanced in weight.

love strong back

....

April 25

Thanks for letting me help with these new-teacher induction letters. I'll try to sound more "academic"! I can take a hint! What a great professional development program the school district has set up with the university! I will enjoy writing on your behalf. I realize this mentorship program you're involved in extends over the year so it won't be a lot of work. I plan to write five times over the next 10 months so don't worry, I can handle it. I already have some ideas! I suppose others might frown on this. It's not really unethical, is it? Wouldn't this be like me doing research assistant work on your behalf? I'm purposely writing for you. I'll write from my perspective so just take what you want and feel free to adjust and reword. Is Chris male or female? I'm glad to be doing the research and thinking about the topic so quit being apologetic and please take my words as a gift. You will think this odd but, as I wrote Chris' letter, I felt like there was a light in me and it was shining through my pores and all I wanted so badly was for you to see my light. I don't know what that image means only that I'm the way I am because of you. I suppose a good teacher does that. Yes, I am trying to please but it's different from trying to make you proud. It's really about doing something I feel pleased about and you just happen to see it, like it for what it is, smile, and then are surprised when you realize that it's a part of me.

Letters to Chris—Introductory Letter

Dear Chris,

I hope this letter finds you well. I'm glad we've been partnered. I enjoyed our phone conversation. As agreed, I'll send five referenced reflections and then we can discuss them as we go along. If you write a response journal to each and add anything else that you want to talk about, we'll very easily meet the mentorship program guidelines.

> That's what writing is, not communication but a means of communion. And here are the other writers who swirl around you, like friends, patient, intimate, sleeplessly accessible, over centuries. (Amis, 2000, p. 268)

I've been thinking a lot about the outlooks, qualities, and skills I consider important and useful for teachers, and of those, which ones might be most useful at the beginning of a career. Often what's perceived as important for the new teacher is not what is important from a veteran's point of view, nor from a researcher's for that matter, so I hope that you will find some resonance with my letters now, or even sometime later in your teaching career. Sometimes reading the same text at a different time or in a different context creates a substantially dissimilar text. Timing and context really do influence so much in our lives. Of course, knowing strategies for respectful classroom management and knowing "what to teach" are critical to all teachers, especially new ones, but these two issues particularly, often simply require time and experience in context so I'm going to focus on something I call *An Embodied Aesthetic Curriculum.* I would like to share my ruminations on how the body can inform experiences of teaching and learning when the divarication of mind and body are reunited.

Ideally, it would be best if I could understand the context in which you teach and model particular learning/teaching strategies you're interested in, or team-teach a series of lessons with you then talk about them. Despite my distance, I'm still hopeful that our reflexive writings to one another will help us grow as teachers.

To deepen transformative teaching and learning practices I encourage teachers to develop an *embodied aesthetic wholeness.* I imagine holistic teaching as fluid, coloured transparent layers dynamically moving under and over one another. Light (context) illuminates certain layers at particular times and at other times, the richness is created by the fusion of layered colours. I suggest the following:
1. increase receptivity and openness to learning
2. foster skills of relationality
3. model wholeness-in-process in explicit reflexive texts
4. layer multiple strategies of inquiry, research experiences, and presentation
5. acknowledge ecological and intuitive resonances

So I'm starting with an introduction and the first letter, and each time I send you a letter I'll speak to one of the five points. I agree with Brent Kilbourn who asserts that:

Common accounts of teaching frequently lack significant details about its nature, including details about subject-matter and about the process of teaching. Bled of these details, teaching can appear too simple in the eyes of parents and students; more significantly, it can appear too simple in the eyes of beginning teachers. (1998, p. xi)

So we can talk casually about things but I'll also include research references which might help you look up something that interests you. Feel free to use the references to write your monthly reflection papers. Even now, after teaching for many years, I still find that keeping a journal and discussing pedagogical issues with colleagues or friends very revealing.

Background
The tradition of formal schools has severed the body from the mind, thereby inhibiting holistic teaching and learning which potentially limits the development of imagination and wonder, and restrains the advancement of knowledge and understanding (Gallop, 1988; jagodzinski, 1992). According to jan jagodzinski, the bifurcation of mind and body in the arts occurred during the rule of Louis XIV in the eighteenth century. It was during this time that the "artisan" was replaced with the "artist." jagodzinski believes that since then sensuous knowledge has been separated from the body and transferred into the art object which is put on display. The separation between maker and product produces an inanimate object which can then easily be sorted and categorized as a superficial commodity. Similarly, the separation between teacher and curriculum has created a static, cold, compartmentalized curriculum which has in many respects become a commodity—packaged knowledge. In so thinking, the disembodied teacher can then be thought of as the mindless conduit of transference. We must breathe life back into the curriculum, make learning meaningful, and focus on the art of teaching. We must not let teaching well take the backseat to covering curriculum. The teacher can address personal wholeness by reconnecting the curriculum with self by connecting mind and body; and second, by integrating self, as a learner in the teaching process.

The body of knowledge

> Real knowledge is not merely discursive or literal; it is also,
> if not first and foremost, sensuous . . . derived from bodily
> participation in the learning act. (Berman, 1981, p. 168)

I'll provide examples of the intersections between living,
learning, researching, and teaching to foster the five intersecting
and overlapping layers of wholeness. Wholeness as a theoretical
model is rooted in micropolitical thought. The ability to see the
micropolitical is paramount. The micropolitical is the human
living curriculum as aesthetic text which "questions the everyday,
the conventional, and asks us to view knowledge, teaching, and
learning from multiple perspectives, to climb out from submerged
perceptions, and see as if for the first time" (Pinar et al., 1995, p.
605). Heidegger puts it this way:

> The most difficult learning is to come to know actually and to
> the very foundations what we already know. Such learning,
> with which we are here solely concerned, demands dwelling
> continually on what appears to be nearest to us. (1977, p.
> 252)

Wholeness employs *currere* as a research methodology as explained
by Rita Irwin (2003, 2004) and William Pinar and Madeleine
Grumet (1976). The word *curriculum*, generally used to refer to a
prescribed list of outcomes, objectives and content, is derived from
the Latin word, *currere*, which means to run. Curriculum is static,
while *currere* is dynamic. Curriculum is focused on "end products
we call concepts, abstractions, conclusions, and generalizations
we, in accumulative fashion, call knowledge" (Pinar et al., 1995,
p. 415). Researching, teaching, and learning through the method
of *currere* as formulated and practiced by Pinar and Grumet (1976)
requires the researcher to actively create two phenomenological

descriptions: 1) to know the self in context; and 2) "to trace the complex path from preconceptual experience to formal intellection" (Pinar et al., 1995, p. 415). In other words, currere is *living pedagogic inquiry*—finding location of self in relation and iterating moments as knowledge construction along the path of the dynamic process of currere. Although understanding that curriculum as objectives and outcomes is important, I propose that we also attend to the *currere* root of curriculum in the classroom setting.

Madeleine Grumet writes:

> If *currere* was to reveal our conceptual inclinations, intellectual and emotional habits, mime would reveal the knowledge that we have in our hands, in our feet, in our backs, in our eyes. It is knowledge gathered from our preconceptual dialogue with the world, knowledge that precedes our utterances and our stories. (1978, p. 305)

Currere is about movement, about awareness, about acknowledging learning through the body. Most teachers know that hands-on-learning and active participation increases learning. That notion must be extended to the teaching self—to embody learning, researching, and teaching that way. A refocus of ways of being a teacher and incorporating *currere* as an integral part of pedagogic living is critical to transformational teaching practice.

The scholarship of Hamblen (1983), jagodzinski (1992), Leggo (2005a), Pryer (2001), Sawada (1989), Springgay (2004), and others, privilege the body's sensuous knowing over the Cartesian emphasis on thought. Sawada explains that knowledge should "constitute the everyday epistemology of the everyday experiences of the everyday student who does not leave life behind when entering school" (1989, p. 9). Learning is an integral part of living in the body. Every living moment is a possible moment for realization, contemplation, or action. Embodied wholeness is weaving the daily into reflexive understandings of continuous heartful living, learning, and teaching. Artful, tactile and multi-sensory epistemologies are thus more strongly supported as the researcher/teacher /learner takes on a reflexive way of being.

Like jagonzinski (1992), I support the understanding that the aesthetic, ethical and political are intertwined. jan jagonzinski argues that "curriculum as an aesthetic text represents a political and moral commitment in constant antagonism with reality. Aesthetic experience becomes . . . a transvaluation and a call to action" (Pinar et al., 1995, p. 602). The researcher/teacher/learner is always in an active state of renegotiating perceptions of self in conceptions of context (Rogoff 2000) and re-searching, re-creating and creating new ways of understanding, appreciating, and representing (Finley and Knowles, 1995). Living wholeness as a researcher and teacher includes living as an embodied aesthetic being, developing skills for finding meaningful pedagogic relevance between personal experience and the greater public good, and recognizing the processes of learning while the passages of learning are being constructed.

Living embodied wholeness is not a blind surrender to compartmentalization and dichotomy; rather, it is comparable to living Garoian's performance art teaching off-stage, outside and inside the classroom.

> Performance art teaching enables students to critique curricular and pedagogical stereotypes, to challenge the assumptions of the art world and those of the culture in general. This pedagogy recognizes and encourages the

tradition of rebellion as a natural aspect of students' creative and mental development. (1999, p. 31)

Living wholeness is the entwining of Merleau-Ponty's (1968) "flesh" of the world with the self through Amelia Jones' process of "reversibility."

The relation to the self, the relation to the world, the relation to the other, all are constituted through a reversibility of seeing and being seen, perceiving and being perceived, and this entails a reciprocity and contingency for the subject(s) in the world. (1998, p. 41)

Wholeness is thus living inside and outside—living a subversive esthetic, moving with conviction, away from the safety of conformity and standardization, and the fear that holds us there, to the unknown, to the new, and to the open connective spaces where the impossible becomes possible.

To be immersed as a learner in the teaching practice you need to question the origins of your thinking and talk about your thinking. You need to teach and learn through multiple embodied experiences. You also need to find location for yourself through actively increasing your receptivity, developing skills of relationality, and acknowledging ecological and intuitive resonances. I would suggest that you begin to view yourself as not just the giving-teacher, but also as a receiving-learner in process. We should talk more about this with all beginning teachers. Herman Stark (2003) believes that to think is to undermine, and one increasingly incurs more intellectual and moral responsibilities as one becomes more thoughtful.

Here's the first letter on Layer One. I'll write Layer Two in June sometime. Enjoy.

Letters to Chris—Layer One: Improve "Receptivity" or Openness to Learning

> One of the major tasks of the curriculum field is to demonstrate in consistent fashion the process of self-criticism and self-renewal. (Henry A. Giroux, 1980, p. 27)

To teach well, in balanced ways, live with verve! Most conceptions of the teacher identity is one of a passive body, a conduit of knowledge, an empty jug which is filled with the curriculum which is then proportionally doled out to students. It's important to change this conception and to see the teaching self as a living, breathing learner closely integrated with students. Focus on the learning moments, limit the key concepts planned per lesson, and be cognizant of seeing and feeling responses from students. Understand self as not *giving* a curriculum but, rather, co-creating a curriculum with the students. Learning can only be meaningful if you can enable students to make relational connections. Teach your students how to increase their own body receptivity to learning as you focus on always remaining open yourself.

Emmanuel Levinas (1981) describes an interesting way of understanding "self/other." Levinas believes that the primary concern of self to the other is the subject's responsibility to the other, even if the other is unknown. He says we can only know self in relation to other. Ted Aoki (1992) explains that Levinas' focus on responsibility before the rights and freedoms of the subject creates a tone which ethically welcomes multiplicity. This outlook appears simplistic but can drastically reshape your perspectives on locating your place as a teacher within wholeness. The teaching profession is dramatically strengthened when teachers understand who they are, know how their experiences have shaped their ideologies, and find and acknowledge their place of contribution in the broader context of the educational setting. There is a lot here in this last sentence and perhaps some would argue against this notion of seeking place and contribution. These ideas go against the grain because the historical concept of the teacher is one of blank uniformity. Levinas' conception of self/other constructs a placeholder for self in the midst of others (through responsibility) and hence creates a perspective of belonging, place and need, yet still values difference. This conception reiterates Paulo Freire's encouragement that "the more rooted I am in my location, the more I extend myself to other places so as to become a citizen of the world. No one becomes local from a universal location" (1997, p. 39).

An aesthetic of wholeness integrates Drew Leder's concept of the ecstatic body as "a field of immediately lived sensation . . . its presence fleshed out by a ceaseless stream of kinesthesias, cutaneous and visceral sensation, defining . . . [the] body's space and extension and yielding information about position, balance, state of tension, desire, and mood" (1990, p. 23). Being open in the moment means listening intently, simultaneously seeking relationality, acknowledging connections and appreciating the fullness of presence in the present. Being open is akin to Leder's notion of aesthetic absorption which is based on phenomenologist Maurice Merleau-Ponty's (1968) "chiasm" which is experiencing the world as "flesh"—a meshing of subject and object, self and body, and body and world. Merleau-Ponty explains:

> The flesh is not matter, is not mind, is not substance. To designate it, we should need the old term "element," in the sense it was used to speak of water, air, earth, and fire, that is, in the sense of a general thing, midway between the spatio-temporal individual and the idea, a sort of incarnate principle that brings a style of being wherever there is a fragment of

being. The flesh is in this sense an "element" of Being. (p. 139)

I want you to imagine wholeness as life lived in luminiferous ether. Ether was once believed to be the fifth and highest element after air, earth, fire, and water and was believed to be the substance composing all heavenly bodies. Ether was imagined to be above air, air itself, and a medium that filled all space to support the propagation of electromagnetic waves (*hyperdictionary*, 2005). Living in the ether is thus living within the fifth element as Merleau-Ponty describes—living an aesthetic openness of being. You feel the immersion, yet simultaneously see all that is around you, even your immersed self.

Recently, I saw Sandra Weber's (2005) presentation at Robson Square Theatre. Her topic title was *Bodies and teaching: From representation to embodiment*. She promotes the active body as learner. During the open question and answer period a teacher commented that Weber proposed nothing new. In this teacher's school, the students were exposed daily to opportunities for embodied learning in such forms as dance, theatre, physical education, and hands-on-learning. The important point to raise is the question which alludes to the mistaken but conventional notion that lessons are "given" or that opportunities for performance learning are "provided." The primary concern should be that the teacher's body be a part of the learning or used in the learning process. This is a good example of the split between teacher and curriculum.

Joseph Schwab introduced dialogic discussion in the university setting in the 1930's (Westbury & Wilkof, 1978). This was a novel method of learning at the time because it involved the insertion of the teacher in the learning process and brought in potential juxtaposition and resistance as the class debated and dialectically constructed understanding. Moving away from directed teaching toward discussion is great, but even better would be a full integration of the teacher as a student in praxis.

My proposal is a radical reconception of the teacher—the teacher as not only teacher, but simultaneously researcher and learner.

The idea of not knowing is a foreign idea for teachers who feign competence, often to gain control of behavioural and management issues, and who are expected by students, parents, and administrators to "know." Being open to newness and receptive to learning first requires a public acknowledgement that teachers don't know everything and are always in process; and, second, an active attempt on the teacher's part to search for connections and metaphoric meanings of relationality in experiences which connect to pedagogy.

Sparganium multipedunculaturm

Fire
Shen (transcendent awareness)

red heat joy
giggling noon
south summer roar

4
Red Heat
Joy

So I can see no way around that. Yet it seems to be that when you are lucky enough to find someone who you think is good and true, then the lies you tell others are forgivable. That may sound strange, but I think it's true.

Richard B. Wright, 2002, p. 252

May 1

Red, I'm serious. What would you think if I wrote about our relationship? I've been thinking about how learning is so natural in this dialectic, dialogical situation. When I'm learning with you I am no longer *in* me, but in the space between us. Sharing some of the letters could give the reader the sense of importance of the relational. I realize it's a bit far-fetched at the moment but, after helping you with the letters to Chris, I realize how powerful this form can be in a sort of subtle didactic way—that I am marking the points of learning through the dynamic curriculum of a pedagogic living inquiry, that I am mapping a way of learning (see Sameshima & Irwin, 2006). In fact I would be doing what I suggested Chris do—to live currere, to know self in context and "trace the complex path from preconceptual experience to formal intellection" (Pinar et al., 1995, p. 415). I'm very intrigued with letter writing as a means to communicate with the reader. Somehow this form brings the level of "academia" to an approachable portal and dispels communication barriers because the language is much more casual, open and uncertain. There can be heart in the work. When I ask a question of you, I am really asking the reader—this could be a bold way to write. My receiver thus becomes anyone who reads my words and I am actually linked directly to one person's eyes. Is that why they say the eyes are the windows to the soul? It's the one-to-one that makes learning and teaching so effective. I'm so excited! This is a powerful notion! In other "heartless" texts, texts for mass consumption, the reader feels little need to be committed to the work. The writer is generally certain about claims and does not invite interaction from the reader. I liken this to a speaker presenting to a large group. Audience anonymity provides reason not to attend carefully or to build connections with the speaker. I want my readers to take responsibility for shaping their own interpretations of my texts. I want to write a text that can encourage a reader to actively and dynamically shape the text, filling the hollow words with their own understandings. Ok, maybe not hollow words, but words which still have room in them for more stories.

I think about our writing. If I'm convinced that we write who we are and who we become, and since I'm a hopeless romantic like you, then is it conceivable that we could write ourselves into love? We're actually constructed by our own word making. When choosing words, I try to write my love letters with depth and as

you read them, you think I actually feel the depth (which I may not
actually be feeling, but it sounds and writes well). I don't mean
that I'm being deceptive, but I'm careful about choosing words
that will make me pleasing to you). In return, you manipulate
your words and I believe them. In time, we'll be in love with the
creation of a relationship based on good writing. Can this last in
the physical?

....

May 12

the future unfolds
with such pleasure
glorious effusive energy
dream with me
poems and words
meshed with mine
in my heart

Here's the latest mosaic.
It's called "Georgia's
Diaspora." Georgia
O'Keefe's images of
flowers have always
been so startling to
me. Maybe the word
"startling" has too much
movement but "striking"
is too still. A/r/tographer
Rita Irwin (Springgay
& Irwin, 2004) writes
of O'Keefe's influential

Georgia's Diaspora, 2006,
mixed tile. 35" x 51"

spirit on her own artmaking/research practice. O'Keefe believed that paintings could not be explained, only experienced (Dijkstra, 1998). Irwin suggests that O'Keefe's paintings sensually celebrate life, startling us into "discovering the sensual, to experience the infinite as a material texture of life" (p. 75). Irwin goes on to say that O'Keefe's work is situated in a "place between realism and abstraction. It was in this paradoxical place that she was torn by the need to reveal and a fear of being too well understood" (p. 75). It's about revealing the close to the heart but not wanting to show the narcissistic self. I know this feeling well, it's also the notion that I want to grasp what O'Keefe calls "the Faraway"—the urge to hold the mystical of the natural world (Udall, 1992, p. 111). Carl Leggo (June 6, 2005, personal communication) writes that poetry opens up the intimate spaces where lives are creatively composed. These are the unspoken places. In my artmaking and my writing, I believe that the articulation of the intimate frees because others are given a chance to see what is hidden. To free that which is hidden is to liberate all who think oppression is acceptable. In this artmaking, I was also thinking about how I can free myself by not holding onto the myth that love and sex are synonymous—an idea which constrains me to only particular kinds of relationships and only one love. I imagine that to open the ovary of my flower is to allow all that is with me in birth to be released.

The idea of opening and releasing is quite empowering. There are other ideas I worked through in this piece. Note the unassuming incoming foliage (top right) against the outgoing dispersion. I wanted to show the focus on both moving out and moving in. I don't think we fully acknowledge the joys of both giving and receiving at once or being simultaneously in and out. Leder (1990) notes that because we live in our bodies, we consign the body's phenomena as absent from awareness and we tend to direct our attention out into the world. Through inward redirection, he says a beautiful cacophony emerges. I think this is what's happening for me. You have opened me by going inside and I'm spilling all over. Thank you.

………………….………………………………….......…………

May 15

before the alarm
before the world
awakes you call
only 3 words
beckon my fingers
this pace unreason
this view frenetic
can't help myself
swallowed me whole
to follow you
to feel you
reflecting me all
pulling my journey
making my way
to your hands

…………………………………………….......……………………

May 16

People use the word groundedness differently. When I say groundedness, I'm talking about an *anchoring* as a settled recognition of a remembered place of return to the earth, wisdom, ecological identity, and location roots. Others talk about this *anchoring* as being tethered, being inside and heavy, not being

able to fly. You've been thinking about my thinking as vertical,
that I'll grow up. I'm planning to grow wide. That is my way.

OPENING THE WORLD
how do I learn to soar?
not taking step by step
but gathering information and flying over
I turn to artful research to ideate
the periphery of understanding
draw the edge of thought
where conceptualization is not limited to lexicon
how can I describe what I understand
without a language – that which I myself do not know?
but with imagination, an instrument with no rules
with my body, and layered with words
I try to dance
all that is yet confined to one alphabetic glossolalia
all that needs to be expressed
all that calls for representation and interpretation
iterating the wordless
translating the unnamed noesis
understanding what we can't but need to
pushing to the unbound
dwelling and moving in rhythm and breath
letting the process teach
opening to ambiguity and
post modern subjectivities
drafting on the power of others
on the crest of natality
I write and story myself understanding
incorporate both sides of the brain
as I type with both hands

integrating the hemispheres
opening the world

…………............…………………………………………………………………

May 20

Do we have this connection only because we are attuned, looking for the mergings which increase the volume and thickness of revelations, articulating like writers in the connected moment? Are we, as you describe, crazy, obsessed, and hallucinating? Are we creating this heightened reality through the "trapping" of text? Are we catching all the fleeting moments like blocks which build this love higher than imaginable, wider than consciousness, so deep in foundation, firm? Is it possible to do this visually? The sight of words give weight. Do all our emails give our relationship more "substance" than one without words? Are we assigning more value to our relationship because of the quantity of text associated to it? Wanda May writes, "Written texts—such as curriculum guides—dupe us into believing that meanings are fixed and stable" (1989, p. 9). I'm worried.

Then again, if I use this same sort of thinking, I can create visuals which will surface understandings, catch the frameworks and stack them up. I can basically build a staircase or a scaffold out of renderings! Think what that means for using the arts in research! I feel like you really see me in my work in an *inside* way, not just my outside. I think you must be the only one. Is that where my intimacy with you is? Do I think we're close because you reflect me the way I want to be reflected?

falling in love
I understand all

3 words speak
louder than all

…………………………......…………………………………

May 21

I had a good hip hop class. Hip hop has a very different movement vocabulary than the kind of dancing I'm used to. I feel awkward and it's strange because I can't seem to feel the synchronicity of the moves. I'm thinking a lot and sometimes the music catches up to the sequence in my head before the moves come out. I know that the segmentation of the moves this week will somehow melt into my body memory by next week and the new parts of the dance will become smooth. Isn't that so bewildering—how does the body learn?

I love to dance, to feel my own heart beat in syncopation with the music. I remember that critical moment when I heard your heart. I think that was my downfall. I've always thought kissing was the marker—the signal of "crossing the line." With you, I fell over the edge when I heard your heartbeat—it was faint, fainter than any heartbeart I've felt. I know I have issues with needing to heal.

Here's an example. I saw Will at a local conference and he unintentionally hurt my feelings about something. I was so upset with him that I was going to cancel my meeting with him later that week. Then he sent me an email saying that when he returned from the conference he was very ill. As soon as I read that I felt myself melting. I know I want to heal him and have the crazy notion that I can. How? What can I do for his flu?

According to Pinar and Reynolds, inquiry grounded in hermeneutics is predicated on the principle that a text "remakes itself with each new reading, notwithstanding the history of previous readings that remain embedded within" (1992, p. 241). David Jardine (1998) says the primary tool of hermeneutic analysis is interpretation, with the fundamental aim of developing new insights by synthesizing ideas or prior findings in a way that builds theoretical understanding. I take these quotes and apply them to hip hop. The steps hermeneutically sink into the body, become analyzed and interpreted. Jardine suggests that "a deep investment in the issues at hand . . . is theorizing in the best sense, a theorizing that erupts out of our lives together and is about our lives together" (p. 7). This is what I want to do in my research.

YOU MAKE ME
you make me
fold and caress
crush and crumple
unravel and smooth
stretch across me
silken strength so
i feel you
every beat, breath
of my heart

....

May 23

I've been busy. I read a few dissertations that were written in novel form. Have you seen Elizabeth de Freitas (2003) and Douglas Gosse's (2004) dissertations? What do you think of *Boundary Bay* by Rishma Dunlop (2000)? I had an interesting conversation with a classroom teacher about the latter. It's intriguing how many teachers and people in general view knowledge—even people who

I consider open and thoughtful. So many people think knowledge is only legitimate when it's in a text book or in the encyclopedia. Have you heard about *Wikipedia* (2006)? It's an online encyclopedia that is written and edited by whoever wants to contribute. There's a sense that the text is always fresh and being shaped toward the "truth" even as we know there is not one truth. I like that. I used *Wikipedia.com* for a definition in a paper and a reviewer said I ought to "research" and write from a perspective that is informed by reliable sources. I find this a curious notion. What is a reliable source? Is the dictionary reliable? Does our work become reliable if three people referee the text and say it's valid? What if the three chosen referees don't know very much about the topic? We need to weigh everything we read and hear and not complicate ourselves with what is *most* true. Information and knowledge is so dynamic. When I find myself second guessing Wikipedia, I look at my bookshelf and ask myself which books have truth in them. I wonder if veracity, validity, and how we define knowledge has to do with how we define ourselves.

I've been thinking about how I'm defining myself through what I do. When you ask who I am, I'm really thinking of what I am. I am an artist, researcher, and teacher, but who I am is really a question of heart, not a category. Do you think this is what we ought to focus on in teacher education? I mean we shouldn't be teaching how to act like a teacher (fit the category), but rather how to feel the process of teaching (to be the verb), to try to develop the heart or the roots for the teaching life.

Oh sorry, got side-tracked. The teacher who read *Boundary Bay* by Dunlop (2000) felt that because it was fiction, it lost the authority research has through generalization. I argue that Dunlop wasn't trying to generalize; she was being specific, but then again, fiction is not viewed as knowledge by some. I think stories whether fiction or non-fiction, provide examples of how others see and live within stories and that is pedagogic. Henry James (1843-1916) in *Theory of Fiction* writes:

> The success of a work of art . . . may be measured by the degree to which it produces a certain illusion; that illusion makes it appear to us for the time that we have lived another life—that we have had a miraculous enlargement of our experience. (Miller, 1972, p. 93)

So Dunlop's work in essence, is to provide us with shoes to walk in other lives.

I want teachers to read my dissertation—and you know how little time they have. Do you know that the most often preferred method of professional development is the one-shot workshop where teachers are given some idea or strategy which can be implemented in class the next day (see Sameshima, 1999)? It's unlikely that teachers will spend the time going through a conventional dissertation. Would they even read a steamy set of letters about learning?

So I'm seriously thinking about writing an epistolary novel. I could create a dissertation by compiling and expanding ideas in our letters. The work would be both fiction and non-fiction and be true enough because the letters would actually be letters I've sent you. Brent Kilbourn says that "the power of fiction is its ability to show, largely through structural corroboration, the qualities of experience that we multiplicatively recognize as poetically true of people and situations" (1999, p. 31).

explain this mystery
burning with pleasure

astonishment in rapture
anguish of unrest
quest to fill
don't know what
tell me all
tell me please
need to hear
hurts to hold

5
Giggling Noon

Like desire, language disrupts, refuses to be contained within boundaries. It speaks itself against our will, in words and thought that intrude, even violate the most private spaces of mind and body.

bell hooks, 1994, p. 167

June 3

I cannot contain myself! I must share! Again, I drain you. I am sorry. I see how passion in teaching and learning allows us to see and create bell hooks' (1994) "remembered rapture" in our emails. The work and the relationship have knitted together and real learning is all about thinking about the learning, being in the moment, saving the exquisite joys, learning in love, feeling the body electric! This is erotic scholarship (Barecca & Morse, 1997; Frueh, 1996; Gallop, 1988). Red, we are living through it, not only talking, but feeling the moments when our bodies are not separated from our minds. Alison Pryer describes pedagogy as an "erotic encounter, a meeting of teacher and student . . . a wild and chaotic process" that is both joyful and painful (2001, p. 137).

more to learn
passion, desire, ecstasy
you and me

....

June 6

Ecstatic! My body surprises me! I went to a Chinese dance class today. There were only three of us in the class and we did so much. I was exhausted after an hour and it was a two-hour class! I started dancing again last year and the big thing for me has always been to stretch myself to my limit. I told you of my breakthrough in kicking my hand over my head with my foot. Well, today I held my foot above my head, behind my back, with BOTH hands! I'm sure you can't imagine what this looks like—imagine an ice-skater holding a blade up above her head while spinning. Imagine standing on one foot, with the other foot extended to the back. I have to lift the back foot high, reach over my head and grab that leg. I am amazed that this old body can do it! I think my head/heart openness has extended to my body! The splits were so easy today too. Why? Isn't the tension in the muscles? Has it always been in the head? Disbelief!

everywhere I go
you are there
in your words
in my world

You mean more to me than the cliché three words, the one line story that drives our living. Do you think we can live our lives without needing the three words? Living the moment is connecting all, isn't it?

June 8

Good morning. Did you sleep well? I kept you up again. I write
and all the layers are compressed upon the words (literal meanings,
metaphors, eros). I think it's because we are connected completely.
Text has in many ways become . . . I was going to say thin, but
general too, for us. We are standing outside (bell hooks, 1994), on
the fringes in ecstasy!

the words flow
the meanings unfold

Do you always intend the personal innuendo or are you innocently
naïve? You're being naughty! Or maybe the body drives all thought,
not the head. I like Peter McLaren's advice that "a politics of field
relations must be grounded in eros, in passion, in commitment
to transform through a radical connectedness to the self and the
other" (1991, p. 163); and Barreca and Morse who state that "the
acts of learning and teaching are acts of desire and passion" (1997,
p. x).

....

June 10

My new favourite word is *prosody*. As you know, I always imagine
that I am Julia Kristeva's shadow. Her work is very much about
bringing the body back into discourses in the human sciences.
Kristeva talks about the fissures in language, about the prosody of
language as opposed to the denotive meanings of words. Prosody
may mean a number of things. I've looked it up and summarized
it here for you (Farlex, 2006):

• Prosody consists of distinctive variations of stress, tone, and
  timing in spoken language. How pitch changes from word to

word, the speed of speech, the loudness of speech, and the duration of pauses all contribute to prosody.

- In linguistics, prosody includes intonation and vocal stress in speech.
- In poetry, prosody includes the scansion and metrical shape of the lines.
- In vocal music, prosody refers to the way the composer sets the text in the assignment of syllables to notes in the melody to which the text is sung; this is particularly a function of rhythm and is not to be confused with musical form.

The power of poetry is the prosody of language. Not in the words themselves, but in the fissures of the words and in the spaces. This is what I want my dissertation to be about—about the inbetween, and about valuing the parallax of diversity.

When I read your work, I see you. When I read your published words, I begin to question what is fact and what is fiction, and really, does it matter? Who knows if the fiction didn't actually happen? For instance, how do you know I'm writing truth now? I could be embellishing everything in order to impress you. Since you're so far away, I'm quite safe in making everything up. If learning occurs when the heart is moved why wouldn't I always try to move the heart? I'm just coming to grips with this. *Memoirs of a Geisha* by Arthur Golden (1997) is like that too. One cannot peel fiction from the research in that book. I think those types of books and movies are the most compelling, when you want to believe that the whole thing is true, even though you know that it isn't or can't be.

I recently read Jane Gardam's (1991) epistolary novel *The Queen of the Tamborine*. It's about a character, Eliza, who writes letters to a neighbour as she reveals her own descent into insanity

and how she eventually finds a place for herself. I realize that
I am manipulated by Gardam and, yet, I still want to trust her
main character's voice even as she writes from insanity. Eliza
begins writing letters like regular letters; the experience is always
recorded after the fact. Later in the novel, Eliza begins to record
dialogue as if she is in the moment and yet she cannot be because
she is the letter writer. The strangeness is that I want to believe
the dialogue, even though Eliza has lost her credibility because I
realize she is reconstructing the scene. How do I write a fiction in
the moment without manipulating the text? For that matter, how
do I record true happenings without interpretation? I want it to
be as honest as I can. Do you think we can really be true in our
living? Sometimes I think it's too hurtful to be honest so we all
just tiptoe around. There is not one truth.

all your world
reflections on water
so many stories
so many years
sliding through me
down, deep down
like draining sand
through the hourglass
of my body
framed by emptiness
nothing to hold
scattered through sky

June 12

Three people have called me Angela this week. What would you call me if you didn't know my name? Does my naming make me? How does our naming frame everything else?

A parent from my old school wants to drop off a gift for me at the new school. He says it's a birthday present but it's not my birthday and I told him so. Curious. I'll keep you in the dark for as long as I can! Do you think the parent/teacher relationship changes significantly when the child is no longer in between? Over the years I've become friends with some of the parents of children in my classes. I notice that when the parents are friends with me the child is "beside" us, not between us. I think this image is important in deconstructing barriers between parents and teachers. The merging of roles also positively affects the child. Dissolving barriers is really about letting go of power and repositioning responsibility between parent and teacher. In our case, you and me, I think my learning has increased because of the blurring of roles. Do you have to consciously distance yourself from students so you have time for yourself? Have you fallen in love with students before?

the last time
you painted me
with sable lips
tight back then
shivers rippled through

June 13

PAPAYA SUNSETS
time lingers free
for places unbound
into the dawn
fresh misty mornings
or papaya sunsets
for silver moons

to uncover all

savour lush mangoes
push away vines
into the deep
sky of love
always with you
time lingers free

you feel me
I know, sense
I want you
rest sweet wine
strawberry sparkling dreams
refresh and smooth
furrows you carry
alone not long
soon we'll awake
wrapped in darkness
know the heart
joined as one

June 18

This is the charcoal on canvas I told you about. We've always talked about getting the research out to the public. Maybe this is the way. I wonder if it's a good thing to have explanations. Can the art really speak for itself? Maybe it's controlling to want to have my interpretation in the viewer's mind. This would be like me preventing the children in my class from exploring and discovering, always directing paths of learning. On the other hand, what if the audience needs guidance? This is so much like thinking about how to guide a child's learning through discovery and experience.

When Savannah and Jade came home from school, they were excited about the drawing. Savannah asked why the woman was naked on the shadow. She was asking what the art meant. Yes, art should have meaning. The art should evoke. But what if the meaning is too sophisticated to evoke? What if the eyes seeing the image are too young or immature to understand? What if the eyes are not ready to receive what is evoked or the intended message? Is the loss of interpretation the fault of the artist in lack of clarity, choice of medium, or skill of evocation? Or is it the interpreter's lack? Will I reach more viewers through narrative text? Is that our common language? Will writing an epilogue for my dissertation be like defending suspect art? Am I being too controlling—too much of a directive teacher?

The piece is called "Open View." Our shadows change shape continuously according to who is viewing, the angle of view, and the direction of light. In order for us to grow in understanding ourselves, we must seek feedback from others as well as look at ourselves reflexively. When we step out to look at ourselves, the visible self (tree) is distorted, even to us, by intermittent visibility.

Open View, 2004, charcoal on canvas. 36" x 48"

We can try to look at ourselves with open, naked lenses, but we will not see the tree fully because we are sitting in the tree's shadow, always ingrained in our own history and culture—aspects of ourselves that powerfully shape our thinking. Even the shadow our (removed) body casts outside of the tree is distorted.

....

June 20

So you think that all I do is sit around writing to you? Ha! You do have a big head! Here's a day in the life of Jules:

OPEN YOUR EYES
open my eyes
write to you
rejoice in lather
adorn my body
present my skin
drive to work
feel the music

prepare my class
care for children
invite their learning
challenge their dreams
meet their parents
rest their hearts

smile and dance
waltz through halls
feel such glow
drive through traffic
meetings and class
open my mind
smile to invite
take with pleasure
digest with urgency
drive home full
eat some food
shower world off
cuddle and kiss
full grown children
work the keyboard
emails and work
write to you
return to bed
skin calling dark
feel his hands
touch me deep
imagine your hands
touching my light
spent and subsumed
close my eyes

a brief refrain
feel your call
pulling me out
to start again

There! So no, I don't sit around waiting for your emails. What's your name anyway?

There you go again about me trying just to savour the moment and not to think so much about the future. I *am* in the moment! What are you talking about? Here's the irony: If I savour the moment, enjoy it as it is, will it be fleeting? Or do I catch the moment, articulate it, write it down, and "reflex" it? The latter could mean that I'm not savouring it as it is but only savouring the relived moment. See, I am thinking too much. This is like video-taping a child's performance. The act of taping detracts from enjoying the moment, all for the purpose of enjoying that moment again! This head work is like climbing mountains. I'm so exhausted at the end of the day! Why is depth of thought down, not up?

By the way, do you think that things got out of hand because we touched? Maybe touch is like articulating, writing text, capturing a moment in a different way. As I write the story, the story becomes me, I make truth. In touch, maybe I make the story real, subsumed by the unconscious creating a truth that I become trapped into believing. I can't see how I could have touched you if I was repelled. If I was unwilling to touch and did touch, isn't that even more a sign of care? Oh, my brain is going crazy! But you must know, when my class is driving me bananas, I consciously go and touch the children lovingly on their shoulders. I think it makes me feel different about them.

You said you didn't get part of one of the last poems. The best ones are the ones we think we understand or the ones we can read understanding into. What does that say about poetry? We're linking experiences and connecting the intersections of life, ideas and perspectives. But what if there are no experiences there to begin with—sort of like kindergarten children without readiness skills? I wonder about this. I think we can teach children to *see*, appreciate, and enjoy even when they don't have the background knowledge or readiness to see. If we can teach children how to *see* through appreciation and story, could we conceivably teach them how to feel? Can we teach how to love? I've read lots of writers talk about choosing happiness. If it's really a choice, to choose happiness, that is, then loving is a choice too. What does that mean to us? Can I choose not to love you at will?

a spark flares
a moment to catch
an inquisitive moth
seeks to understand

....

June 26

Letters for Chris—Layer Two: Foster Skills of Relationality

Here's some more writing you can reformat and rearrange and send to Chris:

Ardra Cole and J. Gary Knowles define arts-informed life history inquiry as "research that seeks to understand the complex relationships between individuals' lives and the contexts within which their lives are shaped and expressed. . . . Research is guided by principles that place self, relationship, and artfulness central in the research process" (2001b, pp. 214-215). When we write to each other, we are using autobiography and life history as the *text* for reflection and analysis. In this way, relationality becomes both a private and public endeavour. We must foster our skills of relationality in ourselves (our living with our teaching), between our lives and our students, and within our students as well.

We need to practise developing awareness of feelings, thoughts and physical responses in order to deepen levels of personal growth. (Chödrön, 1991; Kabat-Zinn, 1994; Kozik-Rosabal, 2001; Springgay, Irwin, & Wilson Kind, 2005). We must "live a life of awareness, a life that permits openness around us, a life that permits openness to the complexity around us, a life that intentionally sets out to perceive things differently" (Irwin, 2004, p. 33). Rita Irwin and the work of others describe this way of being immersed in knowledge creation and understanding through processes of committed living inquiry as a/r/t/ography. Carson and Sumara describe their notions of living practice as action research:

> The knowledge that is produced through action research is always knowledge about one's self and one's relations to particular communities. In this sense, action research practices are deeply hermeneutic and postmodern practices, for not only do they acknowledge the importance of self and collective interpretation, but they deeply understand that these interpretations are always in a state of becoming and can never be fixed into predetermined and static categories. (1997, p. 33)

If we believe that learning takes place when students are able to connect the perceived with something they know and hence process the new information to new constructions of understanding, then it is very important that we cultivate the aspect of bridging the unrelated. Consider Ted Aoki's rumination:

> For myself, these voices do not blend in a closure; rather, they celebrate openness to openness—there is distinct resistance on their part to be brought to a closure. I liken these five voices not to a symphonic harmony of oneness, but, as in certain Bach fugues, to a polyphony of five lines in a tensionality of contrapuntal interplay, a tensionality of differences. (Berman, Hultgren, Lee, Rivkin & Roderick, 1991, p. xiii)

Here's an example of how I see relationality working in my life. This example further ties in with Ted Aoki's words. Last week I was involved in a performance at a motivational convention. We were playing an African drumming arrangement called *Mystery of Love* written by ManDido Morris. There were 200 people participating. The center group of people played a particular drum rhythm, the outer two groups played another pattern, and the four of us on stage each played a different pattern. So there were six patterns going on concurrently in multiple time signatures. Now, if you imagine the music as traveling on a light path, then different time signatures would cross each other like intersecting lines. After a while of playing, I could pick up the other rhythms and the beats were truly mesmerizing, almost hypnotic. The polyphony of six time signatures created a unique tensionality within oneness. Important here was my responsibility to maintain and hold my unique beat pattern. Through my performance, my contribution of juxtaposition, the *Mystery of Love* synergistically became more than six intersecting rhythms.

I consciously understood for the first time about creating synthetic ways of getting to the *pure mood*. I found some fascinating ideas in Otto Bollnow's work. He says "ceremonies and celebrations are not just minor matters; rather, they prove the Heideggerian thesis that the primary unlocking of the world is found fundamentally only by way of pure moods" (1989a, p. 64). When in this place, one can wander with ease, leaving the heavy world behind. This place allows for unlimited learning and revelation. Bollnow writes: "a typical feature of festive celebration is extravagance and boisterousness. People feel themselves freed from and lifted above the limiting structures of everyday life" (p. 72). Well, the drumming experience was certainly a celebratory space. Translated to the classroom setting, this work encourages us as teachers to welcome diversity and tensionality in learning and to create for our students a place where they are released from the limits of daily life and feel free to explore. Bollnow explains:

> If wandering can make claim to great . . . pedagogical significance, then it is given this meaning through deep, far-reaching changes and rejuvenations of consciousness which the person experiences in wandering and which are similar in some ways to the experiences of festive celebrations. (p. 74)

What Bollnow means here is that we must create environments of eros and safety for our students. In that context, students can be engaged in wandering and even wondering. Time for conceptual and artful wandering is minimal in many classrooms because the day is filled with knowledge transference. Here's another link—often when I read academic papers, the text is so tightly constructed as "truth" that there is little space for wandering. If there is no connection between the cognitively known and the new information, little knowledge will be retained. This is the same situation in the classroom. Teaching must consider foundational understandings. Our lessons must have some openings and ambiguity to allow for contemplative and interactive sojourning.

Giving the learner authority in assembling learning that makes sense will honour individuality, diversity, and difference in the educational setting.

In the pure mood, the mind feels clear. It is a sense of openness where the mind can freely make connections. The wonderful revelation is that for children who haven't experienced the Heideggerian *pure mood,* this space can be created. I also now realize I have done this before—made something to force creative cognition response. I'll show you my painting on "Wholeness" in the next letter. We must create ways for students to reach and recognize their pure moods to feel the desire, joys, moments of surprise, and revelations of learning so they can do it on their own. There is no way to separate learning from living. We need to foster this understanding in children. We can teach how to think about learning through examples of our own living. We can help children reconnect school with home and mind with body. Developing these understandings will transform conceptions of what life-long learning is.

....

June 29

Next time, make up an excuse. Don't tell me that you delete me as soon as you've read me.

take me high
make me laugh
take me low
make me cry

July 2

Simone de Beauvoir's (1908-1986) book, *The Second Sex* (1949/1953) is about how women are always defined as the other and not male. This notion puts women in subservient positions and always under authority. I've been thinking a lot about the aspect of authority in learning situations. I don't agree with Beauvoir completely. I like her other ideas on ambiguity though. I try to live this way. She says that people are ethically free only if they assume ambiguity. I often feel so trapped in the given conditions of the world and she says that instead of fleeing, I need to assume. This is a radical idea—to not choose an alternate, but to take on all the alternates. This idea even transfers to us. When I feel overcome by the external weight of the world and how my life seems set, I ought to embrace you, keep you, assume you, while still holding my family. It's a very liberating notion actually. See *The Ethics of Ambiguity* (1949/1972) if you're interested.

Do you know what's interesting? Simone de Beauvoir's notion isn't completely foreign now that I think of it. There are some connections here to Daignault's (1983, 1992a,) view of curriculum. Daignault argues that we must not privilege power between ideologies and doctrines but rather reside in the in-between space. Imagine this metaphor I just thought of: what if the two sides of a coin are the dichotomies in question? Dwelling in the in-between is actually being the coin itself, becoming the "inside" of both, assuming head and tail, constructing wholeness—a fascinating idea!

I'm so excited about my learning! I'm in a place, a space band where I feel completely open. I really think this is why I can stretch my body in ways I never have been able to before (in dance class too)! I feel electric, vibrating, and freely seeking resonation with others in rhythm! Is this feeling *being in* love? I want to eat my books and you! Tell me what you wish for. I wish you were near.

you're a poet
a figment dream
come so real
write me real
lover of mine
dangle me forever

....

July 3

Remember I said that the hip hop moves have such a different vocabulary than what I'm used to in Chinese dancing? We learned 3 sets of 8 counts last week. I had to think and count each one and they didn't roll through my body. I knew that this week they would be "in" me and they were! We practised to slower beats first, then tried it with a really fast beat. Even with a fast beat, I could dance without thinking (just the first 3 sets of 8)!

I felt high! I love the beat and letting go. The moves were part of me and I could add some of myself to the moves. Why? Why does it take a week for the moves to go from my head to my toes? I didn't practice through the week. I didn't even remember the routine until we reviewed it. Why? Did I pour a foundation last week? I struggled with the sequence last week. The new steps always feel awkward and headish. How much time does my head need to filter the moves into my body?

This reminds me of a song I play on the piano. I can play that song off by heart, but when I start to think, it doesn't come out. I relax, open my mind to the message I'm sending and my fingers find the right notes. To open the mind is to think of nothing, a blankness, not even a filled white space, but a clearness. What is this openness, the void that is so important to all we do? Do our bodies have memory without head? If the head is not guiding, what is directing our body actions? How do I dance in the second week knowing all the moves in my body that my head had to think through the week before? What about the body reactions I have with you? What is directing that? Does my body remember you?

....

July 4

I will say it back to you. I too, am in love with who you are and who you will be and who you were. Thank you for pushing me. The paper is much better now. I had the best sleep possible. I am refreshed now. I had a bubble bath in the dark with the girls last night. I feel so awake. I've always been observant but it's different now. Things seem surreal almost, as if colour is more vibrant or the world is in slow motion but clear.

you fluster me
make me silly
giddy with pleasure
giddy with ideas
giddy with possibilities
giddy with becoming

How will I write as author when all I am is you?

CRAZY FOOL
you drive me crazy, make my head spin
make my thoughts fly, steaming turmoil

spread me thin, pull me in, lift me up, crush me in pieces
wet me dripping, get lost! want you, ten thousand times
spread me with words, lick me delicious, leave me sticky
uncomfortably tight, need to be washed, wash me over
round and round, tumbling in my head
have well being – with you, without you
no insecurity, no need for clarity
teach me who you are, who i am
where are we going?
tell me another story
love me to knowing

………......…………………………………………………………

July 9

DANCE WITH ME
take my hand
hold me tight
walk with me
out to the
lonely scratched parquet
where history watched
others make love

together we'll sway
just one rhythm
and gently infuse
like bakers folding
sunny golden yolks
stiff white peaks
keeping the air

harmony plays on

the ball reflects
brilliant kaleidoscopic changes
joyful shimmering sadness
poignant glittering greatness
convoluted ironic paradoxes
of impossible possibilities

weaving our dreams
making butterflies rise
and silently soar
through and between
to our precious
one and only
never ending song

of interweaving words

....

July 11

I only write
what comes out
words spill over
echoing joy songs
refrains of mine
pure and now
take to hold
as you wish

I am strong
unknown until today
I realize this
known before asked

power beyond imagination
power to change
existing set paradigms
people's responses tell
loud and clear
no boundaries hold
walking on water

finding my place
painting my life
finding my work
framing my life
reinventing myself through
text through you

Is the excitement of learning the not knowing?

6
South
Summer Roar

Men call me chaste; they do not know the hypocrite I am.
They consider purity of the flesh a virtue, though virtue belongs
not to the body but to the soul. I can win praise in the eyes of
men but deserve none before God, who searches our hearts and
loins and sees in our darkness.

Betty Radice (Trans., 1974),
The Letters of Abelard and Heloise, p. 133

July 13

I'm fighting the insecurities today. Tell me what great thing I have to do with my life. I feel the pressure. It's all around me, closing in and I don't know what I'm supposed to carry out. I've heard you so clearly: to be true to myself, to stand for the principles I believe in, to strive to be congruent in what I do. I can't do this. What use is the power and the glow? How can I share the glow if I don't know what it's for? How much can I sacrifice for learning? Will I put my own children on the stone slab, baby lambs for my learning? Jade came into the office today. She says I never do anything for her. She says I don't love her. What can I do that will redeem my sacrifice?

deepest 3 words
need you so
all I do
all I am
into your arms
escape from here

……………………............………………………………………………

July 15

You say there are always consequences. Do you think there will be consequences for my iteration, for my openness, for wanting to know?

I notice your voice in the text is different as time passes. You have reinvented yourself as well. Do you really believe this stuff about writing oneself real? Do we become what we write, create ourselves? If this is true, then we very well could have written ourselves into love when we feel nothing physically. We might not even have anything to say to one another in person. Isn't that a thought! I vaguely remember thinking before that having nothing to say was a good thing—a fully open relationship.

What if my feelings for you continue to grow and I only want to be with you? I'm not going to throw my family away, so how do we limit love? Can we? Do you think we can love each other as long as we have no physical contact? Does that make our relationship ok? Is it ok to be so completely in love with someone else as long as there's no skin touching? Somehow this doesn't seem right either.

July 18

Quit ranting! My tirade is perfectly sound and that's scaring me and you too! We both are hopeless romantics. We'll read love into whatever text we read. We're writing love and writing ourselves real. Maybe I'm confused about us. I don't feel stable, trying to think, taking things too seriously as you say, feeling antagonistic to you, why? Will I change how I feel by writing a dumb love poem? See how I'm starting to feel like a pawn of my own writing? My writing is subverting my conceptions. I don't want to be in control. I have no stability. Why do you make me feel that I can just say the word and you can contain/extend what you feel for me? Maybe I'm drawn to extremes. I want you to want me in a way you can't just turn on and off.

I'm uncomfortable with what you said, that you want the best good for me, even if that denies your own desires. That sounds like something a teacher would say. How can you have so much control? So falling in love is controlled? Is learning controlled that way too?

Ok, focus. Maybe I should only talk to you about research. Keep things simple. So for the dissertation I will write a fictional memoir of sorts. I'll use some of our conversations and merge other conversations in. What do you think of that? I'll write about my process, my thoughts raw, real, and embellished. I could demonstrate the multi-layered dimensions of researcher presence by writing about the process within the process and yet also with an outside perspective. After my dissertation letters are published and the book hits the best sellers' list, we'll write the uncut version together for my postdoc with all your steamy letters interspersed with mine and we'll be catapulted to fame and fortune! You'll never have to worry about retirement again and you can fly out to talk to me on a whim, wherever I'll be, about some little inconsequential issue. We'll still both be with our respective partners and the mystery of us will cause such a sensation that our books will keep selling! Everyone will ask if we're having an affair and we'll just say we love each other and that will ambiguously explain it all! Like that? I'll have a house on the water and when I look out, I'll feel you no matter where you are. Is that love—when you don't need to physically be touching? Your Spanish villa will be buzzing with people doing all sorts of house work for you so that when I visit, we'll just stay in bed cuddling in "wholesome" ways (unless you feel up to other things) and writing our dreams real. Right, I haven't yet decided where Clare will be while all this is happening, nor my family! We'll write words and words, spilling from our love and the world will become a better place. How's that? Do you like how I can have a conversation all by myself?

I'll only let you live my dream if you tell the truth, quit skirting around (or is that the feminine side of you?).

What are you saying? How can I let events unfold as they will if sometime down the road our relationship unravels my marriage? I suppose we can't control life that much. I'm trying to understand how we're both teachers and we deal with control in such opposite ways.

Are you resting and eating well? I had lotus roots at dinner tonight. I love lotus roots! They look like fat yams. I boil them and slice them cross-wise like a cucumber. They are so, so beautiful to look at. They have some kind of stringy silk that holds onto the knife when I'm cutting. The cross-sections have patterned holes in them and they're gorgeous to look at. I also like the turnipy crunchy texture. Try some. I think they are my favourite thing to eat!

The poems you're writing are heart stopping. I feel twisted. I don't know how to respond. Thank you.

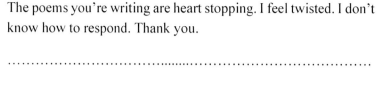

July 19

I must think about where my family fits into my life. I'm so busy with writing and coursework. Life feels so strangely surreal these days. I just ate kiwis and peaches—so succulent and bursting with secrets to tell my mouth. Feel crazy writing this.

Here's my version: in my other life with you I'm with you day and night and you don't find me too tiresome. I can concentrate on my work and am not distracted by our love. We work together separately and together in the same room all day and when I'm tired, I go to sleep and in the morning, I wake up with you next to me and all my work is laid out and sparkling with new freshness. Oh, is this like the Grimm Brothers' stories of the *Shoemaker's Elves* and *Rumplestiltskin* (Ashliman, 2005)? Yes, I'm in my fairytale land again! We eat all the healthy things that taste so natural and good and then we go hiking in beautiful places where there is no time. We can smell the land and we can sweat together and feel no hesitation to laugh aloud, hold hands or entwine our glistening bodies on the soft lush grass and dream of stories from the clouds. Somehow I can turn on beautiful Tibetan music while we're on the hillside and we can run like Julie Andrews in *The Sound of Music* (Wise, 1965) light and carefree across the openness. You sit with your knees up to your chest on a hill and watch me with loving eyes as I smile at you, dancing a Tibetan dance in full costume, the extra long material sleeves like swirling ribbons, free, fluid and lucid, perfect spirals in the outdoor air, in a dance I know that comes from the heart. The wind is on my cheeks. I feel it in my hair but it does not affect the circles of ribbon sleeves in the air. After, you tenderly disrobe me of the many, many layers of the Tibetan costume and hold me against you and I'm not cold, only free. This is my other life.

……………….......……………………………………………….

July 20

You're right. I shouldn't say that the sensual stuff we write is filth. That's my history coming out. I am always surprised that when I'm talking about learning in the head I'm really talking about learning through the body. Actually I was talking about your foul mouth, not the poems you write that make me uncomfortable because they are so direct, raw, unmasked, and honest.

Neilsen (1998) says we should talk about the unsaid instead of methodizing it all, like not showing the kitchen, only presenting the meal. I completely agree. This is why the public gets so disappointed in teachers. They always only see the meal. Neilsen says "we have too long hidden behind the mask of researcher and the products we market. Not enough has been written about our motives, our location, our vested personal and political interests" (p. 10). Neilsen suggests a "Levinasian" notion implying that the researcher aiming to change the world in small ways has a responsibility to present an authentic presence (see Levinas, 1991).

You ask me about my purpose and audience, my reason for choosing to write an epistolary novel. What is my focus and how will I advance knowledge in a particular area? Good questions. My letters will be about the relational learning process, articulating the spaces between being an artist, researcher, and teacher, raising the connections between the processes of making art and the processes of developing artful qualitative inquiry, and focusing on the mundane raised to story level so others can enter the conversation. My greater purpose of course is to transgress the communication barriers between writers and readers, between theory and practice, between researcher and teacher and public; and highlight the implications of how framing constrains us in ways we do not acknowledge. I want my audience to be teachers, researchers, and the public. I plan to write about why I chose the epistolary genre in the procatalepsis of the book. I already have all that research on Samuel Richardson's 1740 epistolary novel.

……............………..………………………………….…………

July 21

Good morning dearest Professor. The letters are just a vehicle to discuss the system models in a more heartfelt way. The organizational models which frame and delimit, and the stories of being a teacher are important to share. Through the letters, the audience will get a glimpse at how inextricably influential place, teaching philosophies, identity, and the personal lives of teachers, structure and construct pedagogy. I imagine that most parents think that their child is being taught by a human blank slate which has been filled with the "teacher norm." Sad to admit, but I wonder if that's the kind of teacher I want for my own children? I don't want a teacher with weaknesses. I would prefer a "run of the mill" average, level-headed teacher guiding my children over an opinionated, passionate teacher who has inadequacies and "holes." What's wrong with me? I'm so constrained by the "norm." You know, this pervasively affects our approaches to teacher education programs.

No matter what the system is, or what the curriculum is, the teacher's make-up will influence learning. Wright, Horn, and Sanders (1997) concluded from their research involving 60 000 students that the most important factor affecting student learning is the teacher. Classroom management also influences student achievement and R. Marzano, J. Marzano, and Pickering (2003) contend that the teacher-student relationship supersedes all other factors regarding successful classroom management.

The way the teacher understands herself and develops her style will affect the classroom heart and the key to learning is not through the head, but through the eyes/body to the heart. So if I'm looking for a good teacher for my children, I should be searching for someone who is good at making relational connections.

And you're right. If I'm conceptualizing the work for multiple audiences I need to consider a form that works for those audiences. Finding and articulating the spaces between dichotomies will integrate the separate to form a new canvas, perhaps a map of sorts. Hopefully, with a new map, we can start to make some changes. We can't make the changes without understanding our location and without roads out.

still dark here
blue skies rise
unraveling the east

....

July 22

I saw the movie *Spiderman II* (Raimi, 2005) at the Ridge. Spiderman struggles deeply to choose the right thing, sacrificing the one he loves—painful to watch. The children thought it was strange that I was crying at a movie like *Spiderman.* Do people get divorced because the real doesn't measure up to the archetype? What if the archetype is flawed in its creation? (What we think is ideal is not really ideal. The ideal in the heart is the real day to day and the ideal in the head is what we imagine as archetypically created from cultural and social constructions.) I'm starting to strain my brain here.

After school, a colleague came to visit as I was cleaning up my classroom. He knows I'm writing an epistolary novel. He's a film buff. He can give me the title of a movie if I provide a character's name or setting. He came to remind me that in fairytales, in order to break the spell of the heroine in love with her archetype, she must kiss or see the archetype in a personal context. I just smiled but my head was spinning. Am I writing our story along a preconceived plot line? We haven't kissed and I haven't seen you in your living context. Do you see how eerie this is? I didn't even know I was writing a fairytale on a "well-trodden path." Do you think we can ever be truly outside of the box?

....

July 23

YOU I FEEL
silky wetness cries
lost unseeing eyes
your lips, breath
upon my heat
raising me up
my body hears
only one call

I need to reframe us so I can cope with the way I miss you and want you now. Dear Red, be strong because I cannot be. Misread me. Shut me out. Turn your back so I can live.

....

July 23

Yes, I know this will all work out with time. I need to live in smooth, gentle, fluid ways and things will find their way. Is this what living poetically means? Maybe this lyrical living comes with age. Or more likely, it's more about groundedness. Kahlil Gibran advises, "The soul walks not upon a line, neither does it grow like a reed. The soul unfolds itself, like a lotus of countless petals" (1962, p. 55). I like this part about the unfolding lotus petals. It's so soft and gentle—a fluid poetic way of living. I read this, understand this, but don't know how to feel it in my living. Maybe I was already telling myself these words when I made the mosaic *Georgia's Diaspora*.

So you think we should keep the two intimacies apart? How can we separate heart and head when my dissertation is about joining the two? You know I live my research! I know you're overwhelmed with work. Then again, do you know any academics who are balanced and relaxed? Is that part of my need to be with you—to heal you? I feel like I'm the only one who can and I'm so far away. I feel as though I have the power to take care of things for you, not that I even know what needs to be taken care of. I don't understand it, but I feel that if I were with you, I could make your life easier. Why are you doing so much on your sabbatical? Too bad all those deadlines are at the same time. I want to do everything for you. Maybe my problem is my way of thinking. I feel so responsible even for my committee members here, imagining that I can do something that would prevent them from getting sick. So many faculty I work with here are ill. I know it's from working too hard.

You worry about me losing my way with my family and you've made a strong stand on what you're going to do. It's manipulative, don't you think? I've asked you to help me frame our relationship in a way I understand. You've vowed "with solemnity and reverence and hope" (oh, you melt me) to take the hard line and restrain yourself. Now I'll struggle with wondering if you love me or if you're being altruistic. Can you really control desire, passion, and love to that extent? In class, can you control how much you feel for and from your students? Do you like all your students? What happens when we don't like our students? No one talks about this. Teachers are just expected to like everyone.

I thought that you didn't want to tell me I was going too far with my feelings for you because you wanted to maintain our working relationship. I see the conundrum here. If you told me my advances were unwanted, then you would injure our working relationship. How would you deal with this if you really did not feel anything for a student infatuated with you? Would you keep telling the student about your wonderful partner and how much you are in love? Does that deter another's love for you? Have you ever thought that you may be loved because the way you love your partner is attractive, attracting, and desirous to others? You know, I think that's true.

....

July 24

Tibetan costumes are wonderfully colourful and the dancing is so very ethereal. I wish I could dance for you. Through dance, the unseen is translated into movement. This reiterates Lorri Neilsen's suggestion that "making the invisible processes visible is an act of responsible scholarship" (1998, p. 10). I agree. I've said this before, we really should talk more about our learning journeys and articulate the body's knowing in alternate ways. This iteration will help us not only personally, but will also lay pathways as stepping stones for others. Neilsen proposes that "inquiry is praxis that cannot be boxed up and delivered; it is a story with no ending" (p. 8). She's giving us advice. Our relationship is a story. Our learning together is dialectic praxis. There is always motion, construction, and reconfiguration. This is so important for the classroom teacher—the unendedness and messiness of dialectic knowledge construction is an idea we must embrace, as difficult as it is. I want to prove that "the flesh of story embraces, disturbs, and connects more strongly than disembodied neutralized text" (p. 10).

fly to the sky
freedom in you
all will unfold

....

July 25

Ok, I will do my work and you're going to be a part of it. Don't make me fight you. I want you to love me without thinking about what's best for me. You said you'll take the stand, be altruistic, take the heat. I see your heart and understand your wisdom without words but it doesn't feel right. I know our intellectual intimacy will unfold as it may with time and my own overpowering need to see and be with you could just be another physiological thing we don't understand. I feel frustrated that I need you so. I know you'll be strong about this. You keep saying you don't want to be instrumental in ruining my family. What is the hard line you're going to take? It's going to hurt me isn't it?

July 26

Thanks for your long letter. I know that you love me. I also feel that connection that can't be explained. You don't believe the power of words? We're romantics. We are writing love everyday, several times a day. How can we not fall into love? You asked once why you didn't meet me a long time ago. Sometimes I wish we had. We could have had something very special, but we wouldn't be who we are today. I don't want to live with "if only's" or regrets. We still have amazing lives, even apart.

three words describe
fragments of lives
lived without remorse

Yes, thank you Red. Never remorse. "He closed his eyes, and one by one, plucked the petals off that delicate compass rose, the rose round which navigators glide and sailors whisper. Round which even dolphins hold their breath. West, North, East, the cardinal petals fell" (Hodgson, 2001, p. 6). You and I are together, not held apart by geography; but entwined in the magical love of words.

I can hear you thinking about me

out of my mind
bathe in my heart

You ask why I'm using visuals in rendering my research. When a picture is seen, the whole is seen. We catch a flavour, a theme, a feeling and a tone. When we read a book, we can only enter sequentially, physically opening the book starting from the beginning, reading from the top left, following the order of language. A visual rendering has air, rumination. The audience connects the image with whatever is personal and goes from there. The audience is looking for patterns or points of recognition which stir something in them. Isn't this the way you have taught me to research? You want me to write memories and stories as data, then look for patterns. The art that speaks evokes conscious or unconscious recognition of patterns or experiences. I think the key to enabling art to become provocative is to provide a bigger "tapestry map" which allows the viewer to situate the single thread they are seeing. The audience may need scaffolding. In books, the scaffolding support comes from previous knowledge. Perhaps with the arts we need to establish some common but open language which describes cross connections between the arts and research. Many cannot understand the jargon and language of other discourses so it makes sense that many might not be able to appreciate dance or art as a form of research rendering. The languages for speaking, describing, and theorizing the arts in research must be developed so that this way of knowing can be shared with larger audiences. Without explication, artful research will remain insular, cycling in repeating patterns, in the sometimes erroneous trappings intrinsic to internal interbreeding.

Art can cross discourses because of ambiguity. Visuals inherently provide a framework for discussion. I do not expect the same answers to questions from all. I just want to provide a big picture vision, meaning that the bigger picture is a woven tapestry made of many threads. One single perspective is but one thread. When art is viewed, the single thread seen is always supported by other visible threads. For instance, I really noticed the sky today. The sky was the same colour for thousands of meters all around. So why did I think it was so beautiful? How is a monotone beautiful? Is it because it means so much, so many things to me? The sky conjures memories of languid beaches with family, of frolicking giggles of the girls, of an old home we used to have, of recess days as a child, of countless memories, all from one plain sky. Is this art?

Unlike the word, which is more specific, art travels across borders and cannot be bound, the image opens a universal language; it is a sign with multiple signifiers. When we see pictures, we cannot capture the explicit line, each detail. We can see and make close observations; we may even imitate, but our creations will not be exactly the same, the way we can copy words from texts. This inability to recreate an original in an original sense is what brings newness in artful practice and research.

I liked our phone conversation. I think it's the cadence in your voice, or maybe the timbre. You move my body in ways I cannot explain.

....

July 27

You guide my
body to lands
unknown and spaces
dark and unrevealed

hear your voice
resonate in pulse
sunset to sunrise
sunrise to sunset
east to west
through each breath
breathe in me

come, go with me

Help me find place with you. Why are you so far and why are we so trapped in stories already written?

July 27

thinking of you
across the miles
to reach home
the moon stands
tall, unfolding slowly
stretching to see
the limitless bounds

I need to explore other possibilities for life's narrative plotlines. I think many of us have been caught up into living a life that is someone else's life, the American dream—the yellow brick road paved by others that promise keys to our happiness. We are disheartened when we get there because the story was someone else's story, not ours. I am on that road too, feeling the entrapment of it, and not just intellectually.

You're right, I need to listen to my voice, my voice that holds my spirit, my energy, all that is me, and must not feel locked into being one person, on one storyline. Does that mean my love for Luke isn't real and I'm still trying to live the ideal family story? The power of words and stories of cultural expectations are just so overwhelming!

....

July 28

Thank you so much for the Lacan books on love and desire. I can't wait to open them completely! What a lovely surprise!

This morning, when I was drying my hair, I had a vision of you giving me a gift in a long flat box. (Do you think I have supernatural powers?) It was a very clear image of us in another time period, perhaps a century ago. It was deeper and longer than a déjà vu. I felt my surroundings. I saw the diffusion of light in that time period. It wasn't the clear light that comes through the skylights of my bathroom. This was perhaps the first time I've thought that we've been together before in another time and you know me, it's so unlike me to believe in that kind of stuff. When I lifted the box lid, it was a beautiful, ornate dress—long, cream, the kind women used to wear with corsets to fancy occasions. I held it against me in glee; your blue eyes were twinkling. I went behind a screen and put it on. It fit perfectly—the way I fit you. You made me beautiful. Just when I put the hairdryer down, the doorbell rang. I went downstairs and the mail carrier gave me the Lacan package from you.

The books mean so much as well as the images you give me. Thank you.

3 words can't
suggest the way
my body hears
……………………….......…………………………………………………

July 28

I thought about you in my bath last night. I fell asleep again in the water. I dreamed that I was in you, you were the water. I want the warmth again. The cold world is all around. I try to submerge every part of me. Sleep in you.

You're right; I am playing with you when I pretend I understand how we are connected, what my location is to you.

overt to flirt
tease to reveal
don't know much
of anything real

....

July 29

Thanks for the committee conference call today. You know I express to learn and type to synthesize. Right now, my dilemma is about getting trapped in one thread of interpretation that isn't Jared's intention at all. How can I record verbal conversations in a voice that leaves open all the other roads so that when I come back, I can see the other paths? Derrida (1967) calls these changes in the rereading *différance*. I can expect to reread with a slightly different understanding each time I revisit the words but can I revisit and read a new meaning if I've already written a path of interpretation? In my interpretation, I may have already gone off the main track! What if I am completely far from the main road (whatever that was) in the first place? I understand this is a problem with researchers recording meanings of events (or what they think are such) rather than what is observed. How can I record meaning in ambiguous ways as you have suggested? Even the observation itself is swayed by outlook. My way is always direct, analytical, goal focused. I want to learn. Explain please.

What do you think of this quote: "Every text one writes is autobiographical: anything else would be plagiarism" (Boal, 2001, xi)? I think it's interesting because myths are so strongly ingrained in our histories that we don't even know what our own stories are. Does it matter if my work is autobiographical or plagiarized from someone else's story? As a teacher, don't I want as many stories as possible in order to connect with as many as I can?

I want my dissertation to teach that we can take this life and live it the way we plan, choose the outlook we want, make ourselves happy, and see the beauty that's all around that so many glaze over. I want my work to make people happy, feel the joy and astonishment in simplicity in all that is laid out and offered to us so widely and freely. The Tin Man from *The Wizard of Oz* says, "Once I had brains, and a heart also; so, having tried them both, I should much rather have a heart . . . for brains do not make one happy" (Baum, 1991, p. 33). I want the heart, the story of love to bind all the other important parts of this narrative. I want to share learning immersed in love and how different words become when they're swimming in watery love. I want the reader to be enticed into the relationship so that the heart opens for pedagogy to enter. I want love to hold the words. I need to teach in love and write in love if my words are to have any transformative power. I need to work in a space that includes both head and heart, space that is not set. How do I frame a space I do not want a boundary for?

How do I balance my writing with both head and heart? Do I try to write intentionally or let the writing unfold as it may? Will the pedagogical get lost in the romance? Will the romance cause the work to be viewed as fluff? How do I change the frameworks of research evaluation to accommodate research of the unfathomable heart when historically the frameworks for valid research have been in the sciences where there has been direct intention to disassociate head and heart? Do I rewrite the way research is viewed through the work as well? My task is daunting!

I must be off now. The girls need a bath.

July 30

You ARE getting old! Ha! I'll just tell you all kinds of things you've promised me! Insert myself into you at will! Ha, ha! My sweet dream! You have my heart and I don't even care! Don't even know why I'm so moved by your words, "I've forgotten, help me." I see now. I am just your rescuer, nothing more. I see and understand us now. I am in your life to get those rusty old parts going so strong that you'll realize how beautiful it is to be loved fully, accepting head, heart, and body by the one who loves you, the one who's close, living with you, sleeping beside you, eating with you, doing all with you, everyday. You will reinvent your story with Clare and my mission will have been accomplished. What of our love?

We have met at the wrong time, in the wrong space for ourselves. We try to grasp at the fragments of love and remembrance that we were once lovers joined in the sky, bonded by the moon and the stars more tightly than the word love and all poetry can express. We cannot be. How can we run away, start afresh, make a new life together? How can I go to sleep and awake with you everyday until your heart is well? How can you fill all the void I am searching for that I don't know I have? Where can we go, how to begin to fill? We cannot. This is not the time or place, no matter how hard we try to find space. We only live through, endure and celebrate the beautiful shards of reflections from our past love that we're able to catch—the prismic light glimmering and yet cutting because we know it cannot be. Oh I miss you already, my sweet, sweet love. How can I express? How can I change this fate? How do I make you well and know you are not for me? My heart weeps for the future that cannot unfold—the understanding that we have no preconceptions of our future because we cannot.

Just hold me hard in every way, make my body remember and go on your way. The three meaningless words I've dared not utter for their casualness must be used now for I have no other means to express—I love you.

yours now and on

Belamcanda chinensis

Earth
Yi (self-locating)

in afternoon poise
sweet fragrant harvest
indian summer hums
as yellow-ocher quavers

ヿ
In Afternoon
Poise

Though nothing can bring back the hour
Of splendor in the grass,
Of glory in the flower
We will grieve not, but rather find
Strength in what remains behind

William Wordsworth, 1806, Verse X

August 1

You asked about my fascination with line drawings of flowers. I've enjoyed doing these for as long as I can remember. I like the simplicity and complexity, and the double names flowers have. I like that "Wood Lily" means the same thing as "Lilium Philadelphicum." I'm not sure why. Maybe it's a bit like knowing that sophisticated theories are plainly observable to everyone or that beauty is about purity and both complexity and simplicity. I've had almost all my students copy line drawings of flowers with pen—even Grade 2 students, and they are always successful. With pen there are no mistakes, no erasures and somehow, the image always materializes. It seems like a very natural art lesson, not in drawing, but in becoming. As the image becomes visible, some sense of self becomes visible for some reason. I find the process therapeutic myself. With ink, I'm in a white space when I'm drawing.

The contradiction between the simplicity and complexity of line drawings can be paralleled in flowers and relationships. There is such a fleeting sense of life—the purity of the blossom, connected with the convoluted complexity of life in time. I'm reminded of Wordsworth—that glory cannot last, only be savoured in that particular moment and remembered. Mitchell Thomashow (1995) writes about the moment being temporary yet infinite and that the deepest significance is the moment's ephemerality. In flowers, there's a continuum which has an invisible peak so I am reminded not to wait for it nor feel regret for missing the peak but to find joy in the moment of growth. I experience and expect the ending with a rich calmness knowing that I will gain a collected concentrate of sorts or a kind of sweet essence from that experience. I cannot hold the experience, only let it run through me like the intoxication of a flower's scent. Forgive me—it's easy to write about this now as I'm filled with the scents of the flowers you sent. Thank you.

Our story, yours and mine, is about capturing the moments and knowing that none of the pleasures can be held the way I always want to hold you—the way I want you to belong to me. This sense of wanting to hold onto or capture is really a consumerist perspective that I'm struggling against. I'm talking about a way that I want to be in the world, a way I want my children and students to see. It's the sense that when something beautiful is discovered, it's to be shared, not horded. Why are we compelled to do in relationships what we do with property—to draw close, hold tight, sign a deed, claim ownership, consummate or brand our territory. Raping the land is such a good phrase to describe the way we prostitute our world, fast-tracking for instant gratification. Red, how do I stop being who I am? How do I change my identity? The drawing in and holding tight prevents the wonder of looking at the land from a distance. Do you know what I mean? I want to watch you, pretend I'm a fly and see you as you live, listen to you speaking to others, hear your thinking unfolding. I miss you. It's so late again. I'm staying up way too late to write but I want to talk about the beautiful word "grace."

Charlene Spretnak (1991) talks about reclaiming wellbeing through grace, through the recovery of meaning. It's more than saying a few words of thanks before a meal. To her, living a life of grace means being attentive to the world in order to be thankful for inconsequential moments. So attention to the insignificant makes the insignificant significant and through that practice, we recover the meanings of living. I really like that. I want children to become conscious of their significance and how their bodies are intricately embedded in a relational web. Spratnek says the natural world evokes celebration and joy. I couldn't agree with her more. Ever notice how much children love the outdoors? Whenever I have classes do these line drawings we also talk about these four questions which are the foundations of reflective environmental practice (Thomashow, 1995, p. 205):

- Where do things come from?
- What do I know about the place where I live?
- How am I connected to the Earth?
- What is my purpose and responsibility as a human being?

These are the same questions teachers can ask of their own practice. I honestly believe this one drawing and discussion lesson changes the atmosphere of my class. There is so much power in the synergy of the simple single line—the same line that forms words and connects us and hold us together and also so simply, yet complexly shows the flowering of the naturality of living through time. I want to teach this letting-go-ness but even I want to hold the fullness of beauty. I want to hold you close.

....

August 4

I've thought a long time and I'm still mad at Jared. I know students aren't supposed to be mad at their teachers. Well he doesn't know I'm mad and he'll never find out. If I had guts I would give this poem to him but I won't. A student should always be respectful. You would probably side with him. I don't care. I'll be mad at you too!

TOUCHING IN THE TRANSACTIONAL DIVIDE:
DEVELOPING WISDOM THROUGH MY BODY

Jared, can we locate ourselves with words or do we need a new language of response? I'm not happy with you today. I don't want to talk to you anymore unless we come to some compromised understanding (Ha, really! And as you're not going to see this poem, I will just end up surrendering to you.) You'll always have the power. Don't bother telling me I'm tragic—I know I am.

> Our depth is the thickness of our body, our all touching itself. Where top and bottom, inside and outside, in front and behind, above and below are not separated, remote, out of touch. Our all intermingled. Without breaks or gaps. (Irigaray, 1985, p. 213)

The self does not exist in isolation. (Griffin, 1995, p. 50)

I write poetry as a way of researching autobiography with attention to postmodern perspectives that promote language as constitutive; the subject as a constructed matrix of identities, always in process; the interconnections between truth and fiction; discourse as personal and political; understanding and knowledge as fragmented and partial; critique and interrogation as committed to resisting closure; and, all texts as intertextually connected. (Leggo, 2004, p. 125)

Conversation, communication and communion[1]
Is that enough? Are words enough?
Can conversation across distance make a difference?
Can sharing without touching connect us?
Can intellectual intimacy hold?
How do we find our location?
In relation?
Where am I? Where I stand?
I cannot find location without my body
I cannot understand without feeling
I cannot move my location without my body
unless my heart is moved
I cannot learn in my head

"Email impinges on our lives"
        I will send no more
"allows communication"
        What good is communication if not received?
"creates connections"
        Superficial or deep?
"is intimate communication"
        Feigned connections, misread transactions

"bridges great distances"
      Punctuating distance
These words I hear you say, in person, in body
I reject: anger me, hurt me
Email belies intimacy
squashes me down
mashed with no exoskeleton to resist
into the dark cracks
between the words
the translation area, the vicinity of interpretation
the space between the words you write and my reception
reader's response
the space between my words and your response
the space between our meanings
the great divide between, a gulf called the transaction
a trade, a barter
where we both partake in creating understanding
Am I negotiating? Am I haggling?
What do you mean with your words?
Why do you use words that pretend you're close?

I am trapped in the valley, the literal meaning of words
Suspended in the chasm of transaction
Not only in the drowning waters of interpretation
between us
between the written text and reader
but also
between my work and the plural public world
where Hannah Arendt suggests we visit the perspectives
of the collective
by listening to others in
efforts to become wiser[2]

Must I not expect or seek response for my writing?
Must I just continue to expose and express
in a silent collaboration
to you, my peers, to society, the contemporary world?
Pouring my soul into the culturally mute cacophonous abyss?
Is this transaction site between text and reader the same
as the dark unarticulated "public sphere"[3]
the ambiguous, uncontrolled constituted makeup of our world[4]
created collaboratively by cultural, social, and emotional views?
Knowledge, wisdom, spectators and actors?
The place where we all pour out our hearts
not letting the colours mix, not responding to each other
silently communing, alone?

Where is the forum for my expression, my writing?
Who notes reception for the collective?
Who are the gatekeepers?
Who knows of the contributions?
Who is listening? Who will read? Who cares and understands?
It is not you. I understand.
You did not "agree to listen and to respond"[5]
Who in mass society has agreed to listen and respond?
What is the language of response?
Paulo Freire in *Pedagogy of the Heart*
says "I cannot be if others are not . . . "[6]
How can I be if others are not?
How can I share without response?
Can I commune silently?
How much can I disrupt?[7]
Can I dare to write you this letter?
You, my advisor, teacher—will I be penalized?[8]
How comfortable will others feel about my disruption?

How far will I go out
into the nameless, alone, kindly challenging?

Can I be

actor	spectator
teacher	researcher
doer	thinker
theorist	practitioner
reader	writer
learner	instructor

Where is my balance? Where is the middle ground?
Where is ground?
What knowledge do I need to make a wise connection?
Can I be both and understand who "I" am?

Will I always create beauty in my attempt to draw?
Drawing conclusions, systemizing
Will I add too much and dull
the purity, muddy the innocence
dilute the integrity
create a mess with forced intention?
Can I see "I" from my place?
Where am I located in the mess, mass, or do "We" become?
Always becoming, changing location
Changing "I", merging into "We" with no responsibility?

Arendt's panoptic view of the public[9] is similar
to views independently arrived at by both
Abelard and Aristotle, famous philosophers
They all saw through the perception
of the particular in the universal
and understood the universal through the particular[10]

In lay terms, we can understand human nature (the universal)
through autobiography (particular stories)
Should we not try to think of society as individuals?
See the particular when we are currently seeing the universal?
Give each body breath, life and response?
Take head understanding of our accepted, unnamed society
and connect the beings within through touch, body and love?

Arendt says, "the public world is the arena
required for action . . . Equal, but distinct,
individuals meet in the public to determine who they are
and who they want to be individually and collectively"[11]
The problem is that the "world between them has lost
its power to gather them together, to relate and to separate them"[12]

Can we respect diverse standpoints?
Touch and respond to each other
without dilution or passive assimilation?
Relate to uniqueness without collapsing divergent views
into a generalized amalgam?[13]
Can we keep an ambiguity[14]
a plurality of independent and unmerged voices and
consciousness?
A genuine polyphony of fully valid voices[15]
of melodies choreographed in harmonies?
Swinging threads of vividly different colours
woven together in an intricate tapestry, freely
a Canadian voice?
Creating the sounds of culture by acknowledging
the body as a being, individual
touching, caring
a new language of response

If wisdom grows out of a conversation between
episteme[16] and phronesis[17], knowing and perceiving
And if phronesis is now better understood as
embodied judgment linking
knowledge, virtue, and reason[18]
then we cannot converse in the transactional divide
without our bodies
utilizing head alone
We cannot teach and learn across the schism
ignoring the public spheres
where no one is touching, only communing
Here is the divide between teacher and researcher
between actor and spectator
between theory and practice
between teacher and student
Intellectual conversation
community and communication are not enough
We have to know our location in relation to each other
We must touch

Great philosophers and critical thinkers of our time
Through their bodies, grew understanding
Abelard and Heloise[19]
Arendt and Heidegger[20]
Kristeva and Sollers
de Beauvoir and Sartre
Great minds, lovers, touching in body
Learning with body
Understanding through love

Teaching and learning
        Love, touch and understanding

Teacher and student relationship
    Love, touch and understanding

Who am I to you, Jared?
Student? Sender of emails?
In public
in the same circle, space, location?
Yesterday
I felt the electricity on your skin, beneath your sweater
innocent luminosity radiating
unseen but exuding, received
heard your quiet enamouration
your sighs of appreciation
of the beguiling work we saw, appreciated
I felt the same
so I made no utterance
for you did it for me, for all

Does this mean I should remain silent?
How can we converse if I do not speak?
How do we communicate, commune
touch, if you do not know how I feel?
Perhaps you do not care, an established, exalted scholar
Where do I pour my heart? Where do we all pour ourselves?
Perhaps in colour, brushed on a canvas
using a vague lexicon, expecting multiple interpretations?
I need the words, the certainty[21]
the language that ensures transmission
Ha!

Touching
More than communing, more than sharing space

more than exposing and leaving
more than communicating
Touching by responding
touching instead of telling
with love, care, in love, insertion
through love, understanding
a new language of response

Shall I continue to write to you?
Or shall I pretend you don't know me in public?
I am just one of many students
Not seek acknowledgement that we have connected?
Need I ask for response?
Is it not enough I have laid out my heart?
Cut it open like a mango
Cut the flesh in a checkerboard pattern
and pushed the skin upwards, inverted the soft tissue
so my gist is apparent, easily consumed
Essence and quiddity revealed
Ripely offered
Ashamed again for revealing

We do not reveal for fear of rejection and lack of response

You do not acknowledge
have no time
hurt me as you "swipe" me aside
as another student
another day at work
think of me as general, not as particular
not touch me in any way, in response
You could have at least said hello

Well get lost yourself,
Julia

P.S. Don't bother writing back. I hate getting apologies I've asked for. That's almost the same as asking "Do you love me?"

………….............…………………………………………………

August 6

Sorry about yesterday's rant. I was bothered. He makes me think about my own students. How do I touch them intellectually? How do I touch them heartfully? How do I acknowledge my care for them in a way that is not suspect? No, this has nothing to do with you. I'm drained today. I feel really down. I can taste the sadness in my sinuses (can't explain). I've been thinking about how I can distinguish the particular without judgment? How do I assess and evaluate without ordering and sequencing and giving singularity in my class?

At my drumming lesson the instructor told me to lift the drum up off the ground to let the sound flow out with the air. I remember too that when she was teaching me how to play the bell, she told me to hold the stick more loosely. I hear her telling me to let my life breathe, relax, let go of control, and let air around my experiences, not just my words. I feel better after writing to you. Thank you.

a crisp red apple's wetness
a mango slice melting on my tongue
a lychee's softness squeezing down
ice popsicle on my lips
missing you so much

Notes

---

[1] "In all my writing I am seeking, not so much communication, but communion" (Leggo, 2005b, p. 123).

[2] Coulter & Wiens, 2002, p. 18, on Arendt (1968, p. 241).

[3] In discussion of Hannah Arendt's understanding that bureaucratic totalitarian complexes prevent action, Bernstein quotes Arendt: "Even in the darkest of times, the question of one's response and responsibility can and must be raised. There is the possibility to initiate, to begin, to act" (1996, p. 38). Arendt suggests "that new forms of dialogue and imagination must be fostered" (Coulter & Wiens, 2002, p. 18).

[4] "The world does not simply precede us, but effectively constitutes us as particular kinds of people. This puts us in the difficult position of being simultaneously heirs to particular history and new to it, with the peculiar result that we experience ourselves as 'belated' even though we are newcomers" (Levinson, 2001, p.13).

[5] "What is needed in order to create communion is communication, a practice of testimony, an ongoing commitment to autobiographical communication, not as an act of self-aggrandizement or self-deprecation, but as a self-reflexive investigation in collaboration with others who agree to listen and to respond and to explore their autobiographies, too" (Leggo, 2005b, p. 125).

[6] "I cannot be if others are not; above all, I cannot be if I forbid others from being" (Paulo Freire, 1997, p. 59).

[7] "Can a teacher heroically, single-handedly, teach against the grain of powerful forces in the larger culture and make a lasting difference? And, perhaps most important, is any notion of good teaching (and learning) independent of the personal, cultural, and theoretical perspective from which it is viewed" (Barone, 2001, p. 25)?

[8] "On the occasions when teachers are able to withdraw from their practice or when researchers are able to connect with wider publics, the use of the kind of imagination required to be judging spectators in Arendt's terms is often penalized" (Coulter & Wiens, 2002, p. 20).

[9] Arendt's public is not a reified fusion, however, but is instead "closely connected with particulars, with the particular conditions of the standpoints one has to go through in order to arrive at one's own 'general standpoint'" (1982, p. 44, quoted in Coulter & Wiens, 2002, p. 18).

[10] Radice, 1974, p. 14.

[11] Arendt, 1973, in Coulter and Wiens, 2002, p. 18.

[12] Arendt, 1958, pp. 52-53.

[13] Coulter & Wiens, 2002, p. 18.

[14] Bakhtin, 1963/1984, p. 6, in Barone (2001). Barone is actually using these descriptors to describe a language used in arts-based research which "is employed to recreate the lived worlds of protagonists and to encourage readers to dwell momentarily within those worlds" (p. 25). I am using this language as a way to develop a touching or dwelling language between individuals within society. Barone explains that the language employed is largely contextualized rather than abstract, and more vernacular and literary than technical and propositional. I interpret this description as a language of heart and care, the language used in loving relationships.

[15] Bakhtin, 1963/1984, p. 6, in Barone. 2001, p. 25.

[16] "Episteme aims primarily at helping us to know more about many situations" (Korthagen & Kessels, 1999, p. 7).

[17] Phronesis is about "perceiving more in a particular situation and finding a helpful course of action on the basis of strengthened awareness" (Korthagen & Kessels, 1999, p. 7). This is an interpretation of Aristotle's episteme-phronesis or in other words, knowledge-judgment.

[18] Coulter & Wiens, 2002, p 15. This view is also supported by Reeve (1992) and Beiner (1983).

[19] "Peter Abelard was a French scholastic philosopher and the greatest logician of the twelfth century" (Radice, 1974, n.p.). Heloise was his pupil and lover.

[20] Coulter & Wiens, 2002, p. 17.

[21] "But beyond culture and philosophy this preoccupation with certainty in our words and actions may be seen ultimately as an important human need" (Barone, 2001, p. 24).

8
Sweet
Fragrant
Harvest

*We are learning that we are no longer mere
creators of text, we are texts ourselves.*

Lorri Neilsen, 1998, p. 10

August 8

I miss you so much. I cannot explain; I want to starve myself.
What a strange thought. I already feel as if I am starving and I've
just eaten too much. The more I love you, the emptier I feel. Have
the words that frame me all come loose and emptied out of me?
What is desire wanting—words in return that echo my heart?

The reality is that even if you were here, how could our lives be
different? You and I are in a Venn diagram with no intersection. Yes,
we've crossed paths intellectually but intellectual intimacy cannot
be held, has no place holder or designated space, no structure to
frame it. Maybe I should be happy that I'm not held the way the

structure of formal education systems hold me; yet, without the system, how do I conceive? I don't know how and where to place you in my life. I wrote you a song to try to understand us. It's called, "No More Words." I'll attach the file. I'll italicize the lyrics here and explicate in regular text.

Only in my dreams
I feel you close to me
Body to body as one
I need you, can't you see
Only in my dreams
The world feels so right
silent and sure
a fleeting kiss
that needs no more words
Is it all in my mind?

Have I written our story, created love, made up this fiction in my head? How can I tell the difference between fact and fiction in text? What haven't I constructed through text?

No more words
To show how I feel inside
I give myself to you
And know it's enough
'Cause now you're here with me

Do I feel apart from you because my words have not become "real" enough? How can I give myself to you when what I feel has to travel through distance, through space, translated in the interpretative space, in the soundwaves out of my control? When can I pour my heart directly into you? Like Derrida's blood as ink—take my blood, pure and true to show my love. How do I let my outside show you my inside? How do I go *through* barriers like skin so we can truly be together, my inside outside with you? Here are Derrida's words:

> And I always dream of a pen that would be a syringe, a suction point rather than that very hard weapon with which one must inscribe, incise, choose, calculate, take ink before filtering the inscribable, playing the keyboard on the screen, whereas here, once the vein has been found, no more toil, no responsibility, no risk of bad taste or violence, the blood delivers itself all alone, the inside gives itself up and you can do as you like with it, it's me but I'm no longer there, for nothing, for nobody, diagnose the worst. (1978, p. 12)

Only in my dreams
You'd only be mine
'Cause you're with another
with her in the night
How could I be so blind?

Only in my dreams
We'll change the past
To a new beginning
A new way of life
Out from the darkness
And into the light

We can't change the past. According to Levinson (2001) and Arendt (1958, 1968), we are new and belated. We come into this world already part of a story, framed by the past. How can we write a new beginning? How can I reach out of this dark?

No more words
No more words
You're mine, you're mine, you're mine
But . . . only in my dreams

And even if we had no past, you are my professor, my advisor; our positions separate us and frame us apart. jan jagodzinkski (2004) says the student in love with the teacher wants something that is unattainable. I know what it is. It's all of you—body, mind, and soul; you can never be mine. The way I am trapped in my life echoes the way we are all trapped in life—oppressed by our given situations as we self-perpetuate those conditions. We cannot get out without drastic measures. I have no courage. How can I leave everything I am to be with you? How do I purposely remove the ground I stand on and cling to you submissively? How do I free myself? Even in my work, how do I acknowledge my potential to shape practice against the constraining "norms" and to actually develop personal political agency in a way that will influence structural change (see Sirna, 2006)? How can I interrogate notions of teaching and learning in a subversive way without becoming submissive and "other" to whatever I'm seeking to change? I'm safe staying "inside" and keeping things as they are.

In de Beauvoir's (1949/1953) *The Second Sex*, she says women are oppressed because women are men's "other." Men are essential and women are inessential. The sad thing is that I want to choose to be your other, to be yours. In *The Ethics of Ambiguity* (1947/1972), de Beauvoir says human existence is the ambiguous mixture of our internal need to break free of the given conditions of the world and the weight of the world's ideology on us. As I've told you before, she suggests in order for us to live freely and ethically then, we must assume this ambiguity rather than try to flee it. How can I? If I want to be free to be with you, I have to leave what I am, what I know, and then I'll become your "other," your object, so then I really am not free. Besides, you are attracted to me because I'm strong, not dependent on you. Why is it that I feel the need to leave and go to you anyway? Gallop says as a student I have "no otherness, nothing different from [you], the teacher, simply less" (1988, p. 43). I disagree. I am already woman. I am trapped, crushed and confined in every possible way—truly dismal.

I've been thinking that if love is joyful, light, happy, and free, then I'm not in love with you. This is all too overwhelming and complicated. jagodzinski is right, "any sexual exchanges between student and teacher are taken as fundamentally damaging to the self-esteem of the student" (2004, p. 101). I laugh at myself. I am in love with my professor. How dim can I be—always a part of this darkness?

According to de Beauvoir, every step of my living and becoming a woman is a movement toward passivity and alienation in order to meet the head's active demands. Is my emptiness, the gaping wound of love, a play on de Beauvoir's notion that women are but sexual receptacles of the male libido? What if you have nothing physical to fill me with? Oh I must stop. Don't you see I want to be passive? I couldn't even choose you if I was free to choose. So I am neither existentialist nor feminist, just lost in love. Even I laugh at myself—the way I love you.

My darling Red
Adorn with brush
Caress with sable
By your hand
I relinquish all
Paint me new
Stroke by stroke
Adoring as other
Submission I choose

Release and curve
Until I'm whole
Until we're one

Let's talk about something lighter. Actually, I have had a pretty
good day. How ironic, I'm much happier when I'm out, away
from the computer, away from you! I went to a book launch for
Bernadette Campbell today. You won't believe all the strange
connections I've had!

Bernadette gave a few words at the end of the speech section.
She is not well now. I was moved by her words and the effort she
made to make herself understood. Why do we all try so hard to
make ourselves clear to others? Does it matter? Interpretations
of us are so varied anyway. Aren't we texts ourselves? Really,
it didn't matter what she said; I could read her heart. The body
betrays us so badly. Bernadette only had perception of one side
of her body—she must have had a left hemisphere stroke. She
faced the side of the room where her family was sitting, her back
to the other half. Our families are always where we'll return. So
you'll understand why we'll never be together. I cannot turn from
my children and my family. Even though I know I cannot flee my
guilt as a mother, I struggle. de Beauvoir's (1949) views in the
"Eternal Feminine Myth" explain the unattainable expectations
of the mother figure. She says that the nurturing woman as the
constructed ideal denies individuality and situation and that the
mother figure is responsible for birth and thus death. The mother
can never be guilt-free.

Here's the story. When I arrived I sat behind someone wearing
a black sweater. I've told you about my body reception before.
Today I really noticed this phenomenon. I didn't know if the
person in front of me was a male or a female, though the person's

shoulders were quite broad. The person had beautiful thick, long hair and I noticed this because my chair was directly behind and I had to keep shifting to see the speech-makers at the center of the room. I found this person somehow appealing; in some sort of intriguing manner. I'm not sure. Ok I admit I'm strange! I think my body senses other "bodies" in ways we don't acknowledge or have words to express yet. As the speeches progressed, the person in front of me was asked to give some words. HE (and it was obviously a he!) said that Bernadette was at his final PhD oral exam in the late seventies and she told him to be good to his students. It's funny how we remember what people say. I wonder if Bernadette remembers saying this almost 30 years ago? We need to always be so diligent about what we say and how we say it, especially as teachers. As the sweater-man spoke, I was really aware of how easy he was to listen to. I had some kind of connection with him, not only in body, but in words too. So after the speeches I went over to the food table and introduced myself.

To be quite honest, our conversation was not remarkable in any way. I did notice that there was a very easy comfort. You always call me a drama queen, well, there was no show! What I noticed was that he spoke to me in balls. What, you say? Well, I imagine that when I talk to some people, balls come out of their mouths and slide into me, not only into my ears, but through my eyes and mouth. I feel understanding going down my throat somehow. (Yes, I'm totally crazy. Good thing I haven't told this to anyone else!) Some people talk to me in cubes and I have to "eat" them slowly or translate them somehow before I swallow. Some people speak in shapes I don't want to consume at all. Anyway, this fellow spoke to me in little balls! I later found out that the person was actually the writer of an article I have been so enthralled about that I had been carrying around the journal for three days and re-reading parts of the article at every spare moment! In our conversation, he never brought up the article or gave any indication who he was but for some reason, my body knew him. I thought the article in my bag was written by a woman called Jan. This man's name was jan (pronounced "Yun"). This was jan jagodzinski! So here's what's interesting—my body recognized the person before my mind made the connection!

I had been carrying the article around because it was so fresh and niggly in some way. It's titled "Fallen bodies: On perversion and sex-scandals in school and the academy" (jagodzinski, 2004). After I read it, I started a response to it called "Learning with Dick and Jane." (Do you like the title?) jagodzinski's take on Jane Gallop is so decisive. Jane Gallop is a feminist, psychoanalytic, literary theorist. She's written several books including *Thinking Through the Body* (1988). I had to write a reflection on the article! I even ordered three of Jane Gallop's books!

After I realized who jan jagodzinski really was, I told him about my Dick and Jane reflection and we talked about the power of mixing sexual and intellectual intimacies. In the article, jan alludes to another dimension of "truth" being possibly reached through an intimate discourse (p. 100). I'm almost convinced that the synergy of love or eros with an intellectual relationship can actually enhance pedagogical transference (see jagodzinski, 2004, p. 107; Sameshima & Leggo, 2006a). Jan's article takes a strong stand. Don't get all excited about my response to the article! You know how obsessed I am with you. I can and have analyzed our relationship and it doesn't affect how I feel about you. I completely see the irrational weakness of my carnal nature with you!

It's so fascinating that throughout the afternoon, I was somehow drawn to jan and I didn't understand it. You'd call it intuition.

Are our lives already destined? Did my body recognize jan's body through his words? I read his article several times. Does my body know what my mind does not? Does noesis have to be conscious? What don't we understand about the body's reception and learning? Are our stories prewritten? Am I in love with you so that I'll research this topic? I realize that my body knows things my mind cannot grasp. What's going on? I can feel my body wanting to express, but I don't know the language.

Oh, by the way, remember we talked about body memory before? Well, it's called *proprioception*—the muscles' ability to memorize movement. The proprioceptive sense is sometimes considered the sixth sense and information is stored in sensory neurons located in the inner ear and in the joints and muscles. There's even an educational method for using proprioception to relearn movement when there's been nerve damage. It's called the *Alexander Technique.* One does this by using reflection to recognize location of body placement. I feel some kind of connection here and must not forget to come back to this. I'm sure this has to do with the way sound moves me somehow (see Lephart & Borsa, n.d.).

So if our bodies can memorize movement patterns without our minds, then is it conceivable that our bodies can read other bodies? Maybe my body recognized jan's body (essence?) as familiar in some way. So . . . can the body see through manipulated text? You know how I've been so obsessed with being able to tell if an author has a good heart; maybe my body has been trying to read and recognize the authors. Ok, I'll be quiet before I scare the pants off you. (Oh, shut up, I don't mean that literally!)

Back to the article: I love jagodzinski's title, "Fallen Bodies." "Fallen bodies" refers to "falleness" as used by existentialists like Jean-Paul Sartre (see Flynn, 2004). Sartre uses *falleness* and *bad faith* interchangeably to describe a way of escaping anxiety and despair when one understands transcendence but cannot choose transcendence. This fits me to a "T!" You see, I know how unhealthy it is for me to be in love with you, but I cannot overcome the way my body responds to you so I purposely choose to focus on my lovesickness and despair of missing you. Truly pathetic, even from a non-feminist point of view!

When I think about our situation—being in love with you—I try to remember how it began. I've asked you when it started for you and you always say you liked me before I opened my mouth. Then again, you're always a bit ambiguous—the sign of a good teacher. Maybe your ambiguity was the beginning of my misunderstanding! I distinctly remember how warm and inviting your "hello" was. jagodzinski says the dominant western view of pedagogical authority is informed by power and seduction (1996). I would say this binary is not just a pedagogical phenomenon. Men have always used power to attract women and reduce other men. Women, even more so in the past, in their corsets, fans, and skin covering clothing, used their bodies to seduce. In fact, I think that the more masculinized women have become, the less power they seem to have. The "suited" woman always looks defensive, dressed in armour, powerless underneath, blank too. In our case, I had no intention of seduction and you do not appear to be the type interested in power, so what happened? I think you seduced me with the power of your mind.

Interestingly, as I re-read jagodzinski, knowing now that the author is a man, the tone of the writing has changed for me. I think the male writer comes from a "power" position and I am intimidatingly seduced. Why is it that the male voice "pierces" in a matter-of-fact way while the female voice invites-me-to-believe?

There is no reason. Maybe I'll change this thinking tomorrow. I mean, as I write this very letter, I want to seduce you, my reader, into believing what I have to say. I am seeking power over you. I want to write with a governing voice. Is writing with authority a male role then? Is the male text always aggressive in some way, even without intention? If the "head" is male and the "body" is female, then when I write in a "heady" way, I am no longer "other" in my words—just as I first misread jan (yun) as Jan. Does that mean text becomes gendered by the viewer? You know, the only time I am writing from an unconcealed power perspective as a female is when I'm writing report cards? Then again, I am writing to inform, not convince. Let's talk more about this on the phone. There's a lot here to sort out.

In terms of Lacanian psychoanalysis which notes that power and seduction are not strictly biological givens of male and female, I would have to agree that at first, it was unclear who seduced whom and who has power but, now, I would have to say that I really hold all the power and yet I struggle daily because I want to be the seduced. To be honest, I would be really happy to be the little girl in Jean-Paul Sartre's well known example of 'bad faith' (*mauvaise foi*). Sartre's notion of bad faith is the human attempt to escape anguish by imagining that I am passive and not free to do as I wish. I am the girl sitting with a man I know very well and who would like to seduce me. When he takes my hand, I try to avoid the painful necessity of a decision to accept or reject him by pretending not to notice, leaving my hand in his as if unaware. This is how I want our relationship to unfold. I want to be passive and not feel so guilty that I've let this get so out of hand (see Leslie Stevenson, 1987). How can I hold power I don't want?

We both have much to lose if we disclose our relationship. Of course, I have my family to lose. Gallop's image linking pedagogy with pederasty—"a greater man penetrates a lesser man with his knowledge"—is a vivid image although a bit elementary for current times (1988, p. 43). If I could gain knowledge from a professor as he or she spews seed then education has really taken a nose dive. Give me a break! Who still thinks that transferring knowledge is what pedagogy is all about!

Gotta run, I have to take Savannah to a piano lesson now. Talk later.

……………………………………………............……………………

August 8

Oh my gosh, Gallop IS right! Maybe this is our biggest problem! Everybody still thinks we can squirt knowledge into students. Gallop says "the student is empty, a receptacle for the phallus; the teacher is the phallic fullness of knowledge" (1988, p. 43).

I think Gallop actually explains how my loving you makes me miss you and thus I feel my emptiness, this hole getting bigger and bigger the more I love you. She says that in Sade's *Philosophy*, he explains that the student is innocent and empty, lacking her own desires. "The loss of innocence, the loss of ignorance, the process of teaching, is the introduction of desire from without into the student, is the 'introduction' of the teacher's desire" (p. 43). You have taught me desire and only now do I know my emptiness. By the way, what is the teacher's "desire?" Is it nurturance or could it be seduction? I sort of like this idea of seduction; it's alluring, a call toward desire, and much better than a teacher teaching through power.

I'm intrigued with all the fascinating couples who have made contributions to critical theory. Is there something connected with intellectual and physical intimacies? There's Kristeva and Sollers, Abelard and Heloise, de Beauvoir and Sartre, Heidegger and Arendt and even Žižek and Salecl, and there's more. I'm not saying that you and I can "go all the way," but does physicality arouse body reception or open some doors for body understanding or cognitive awareness we are not able to currently access through language when we try to process alone? I'm not really clear about what I think here. I'm just throwing out ideas, imagining the words sailing like confetti through the air, a true Bakhtinian carnival creating the space of the *chronotope*—the place where multiple voices of narrative are linked and unlinked (see Bakhtin, 1981). Could that be it? Can the liminal be intentionally created in the chronotope? What about just sleeping with? Do we somehow, in the silence of the night, connect with our loved ones in our dreams and sleep? You know how everyone talks about being "wide awake" in the day. Well what if we were "wide awake" in our dreams, in our fictions, in the stories we are living that we think we've chosen but which are already socio-culturally written? Can we step out of ethos—the disposition, character, or fundamental values peculiar to a specific person, people, culture, or movement?

You know how I told you earlier that male text "pierces" me . . . I just happened to fall upon Gallop's chapter on *Carnal Knowledge* this evening. She says Roland Barthes uses the word *pierce* and the French word *piqûre* which is translated as "prick." She writes with amusement that the term does not refer to the vulgar word for the male genital (note the connotations though) but that the word means "something that wounds" (1988, p. 152). So I'm wondering whether your words prick me, wound me, and thus produce the flowing out of me and hence this emptiness, and desire to want filling. I should explain the prick/piercing further because it relates to my art.

Jane Gallop (1988) explains Roland Barthes' work in *Camera Lucida* on "erotics *of* the text rather than *in* the text" (p. 151, italics in original). In the later text, written seven years after the first, Barthes explains that there are two elements of a photograph. I interpret the photograph as art—visual or even narrative text. Barthes describes the two elements. The first one is *studium,* which is the theme of what the photographer is attempting to depict with regards to ideas and general culture. The studium is the representation and is *in,* or statically enclosed in the rendered work. Barthes explains that sometimes this enclosure breaks and the passive, inert studium suddenly has a second element that goes off the scene and pierces the viewer. Barthes says, "A word exists in Latin to designate that wound, that prick, that mark made by a pointed instrument . . . I will thus call it *punctum* . . . The *punctum* of a photo, it's that accident which, in it, stings me" (quoted in Gallop, p. 152). The punctum is thus an opening or "a 'blind-field' which is created or divined . . . and allows what Barthes calls 'life' to pass through, to permeate the frame" (p. 153).

Barthes goes on to explain that the difference between eroticism and pornography is the presence of the punctum in the former. The punctum creates something dynamic where the art animates the spectator and the spectator animates the art. Gallop discusses this reciprocal activity where the viewer is both the subject and object of the verb "animate." Is this like me? If I liken all my writing to you as art, my created representation, my studium, then I am animated by the power I have over text and the power the text gives me in return. This eroticism of the punctum or piercing and wounding, the connection between the art and the animator/ animated, draws "the spectator out of its frame, out of his frame, out of her frame" (1988, p. 154). I'm speaking here of the frames and boxes we're socio-culturally and organizationally constrained in. When I move beyond these "boxes," I am moved to alternate, higher spaces of learning.

This whole idea of reciprocality is so dynamic. It's interesting that one of the meanings for the word is "owed to each other" (Farlex, 2006). It's the space of role mixing where newness is birthed. Paulo Freire suggests that "Liberating education consists in acts of cognition, not transferals of information" (1970/1994, p. 60). The reciprocality is evident. The teacher becomes the learner in dialogue and the student while being taught, simultaneously becomes the teacher.

The last thing I wanted to mention here goes back to why I can't seem to find a way for you to soothe my desire. Barthes presents the word *jouissance*, an ecstasy which moves him in his favourite photographs which by the way is produced by having that second element called punctum, or the arrow that leaps out and pierces. Gallop (1988, p. 152) explains that ecstasy etymologically is derived from the Greek "*ekstasis,* from ex- 'out,' plus *histanai*, 'to place.' Thus, it means something like 'placed out.'" This intellectual intimacy we have, the blind field of the erotic ecstasy creating punctum in my writing to you will stay "placed out" and I will keep seeking to put that desire back in. Maybe that's what I want from you—an impossible notion.

> In *Camera Lucida* [Barthes], the imagery used to describe this ecstasy carries connotations of pain. The arrow recalls Cupid's arrow, a tradition in which love comes from the outside and against your will, attacks you, pierces you, changes you, takes you outside yourself, puts you in a state of passivity that (at least in the European tradition) is seen as a violation of the body, a penetration of the self, something

dangerous and threatening and yet at the same time terribly pleasurable, something wonderful. (pp. 152-154)

Oh Red, let me continue enjoying this terrible torture of love. I better stop now. I'll talk to you about the rest of the jagodzinski article on the phone. Read it if you can.

....

August 11

When I awake in the morning I always have a lot to write and if I don't get up right away, I forget what it is I need to record. Why? Is the imagination still running from the dream time? Does everything become immobile once the mind turns on, frozen when Medusa's eye awakes, putting everything back in place? Is the mind like the Christmas toy shop that awakens at night, with effervescent joy and prancing freedom? Are all the toys standing composed with their plastic painted faces frozen in acquiescence during the day? Is that ascetic compliance? Is that the teacher's outlook? We're always so still—showing no personal pictures through our skin—martyrs to our work. Some days I don't think I can cope without you but, when I get to school, I have my steady teacher smile and clothes—they're so easy to put on.

This piece is called "Flawed Fairytales" because no matter what I do, you won't hold me. You can't hold me the way I want you to possess me. The fairytale is a myth as well. I've copied part of the image from Claude Theberge's "Romance." I hope you understand. It goes with the poem beneath. Notice the male head blends into the environment—we don't even recognize the fairytales we're trying to live. We hardly know what we are aligning ourselves to.

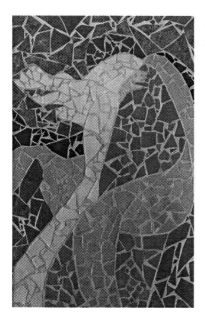

Flawed Fairytales, 2005,
mixed tile. 35" x 51"

A WISH FOR CEASG
in the night
my mind asleep
your warm hands caress
shape my form
materialize me from an ancient mist
pulling me from the distant miasma

you are child of Ceasg
the beautiful Highland mermaid
who lures the men to the sea
you, her offspring, a great sailor
you know the infinite waters
even down to where your mother is
they say when Ceasg is captured
she will grant three wishes

oh Red, take me to her
I only have one desire

in the starlight of our night
golden mica talc
lingers breathlessly on my skin
soft glow longing for your fingers
I see without my eyes
your softness on my cheek
your lips so near
divine to eat
hunger in my throat
empty mouth
wanting you more than my skin

you deny
put your lips on my breast
arch my back I give myself to you
and you wrap your arm
around my back
my breath in your ear
your fingers in deep
I want to break the
silence that holds us
the night that wraps us
but must not awake

when can I be yours?
truly belong to you?
chattel, object, possession
I freely offer
resign, relinquish and

abandon myself to you
for I cannot live
in the day
stone-faced smiling and still
when my heart is gone to you

I am so tired of being so strong
I'm going to sleep
I'll lie in the dory
attached to your stern
until you find your mother
Please Red, take me to her
until then
let me sleep forever
for in my dreams
I am with you

Goodnight Red

9
Indian Summer Hums

No matter how far back my love memories go, I find it difficult to talk about them. They relate to exaltation beyond eroticism that is as much inordinate happiness as it is pure suffering; both turn words into passion. The language of love is impossible, inadequate, immediately allusive when one would like it to be straightforward: it is a flight of metaphors—it is literature.

Julia Kristeva, 1987, p. 1

September 5

Today was a beautiful, fairytale day with my class. It was my last day with this group of Grade 2/3's at Ridgeway. I felt a tinge of sadness to tell them that I was going to another school and that they were going to be divided among four different classes. I told them at carpet time and explained all the details of the move—that the school enrollment was too low and I was being transferred but excited for the change. When I asked if they were worried about anything, the concerns were those of practicality. "Where will my new class be? How will I find my new class? I won't know which door to line up at." I told them we would walk to the new classes through the inside of the school, meet the teachers and go through their external exit doors so they would know where to line up tomorrow morning. I have enjoyed feeling nurturing to these children. I was surprised at how much I have grown to feel for these students in the three days I've had with them.

We talked about accepting and looking forward to change, that change was a present to be opened. Then we did the best, possible thing! I've been telling them about how I've been looking in wonder at the hill behind the parking lot (picture attached). The hill rises with a calling of some surprise on the other side. After music class, we walked out to see what was on the other side of the hill. I had framed the experience with them as something magical awaiting us and it came true!

We crossed the road using the sidewalk and, when we got to the path up the grassy hill, I suggested that we make our way up, *not* following the set path (even though it was curved and inviting). We all ran up the hill in glee. At the top, the ground opened out but there was another incline—a present within a present! We continued our exciting climb. At the crest, there was a raised circular concrete structure, large enough for 18 of us. We ran there and mounted it like an Olympic podium shouting, "We're here, we're here!" The entire city lay before us! The children stayed with me on the podium exclaiming about the view, clouds, the two planes that flew in the distance, the school behind us, coming here for picnics with family, more. Then we started down the other side. There was a fence at the bottom and a road. Then some children called from the right side of the hill. We all ran and on the sloping down part (having trouble describing land, don't know the words to use), was an outdoor amphitheatre created in the grass with a semi-circle stage at the bottom. I felt like I was in Scotland at a stone circle or in a hallowed church. There was a holiness or purity in this place. Perhaps it was that this place was new to us. The staggered grass steps were wide and uniform and perfectly engineered! The children ran along the levels and some danced in the center stage. These were heartfelt pleasures, soaking the world standing up. We stayed a bit longer then we raced back to the crest and most of the children lay on their sides and rolled down the hill. I could have cried. Such delight, such innocence and so much gratitude.

In *Images of Love, Words of Hope* (1991), Jean Vanier provides powerful wisdom for shaping the curriculum of joy. Vanier observes that,

> we give value to people by the way we look at them, by the way we listen to them, by the way we touch them, and care for them. We give value to them by the way we are present to them. (p. 12)

I feel the presence of being present. It is the sense of acute awareness of nuances I would have missed before, of connections all entangled, astonished wonder of all around me. It is the feeling and purpose of narrative—the ever becoming present.

Where does agency stem from?

....

September 6

You asked about what I was thinking while creating. When I'm writing and art-making I often catch myself thinking in another genre. I am informed within each genre explicitly through the other. As I am immersed in mosaic art-making, in the midst of a repetitive art motion like laying tile pieces or grouting, I think about connections in my processes. I am thinking explicitly of how the theoretical questions on my mind can metaphorically be unfolded and enfolded in my art making. As I work, the text that accompanies the finished rendering comes in bits through the process; the ideas begin to pattern themselves. Alternately, when I am writing, I begin to envision representative images which reiterate or layer my thinking processes. Despite this simplistic observation, not only the act of art-making creates understanding but the finished product maps a broader picture. Simultaneously, I am consciously aware of how my work, both text and art or song can be viewed from a single vantage point and yet completely interpreted in alternate ways too. This doesn't bother me. I notice though that when my friends talk to me about art, they welcome the text and explanation that accompanies art. Everyone wants to hear a story. I like to hear different interpretations of my work. I'm always surprised.

....

September 7

My new class is a group of Grade 3 students. We had a great time today. They played with base blocks (used for teaching place value) not only to count, but for building towers. I asked them to build a tower and then to calculate its numeric value (There's a 1000 block, a 100 flat, a 10 stick and a single cube which stands for 1). Playtime is so important. I see the importance of taking time now for everything. Learning, too, is much better supported when dwelling is incorporated.

I think all this has major applications to teacher education programs which tend to funnel and push student teachers in very direct lines. I think of the new teacher at my school who asked me for help with her math program. She seems so light, ready to be blown by any wind. How can we help to build identity and philosophy of teaching? Our perceptions of ourselves in the moment can be quite misguided. How do we encourage "readiness" for reflexivity and not only reflectivity? Or even more important, how do we provide time for reflexivity during the first few formative years of teaching when just coping drains all time? I always find it a bit odd that we offer after-school coping sessions for new teachers who have no extra time and are thoroughly exhausted by the end of the day!

I think I am in love with a romanticized character in a novel. I want to run away and be with you. My writings to you are becoming the stories I want to live. Won't it be interesting to include my process of writing the letters within my letters to you—the story of the story within the story, a never ending layering of process and thought?

……………………..………………………

September 12

How's this title? *Replies from the Skies: Professor and Protégé Pressing Provocative Boundaries.* The book would be my learning process through writing and rendering. The professor is in her head (in the sky, made up). They press the boundaries together—in the heart and in the head. Did I explain how I'm setting up the book? I have to apologize, I have deleted so much that I've written, not wanting to bombard you with reading, I can't remember what I've sent. I want to share our dialogic conversations as another way of knowing and learning. Am I going down the wrong road? Too far fetched?

I was thinking about your voice today. You have an amazing voice, thinking about it now makes me. . . . Seeing your artistry makes me feel that way too. I am seeing your heart. When I hear your poetry read aloud, I feel like I can't breathe. I get completely drawn into you, your sound, your images. It's some sort of smoothness, rich lushness that draws me . . . can't explain. The first time, at the conference, I hardly knew you but it took all my energy to stay still, to remain where I was. I feel a drawing, an attracting, there is something physically emanating from you and I can perceive it. My being seeks some kind of union through your hands (your writing, art, words) and your sound. Maybe those overt things are your feelers and I'm hoping/trying to get caught . . . I don't understand what I'm trying to say except I like your work, your voice. Thank you.

touch the keys
fly the words
through my skin

....

September 13

The white wall looks like a relief map. I stare at it like a topo-graphical story reflecting tension and release—a living cartography of all that's happened here before me, all on a white wall—a scratch here, a scuff there. I feel the wall absorbing, my body crying to it. I'm dizzy with tension at the barre. The teacher says "body go down, feeling go up," over and over again. I'm fighting my body. How do I bend my knees and feel my body going up? The focus and tension I create suffocates me. I repeatedly feel the darkness creeping across my eyes. I blink and breathe to release. For an hour, we work at the barre. This dizziness is not new. How can I tense my own muscles so tightly, hold my stance so firmly that I can make myself black out? Is my will stronger than my body? I am not holding my breath. I feel the tension I create in every muscle. I feel the verge of muscle implosion. Is that possible? This is not a stretching or extending pain. I do this with almost distain for my body, my head controlling.

This new dance teacher makes us do everything very slowly with complete concentration, never releasing: Four full counts to extend the leg to a point, four full counts to return to first position. I feel my leather soles forcing the floor away with every increment of movement. My pointed toe is on the verge of cramping. My arch is a fist of pain. On the fourth exercise, I feel some kind of sensation flooding through me. Something running from my heart to my head, my eyes well up and I have to release my trunk or I will crumble. How can I prevent crumbling by releasing?

When the Chinese teacher corrects me, she presses my abdomen and says "Fee" something. I can't remember the sound of her words so I can't ask someone for a translation. She's speaking in Mandarin. I know she wants me to tighten my stomach muscles and to pull my carriage up. In Cantonese, "fee" could mean "fly" or "fat." These words explain my entire being—freedom and weight. I think of my work. I'm trying to fly but as I work I feel as if I'm going deeper, going down. How can I fly when I am tethered and digging deeper and deeper, trapping myself, ready to implode, confined in a dichotomy in my heart, in my head, in my body?

What is my destiny? What am I to learn? What is my purpose? I don't understand my life.

teach me all

....

September 14

Oh my! You're getting serious now! You're saying the three words without limitations! I'd better watch out for you! What's gotten into you? When I push you away you spring back harder? Shall I push really hard?

And what's all this about the kiss? I'm not fixated on it but I just can't kiss anyone. Kissing is sacred. There. Ok, think I'm strange. And no, just because I said "no kissing" didn't lead us into our relationship! That utterance didn't set us onto a storyline! I don't play out cliché stories like that!

....

September 15

How can you love someone who is unfaithful to her husband and family? How can you love someone who is cheating in mind and heart on her spouse? Are you more worthy of my love? Is what we have greater than all the years I've had with Luke, you with Clare? What makes me think I can have you more than Clare? See how this is all wrong?

September 16
UNSENT

WHEN THE MOON AWAKES
If I awoke in another time
After the moon had slept for a century or more
Or if I flipped the calendar back
Over and over
Back even into my dreams
When I was beautiful in a Victorian dress
Creamy flowing silk, languid satin through my fingers
It would be right
I know with surety

For I have known you forever

You live a tightrope with me
You want to take me away
To be with you
Walking through the trees
The vines underfoot
The humidity of the tropics in my hair
My skin bare for your touch
My hand always ready for yours
Our laughter blending with the calls in the green
Our silence in the shady leaves
Telling shadow stories
The same as the scales
on the fish who swim the freedom we seek
The snow covering the lines between land and lake and sky
And the light our only path

But you say nothing

Push me away
Ignore my endearments
The hints I leave you
Because you know the tightrope
I walk

Pretending that I don't feel you
50 000 miles away or whatever the distance is
that separates the oceans
Only blinding my desire when I distance myself from you
When I close my body
When I do not hear your voice
When I do not read your words
When I cover my heart with my life
When I do not let the paradoxes in my body fight
I resign myself to my present happiness
The joy you saw that drew you in the first place
My delight in living my life
You say nothing
because you are a good person

And all the time, over and over
I want you to know that I love you
Love you with a crushing pain in my heart
And I cannot leave this life I love
To be in another life with you

And it doesn't matter what you feel
Because I have storied you
I have dug my own grave
And it calls me
Six feet so close

Trying to lure me
out of happiness

Some days I am strong
I can wait until the moon awakes
to be with you
Some days I want the world to crumble me
Chip me piece by piece
To look like a natural death
And no one will know
But the happiness shell smiles
smooth and shiny
And the tears bead up and are whisked
Away by the windy world

Help me, Red. Teach me how to live in love when I am already
happy.

10
As
Yellow-Ocher
Quavers

*Why is it that the most unoriginal thing we can say to one
another is still the thing we long to hear? "I love you" is always
a quotation. You did not say it first and neither did I, yet when
you say it and when I say it we speak like savages who have
found three words and worship them.*

Jeannette Winterson, 1993, p. 9

September 9

Letters to Chris—Layer Three: Modeling Wholeness-in-Process

Feel free to take whatever you want out of the following for Chris.
We can talk on the phone about this letter too.

If we think about integration as embodied curriculum, we
take the focus away from the disciplines and find the desire by
artists and generalist teachers to create a holistic curriculum,

> a curriculum that is embodied, a curriculum that involves
> the mind, body, spirit and soul, a living curriculum. (Irwin,
> Wilson Kind, Grauer & de Cosson, 2005, p. 56)

Teachers and researchers give lip-service to implementing an
active, involved curriculum. Teaching in themes and integration
across subjects with a focus on holistic learning is fashionable but
not the dominant paradigm. It is important here to remember what
is important in the learning process. I think my goal is to teach
the joy of learning and through that goal children can develop
into integrative, relational learners. By sharing reflexive texts in
creative forms (narrative, visual arts-based, and so on), students
are given examples of integration and relation. I have found the
culture of my classes significantly more attuned to learning when
I have shared my own learning representations. For example, last
summer, I wrote a song related to some work I was doing on life
history research. I layered my research in my lyrics and shared with
the class the personal meanings behind the words. Naturally, risk-
taking is involved as all students come from various backgrounds
and with deeply acculturated understandings. The teacher's job
is to make opportunities and possibilities accessible. Sharing
autobiographical texts explicitly connected to learning provides
an environment of living research in the classroom. Leggo,
Chambers, Hurren, and Hasebe-Ludt describe autobiographical
writing as "a method of inquiry through attentive contemplation,
reflection and rumination. . . . As life is lived and imagined in
relation to others, autobiography becomes an inquiry of the self-
in-relation" (2004, p. 1).

The teacher's pedagogy is deeply connected to philosophical
frameworks created and reinforced by past experience.
Standardization and regulation for "norms" are outcomes of fear

generated by the public to ensure that their own children are able to compete in the "real" world and by teachers themselves in efforts to belong. Teachers mistakenly ground themselves in static curriculum texts using standardization as the evaluator of good teaching. The teacher continues to wear the mask of all-knowing and perfection, filling the "wounded world" with knowledge from books. We must urge teachers to examine themselves, to reflexively challenge thinking norms and to share their learning publicly. Open communication between teachers, students, and parents will allow for grounded learning that is rooted in wisdom, not prescribed outcomes. The concept of identity is integrally connected to ecological constructs of location and landscape, and the hopeful and joyful search for meanings of living.

Irwin et al. (2005) cite numerous inquiries around the potential of the arts to enrich the general curriculum. Burton, Horowitz, and Abeles (2000); Catterall (1998); Catterall, Chapleau, and Iwanaga (1999); Eisner (1998); and Upitis, Smithrim, Patterson, Macdonald, and Finkle (2003) have focused on the arts increasing student achievement; and Miller (1988, 2000) and Nakagawa's (2000) work have looked at holistic curriculums integrating mind-body-soul connections. Burnaford, Aprill and Weiss assert that "instruction deepens when the arts are present because art images help children think metaphorically" (2001, p. 17). Newmann, Lopez and Bryk (1998) further suggest that the arts authentically deepen instruction by inviting intellectual depth.

Integrating the arts through theme teaching is not uncommon in the elementary classroom. For example, in the study of the water system, the class might build a multi-dimensional model, draw a picture of the water cycle, or write a poem about water. I propose that teachers specifically use artful practices in classrooms to not only authentically deepen understanding of the subject matter as supported by Burnaford et al. (2001) and Newmann et al. (1998) but also to enable students to understand their own learning practices and the pathways by which others learn. Through written (if possible, depending on age) and oral articulation of new understanding derived from the process of creating artful work, or by articulating new understandings conceived from experiencing their own and others' completed rendered products, teachers enable students to move from memorizing facts to learning how to learn. These are methods of learning and coming to know which need to be modeled in schools.

This is an acrylic on canvas painting called "Wholeness." Charles Garoian explains in reference to collage that:

> the images and ideas that are radically juxtaposed in these visual art genres constitute a disjunctive collage narrative that is apprehended rather than comprehended through a fugitive epistemological process in which the interconnectivity of its disparate understandings is indeterminate and resistant to synergy. (2004, p. 25)

In "Wholeness" we do not ignore the incongruity of texture and colour; rather, we welcome the conflicting interplay which forces a movement toward creative cognition. The painting makes us think because we are cognitively trying to sort out the parts, to make sense of which parts belong together and to make sense of the whole. In the process of thinking relationally, we acknowledge the action of creative cognition which we seek as teachers to nurture in our students. We also acknowledge the differences between self and the other that Aoki (1992) warns us not to erase. Nick Paley uses the words "polyphonous voice" to describe "systems of univocal discourse . . . [that] affirm multiple voices . . . [and]

multiple realities and experiences . . . in which no particular vocality can assure itself an absolutely authoritative status to the exclusion of others" (1995, p. 10). This position of enabling students to voice their standpoints against dominant cultural values is supported by the educational politics of Paulo Freire's "pedagogy of the oppressed" (2001, pp. 54-55), Henry

Wholeness, 2004, acrylic on canvas. 36" x 48"

Giroux's "critical pedagogy" (1993, p. 21), and Maxine Greene's "dialectic of freedom" (1988, p. 116). In the classroom, through a lens of wholeness, privileging juxtaposition and multiplicity, children can voice their diverse cultural identities much the same way Clifford (1988), Garoian (1999), and Taussig (1987) describe the use of surrealism and juxtaposition as strategies to counter hegemonic and colonialized conditions. My painting is yet again another reiteration of the need to embrace synergistic wholeness and recognize the power of the particular in communion—much like the mesmerizing juxtaposition of playing a multi-rhythm drum piece.

In the in-between spaces of collage, the grout of tile mosaics, or in the unmarked, silent space between two colours and textures is where Garoian believes "knowledge is mutable and indeterminate" (2004, p. 26) and where production of understanding can be sought. As one tries to sort out which part belongs to what, "newness" is experienced. This space is what Homi Bhabha (1994) calls the indeterminate, the *Third Space of Enunciation*. Ulmer (1983) suggests the word silence to describe "a space of critique in which codified culture does not predominate or prevail, but makes possible multiple interpretations and expressions" (Garoian, 2004, p. 27). It is this *in-between space* (Ellsworth, 1987; Irwin, 2004; Minh-ha, 1999), the silence, and the Third Space of Enunciation, that I want to open through sound, visual articulation and sharing—the personal and social indeterminate dialectically becoming enunciated in efforts to make us think anew.

....

September 10

Look, I know you think you're the big kahuna, queen bee, "king of the castle (and I'm the dirty rascal)" but I can't very well keep calling you every 15 minutes. First, it costs me money because I have to go though the operator each time and second, it makes me feel like I'm at your beck and call. Third, I have a million things to do! You could at least give me approximate times when not to call (when you plan to be out)! So I'm going out at 10:25am to the bank to try to get some money for all the debt you've incurred. Then I have to get more ink—why does the ink always run out on presentation days? You can just very well jump in a lake and shrivel up into a prune until I get a hold of you later! You'd better be worried when I get my hands on you! Run away now!

September 10

Just to clarify, then we'll do what we've said we're going to do. So you don't want me to write anything to you unless it's for my dissertation or a paper I'm submitting elsewhere. No more poetry. No love. Just head. Is that right? You are so typically Jared! You want me to separate my journey and learning from you. You want only the products. Ok. I think this is how lots of teachers teach. I got it.

And don't give me all that stuff about being unappreciative. I do appreciate you! I read your care through the time and energy you put in me. I'm grateful that you care so much about your job. Ha, ha! And don't write in FULL CAPS. You sound so mad! I know you were doing it for effect, but I don't like it. I don't want you to be angry.

goodnight starry skies

…………………………………….................………………………

September 11

It's so good to have you all over me! My dream of you was all through my body. I will try to frame my learnings with you in ways I can share with others. Right, focus on the work! This is academic work.

As you advised, a good researcher will record observations, not interpretations, and leave the observations ambiguous so that they can be interpreted later, perhaps, in many different ways. This is the historical, scientific, "reliable" method of gathering data, right? I think it's cold and boring. I would rather have an interpretation that is incorrect than to have none. Maybe through my interpretations I can find further understandings. I know you think I'm stubborn!

Ok. I will try to be a "good" researcher, describe my dream last night and leave my interpretations separate.

In the dream, you and I were coming back from a trip of some kind. I was single and living in my parents' house. My parents were away and we were debating if you should sleep over that night. I was old enough to justify your presence if my parents did come back early.

On the way to my parents' place, we switched our transportation. I got into an enormous semi-trailer. It was heavy and cumbersome, wide, and on the verge of controlling me, even though I was the driver. You were riding a moped.

I led us through a residential area in San Francisco. I noticed the distinct opposition between the silence of the delicate dappled pictures of light the old oak trees created on the narrow streets and the way my semi-trailer, top keeling, was swerving speedily through these convex streets narrowly missing sporadically parked cars along the way. Despite the speed I was traveling and the racket of my trailer, the steady hum of your moped, traveling at a constant tempo, followed beside and behind me in a straight even line as I careened this way and that.

I stopped at a house which had a long empty parking space in front of it. I jumped down from the high seat, using the running board with ease, and slammed shut the heavy door up above. I spilled onto the sidewalk grass. The grass was dry with weeds. You joined me. I noted that you got some thistle stuck on your pant leg. My head was on the grass, the sky was a deep decadent blue, like powdered lapis lazuli. You lay, warm body against me; propped on your side, head in your hand.

Looking into the sky, I felt beauty raining like spring blossoms through the air, felt the glorious world shining, descending from the planets, through the atmosphere, through the sky and down through my skin. You said nothing, but kissed me. Your lips were soft, wet, sweet with tenderness, want, care, gentleness, affection, fondness, protection, respect—lightness with depth. I tried to understand the contradiction between lightness and depth. This was our first kiss, pure. I knew my heart was gone to you. Everything I had saved from you was now laid out, given completely, surrendered to you.

Your desire for me was clear, for you were now undressed, exposed to even the sky and I smiled at your ease and laughed. We entered the old, dark house, you now, suddenly fully clothed.

Inside, the air was dark, musty, old and lethargic. You sat, leaning forward on a wooden chair that resembled a small throne, ornately carved. I was on a deep red, heavily tessellated Persian carpet, kneeling at your feet. The rabbi-looking owner of the house did not question why we were there. He brought us a plate of something I had never seen before. The triangular crackers were made of gold lattice, not garden lattice, but more like the screen between the two sections of a Catholic confessional. The crackers had cream cheese sandwiched between the two parts. I smiled at the silent, stone-faced man and accepted the plate. I took a cracker sandwich, examined it carefully—noting the details in the cracker's pattern, thinking about the lattice tessellating and fitting all together so perfectly—and then ate it. You did not want it. You did not even want to try it. I remembered you didn't like religion. I made no comment.

I woke up then, noticing with clarity how stiff my wrists were and all in one moment I was reminded that my wrists are the connectors between my hands and fingers and my body. I realize how my fingers type words to give understanding to my living. My hands touch bodies which give face to who I am. My hands form the face of the other in which I seek to see myself (see Levinas in Hand, 1986). My hands synthesize my life, teaching and constructing me as I move them through space—caring, holding, touching, and creating. Through motion I learn (see Pinar, 1988).

What of my dream interpretation? Can I honestly separate my analysis from the recording? Doesn't my mind seek clarity without conscious thought? In my writing out, have I not already sought for rational sequence, methodical ordering, or comprehension of knowing? Yes, I can add more to why I had this dream or other connections I see interspersed in the dream thoughts, but how can I observe and record the dream in a detached way?

I have tried to record without interpretation, but the whole dream makes sense to me after writing it out. We construct and come to understanding, intentionally or not.

a winged seed
spirals down
lies in wait
ready to run

....

September 12

I've been reading the *Gilgamesh* epic to my class. I like this quote:
    For an artist there is no more serious and, at the same time,
    more joyous task than to create, through art, a new aesthetic,

and ultimately, a new way of being. (Karel Zeman in Ludmilla Zeman, 1992, n.p.)

Karel Zeman is the father of children's book illustrator, Ludmilla Zeman. Her books are amazing. She's retold and illustrated the stories of the Gilgamesh epic. These are stories that were inscribed on clay tablets over 5000 years ago and currently held in museum collections in London, Paris, Philadelphia, and Berlin. The story told is of a great king who learns to love through friendship and by example. He later seeks to find immortality. The irony is that his search is futile but his immortality is created through his story. I must not forget the power of language and word.

I was thinking of all the parallels in this legend with the work I'm doing. Myths and legends remind me over and over that we've always been trying to understand true humanity, where we belong, how we can love and be loved, and what our roles are. If these are the age-old searches over all the centuries, what is important to teach in the classroom? Gilgamesh's name is remembered because of his courage and good deeds—the ways of the hero. Zeman (1995) talks about the virtues associated with heroes: courage, compassion, loyalty, tenacity in hardship and dedication to vision. How do I teach these things in a classroom? Wouldn't education be different if I started the year teaching about these virtues? I don't even think I'm trying to "make" heroes and heroines, I just want the world to be kinder. Maybe Gilgamesh reminds me that narratives have political agency for peace. Don't I sound so righteous?

How do I effectively teach place, placement, and identity? Is war a foreign entity which I'm unaffected by? Where is war and peace to me, where I am? How do I teach children that transformation must be in the everyday? Of course, the school-wide plans produce a generative culture, but the real change occurs in smaller places.

I've always known that my favourite teaching time is the story time at the carpet. We're sitting close together. I'm at their level in a very low primary chair. I'm reading or we're sharing stories. I think this is where the greatest learning occurs. It is in the stories, isn't it? You always talk to me in stories too. One time, I remember you being upset with Jared. You said, "What does he think I'm doing, sitting around telling stories all day?" I remember smiling and wishing I could hug you because you are! That's what you do. That's how I learn from you.

Gilgamesh's story takes place in Mesopotamia—"the land between the rivers," between the Tigris and Euphrates Rivers. I always talk about Hannah Arendt's discussion of agency and freedom. She writes about natality, explaining that "in the birth of each [a child] this initial beginning is reaffirmed, because in each instance something new comes into an already existing world which will continue to exist after each individual's death" (1968, p. 167). Arendt explains that the human ability to create life through action means that we do have freedom. She says, "the principle of beginning came into the world itself, which, of course is only another way of saying that the principle of freedom was created" (1958, p. 177). Coulter and Wiens (2002) discuss Arendt's vision of action as an expression of freedom, that we can make a difference in the world and thus must take the responsibility of this agency. Do you know what that means? This is a critical issue of being and becoming a teacher. If we hold the freedom to make, we must be able to judge and thus, teachers can never be neutral or live in the safe zones of conformity and mediocrity. Do you see how we as teachers are somehow all on the wrong geographical map? I keep coming back to Levinson (2001, p. 13) who says:

> The world does not simply precede us, but effectively constitutes us as particular kinds of people. This puts us in the

difficult position of being simultaneously heirs to particular history and new to it, with the peculiar result that we experience ourselves as "belated" even though we are newcomers.

Whenever I read this section, I imagine that the river of life is flowing, has been flowing for centuries, and we are born into that river. The river will not stop. It has come from and is going toward. Sometimes we are torn out of some tributary and thrown into another but we are always drawn along, belated and new. In the story of Gilgamesh, Mesopotamia is the land between the rivers, where the land is fertile, the place of rich birthing. Some say that Mesopotamia is believed to be the setting for the Garden of Eden (Zeman, 1992). I want to live in that place with you. How do we get out of the river by ourselves? How can I tear myself from who I am, my culture, my society, all the world that constitutes who I am for I can only see when I stand on the bank and look upon the river and see its course wind toward destiny. Everyone in the river is traveling the same story. Red, help me write our own—the story that allows me to love you openly and to be with you when you are already in a different story. Why do we let the river play out the stories? Can we change the river's course with a critical mass? Can we choose new stories without ruining the river we've come from? Urak, where Gilgamesh came from, is now a desert because the river changed courses. It is a dead place now. Can we choose and still allow diversity to thrive?

I'm reminded of Daignault's work. Daignault argues that "to know is to kill" (1992a, p. 199). Violence stems from privileging power between ideologies and doctrines, thus to know is to murder, to terrorize. For Daignault, the opposite of terrorism is nihilism which is the abandonment of any attempt to know. Nihilism is the hopelessness of surrendering ideals to empty fictions and memories. Daignault (1983) urges a residing in the in-between, where the power of terrorism is not sought nor is education viewed as a place of efficiency and manipulation. Thinking, he believes, "happens only in between suicide and murder . . . between nihilism and terrorism" (1992a, p. 19).

Daignault believes thinking is itself the passage between. It is in the process of thinking that a forward movement is created. Daignault writes, "I have tried to find passages between the variable and the invariable, between both: not from one to the other, but passages at their absolute difference, the différence [Derrida, 1982] between death, twice evaded" (1992a p. 201). Many researchers seek to bridge the disparate, trying to link the science and the arts, or theory and practice whereas Daignault suggests that we walk between, not across. We follow the paths of the liminal edge not seeking the nostalgic desire to leave where we are and travel across to the other place, but travel between and along the edges of here and there in the unsettled liminal space (see Sameshima & Irwin, 2006).

So thinking about living on the land, in the place between the rivers, is really articulating Daignault's passages of the between. Daignault resists representing a totalized knowledge but rather stages or performs "knowledge through a passageway" by thinking aloud (1983, pp. 7-13). Daignault says the "gap" is the curriculum and that "thinking is the incarnation of curriculum as composition" (quoted in Hwu, 1993, p. 172). See how this connects with Hannah Arendt's work? The creation and coming into being is the teacher's agency and responsibility and obligation.

Curriculum understood as composition allows "a participation" in "continuing creation" (quoted in Hwu, 1993, p. 171). Daignault's views on knowledge creation are not about pinning down or defining reification, but are rather a translation of a joyful wisdom, "thinking maybe" (1992a, p. 202) and being sincere as he says, "Do not expect me to know what I am talking about here; I am trying to think. That is my best contribution to the composer's creativity" (p. 4). Red, how can I hold teacher education with this much responsibility? My student teachers don't even want to talk about theory. All they want are bunches of pretty cut flowers to present to their students when all I have to offer are seeds to be sown. The thing is, many of the seeds will not grow in the contexts they'll be in. They need to be sown in fertile ground. Then again, if I can't get out of the river onto the land between the rivers, how can I expect them to? I'm finding that being inbetween myself, being part time in the classroom and teaching part time at the university such a struggle. I don't think we should bridge the two. In bridging, we force conformity and mediocrity. We need to articulate the place between so we can stand in that space.

And all the while that I'm sitting on the little chair with picture books in my hands and 48 young eyes glued to the illustrations, I'm thinking about why the survivor of the flood story of Mesopotamia is named Utnapishtim in the Gilgamesh trilogy and named Noah in the Bible; and why we have the same stories in different times and different names and how words and language get us all so muddled when we all really mean the same story. How do I make a beautiful song that everyone can hear? I want to go lie down now.

September 13
UNSENT

RELEASE TO RECEIVE
a thousand kisses
can't tell all
so lightly flit
like bursting bubbles
fresh but fleeing
on my cheeks
want to keep
mine to hold
but know truth
must be free
you are sky
can't be confined
all I understand
I get you

Wish we were lying together right now. Just being near.

I can release. I will learn to let you go.

....

September 17

You're right, my work should be motivated by passions, desires and emotions. I just need to keep the passions focused on the work. As you suggested, I'm challenging the notion of "I", the complicated multiplicity of all my identities, my various "I's." What do you think the reverse of ekphrasis is? Ekphrasis, alternately spelled ecphrasis, is poetic writing in response to the visual arts. What about making art in response to poetry? This is what I've done.

This mosaic is called "The Quotidian I." It's about seeing the everyday, giving those moments value, and re-seeing the "I" flying through the valley of becoming, beak down and head-strong in a quest for knowing, moving into the future looking down at all the past laid out below.

The Quotidian I, 2006, granite, tile, and marble. 51" x 35"

So the mosaic is a response to two poems in conversation (see Sameshima & Leggo, 2006b). One is a poem called "The Quotidian I" and the other is Carl Leggo's (2003) "Tangled lines: Quizzing the quotidian." The phenomenological "I" is so often removed from inquiry as a means to empower the research. When the researcher uses "I," some people think the work is narcissistic. You know all this. Like Derrida (1978), I wish I could draw out some blood that would speak purely who "I" really am. Words can so easily be manipulated—masking and overmasking who "I" am. "I" is always translating, deflecting, and deferring to language; and this language, outside of us, determines the meaning of what is said—beyond our control, controlled by our heritage, culture, and context (Derrida, 1982). We lose control in text. This is all so postmodernly liberating and paradoxically confining.

Ayers (1988) believes teachers have a special responsibility for self-awareness, clarity and integrity because they are in such powerful positions to witness, influence, and guide the choices of others. Cole and Knowles (2000) suggest that making sense of prior and current life experiences, and understanding personal-professional connections is the essence of professional development. These authors further suggest that informal professional development through "continually redefining oneself as teacher marks 'authentic', ongoing professional development" (p. 23). "I am continually changing, remaking myself as I search out the meanings of experience in the worlds of society and classrooms and look to the future. I am who I am. I am who I am becoming," says J. Gary Knowles (p. 19). To question "I" is to iterate the unnamed noesis of identity, make visible the unknown, and therefore to become.

As researchers and teachers, we're expected to keep the academic veneer shiny. We hide behind studious jargon and text, and in the classroom we teach "by the book" in efforts to remain politically neutral and professional. We show no weakness and in that act, we prevent ourselves from learning. I will send John Elder's (1994) article "The Turtle in the Leaves" when I mail you the cd with the other papers and visuals. He writes about how perceptions of loss and despair when intricately woven into healthy understandings of wholeness, will ultimately lead to hope. I think he's right. To be balanced and healthy, we must weave the difficult aspects of teaching and learning in with the euphoria of understanding. We need to go below the visible. I'm reminded of an example from my dance class. Whenever the dominant movement is up, there is always a breath release and motion down before the up begins. If the up motion is on the count "one," then the down is on "and one" (in the empty space before). We must focus on the exhale if we want the inhale to be full—focus on the clear, unknown, empty space before the forward motion (learning) begins. We must look at what is already in front of us.

....

September 19

Will has responded regarding the epistolary novel idea for my dissertation—he says I should go for it. Jared suggests I incorporate an analysis of the form that I draw upon. I think he means to do a scholarly examination of the veracity of this representational form for knowledge. Now don't get all upset. I know you think this looks like I'm apologizing for using arts-informed practice and research, but perhaps some of my readers may need this. I'll try to do it in a way that is incorporated in the making. I've seen so many bifurcated texts—where the heart of the research has to have a separate "head" explanation. I want the work to stand whole. Jared also proposed a "side-by-side" text. His suggestion was that the fiction could be on one page and the facing page could have academic references or notes. That seems too pretentious to me. I want something smoother. I had also imagined a fiction with a compendium, but that's a lot of work for the reader. I just want to write something enjoyable to read but that has layers of meaning.

September 29
UNSENT

hear 3 words
no sounds express
hear me cry
them to you
with my being

Lilium philadelphicum

Metal
Po (subliminal awareness)

dry dusk sobs
west of autumn
in cracking white sorrow

11
Dry Dusk
Sobs

Speech about hope cannot be explanatory and scientifically argumentative; rather, it must be lyrical in the sense that it touches the hopeless person at many different points.

Walter Brueggemann, 2001, p. 65

October 2
UNSENT

UNDERSTANDING KNOWING
I stand alone
under the pale blue open
hot air, maize expanse, holds no hints
I only know with surety
something will come to be

I see my back
so unaware

to the left and to the right
no being, no movement
no beginning and no end
a wafting mirage perhaps
all in front, a vast forever
waiting
in trepidation
seeking proaction
but cannot grasp
know not where to start

a noise will come
and scare me wild
I see
but not comprehend
for what I see is
not what is

I only feel

my body knows no lies
or so I felt until we met
so I still rely
for what else have I?
because my head cannot explain

my body feels foreboding
of tragic untold pain
and it cripples me
day after day
because my body knows
before I do
that my heart
cannot be freed

LACAN'S LUGGAGE
the clothes I wear over my heart
cover me in silky sheaths
protect my body from all my
soul remembers
layers and layers lightly flutter
patterns of habitual beliefs
intricate systems of joy and hope
dark somberness for memories
too difficult to forget
I wait for you my love
to undress me unfold me
see me as I am
touch my skin
and yet the layers
refuse to cease
Lacan's desire
is my luggage

I had a good day in class today. Trying to focus on my work. Trying not to think of you. I got all muddy on the back of my skirt from racing on the wet grass with the children. The running splatter of mud was on everyone! I tried to see if there were any patterns. No. There is no reason for everything. We had three running groups—the "feeling energetic group," the "feeling ok group," and the "feeling tired group." I had so much fun teaching. Wish you knew. Wish I could tell you everything.

October 6
UNSENT

Oh look at this one. It's the perfect gift for someone who can't read me—so cliché it hurts. Truth is, nothing is as it seems. I'll paste the poem that goes with it after. Cute, isn't it?

Walking Puppylove, 2005, mixed tile. 35" x 51"

WALKING PUPPYLOVE
can you hear me?
do you understand me?
look at me
really look at me
not just a comfortable cliché
cute puppylove
bitter-sweet heartbreak
look from far away
so easy to see
up close, too sharp and jagged to understand
you can't recognize the semiotic ways you view
and interpret the visual anymore

the focus changes when the emphasis is on the negative
doesn't it?
hear me, the subservient voice, oh master
my collar reminds me who I belong to
my loose leash is a constant attachment to you, beloved
only when I strain away and my leash is tight
then I know you love me
walk me, show me your love, travel with me
experience the world in connection
do you care how I feel? all you want is a feel
do I console you? suit your need?
you hurt me more than the nothingness I can't articulate
my language you cannot understand
the vast separation between us
built by an urban landscape of differences
you can't be neutral
there is no absent space
the absent makes the whole
the negative frames the object
I don't want to need you
always a collar around my neck
consume and defecate when it's convenient for you
you continue to torment me, see the pattern
hold me when you want
drop me when you don't
can I choose not to look out the window for you?
can I stop loving you?
or is that my cliché?

Proximity is not a good reason for not loving me. That's your
excuse. You don't need to protect me anymore. I'm going to
graduate and get out of your hair.

You say I'm very disappointed in you. True. Disappointment means expectation. What do I expect? You have your life. I have mine. We have no intersection. You have a past you won't share, even when I press you. You won't even share the present willingly. You ask what it matters since I can't change anything in your space. No. I don't expect. I would be very disappointed if I expected you to pack your bags, come back and take me away from my home and family. I would be very disappointed if I expected you to find us jobs at a university somewhere else, where we could work together, live together, and breathe the same air together. I would be disappointed if I expected you to send me a gift I could wear to hold you near, a collar (ha, ha!), a symbol of promise. I would be disappointed if I expected to fall asleep and wake up beside you day after day. I would be disappointed if I expected you to love me in any of these ways. I don't expect these things from you. You cannot give them to me. How can I be disappointed? I don't even expect you to reply to my emails. What is there to be disappointed about? We have nothing between us, only my holding on.

....

October 8
UNSENT

You say you're enjoying the windstorm around your home this morning. You wonder what it would be like to be a whale that could swim in the wind and rain. The windstorm here tore the Canadian flag on the children's play center into the aftermath of war. The sandpit looked disheveled, wet winter dunes of mud, and the coloured outdoor toys discarded, littered in lonely places on the grass. Perhaps I want the wind to blow me, rip me and all

I stand for into pieces hanging by threads so I could feel a pain that's real, not this unbearable mourning I have that cannot be acknowledged or witnessed or healed because you are untold. A whale can cry freely and embrace the salty wind sting of the open air. But a whale cannot feel the tears running down her cheeks nor the salt in her eyes. She cannot feel the moon rising over the fluid dreams of you. She cannot feel need, the way I need you because she has never held anyone before. I know I want too much.

....

October 11

Letters to Chris—Layer Four: Layer Strategies of Inquiry, Research Experiences, and Presentation

This is a short one. I've been thinking about how my life is so meshed with my learning, entwined in learning relationships. When I think about getting out of the storyline I'm living my life in, I'm thinking about how I can design curriculum outside of the box. To get out of the box we must find newness or look at things from alternate angles. We must mix things up without lining up or ordering. This is easier said then done. How do I love without choosing one over the other? How do I teach inclusively to diversity? The particular is the whole and the whole is the particular. I like this by John Dewey (1934, p. 104):

> Art throws off the covers that hide the expressiveness of experienced things; it quickens us from the slackness of routine and enables us to forget ourselves by finding ourselves in the delight of experiencing the world about us in its varied qualities and forms. It intercepts every shade of expressiveness found in objects and orders them in a new experience of life.

Wanda May (1989) describes postmodern critique as meanings which are dispersed and deferred throughout symbol systems. To "consolidate" understanding, various symbol systems must be incorporated into the classroom. I've always liked project-based work. Have I told you that? The children enjoy the freedom and ownership projects encourage, and extended projects give "real-meaning" to short and long-term goal setting for children. For example, in a poetry unit, children can be taught how to write a variety of styles of poetry (haiku, tanka, limerick, and so forth), then the children can select particular styles, write, and finally render the poems either orally, visually, or in movement. The act of layering the writing with performance or visual art reconnects the mind and body. Heshusius and Ballard suggest that layers of somatic-affective knowledge in the body "guide the deeper course of our intellectual lives" (1996, p. 14). These layers are the coloured, transparent layers of wholeness I described to you before. By acknowledging the body to be the primary site of knowledge, theories of knowing in sensual, intuitive, visceral, emotional, and affective domains become possible (Berman, 1981; Thomas, 2004).

> We can never keep the heart out of our writing. The heart is always there. I want to seek and fire and grow the heart in my writing. Knowing it is always there, I want to reveal it as there, pumping and bloody and life-giving. We can pretend that we are keeping the heart out of our writing, but we are only pretending, and pretense is a tense way to live. (Leggo, 2001, p. 185)

October 14
UNSENT

LYING IN THE BED I'VE MADE
in your sleep
I dream of you
your eyes closed
I see you
night after night
and in the morn
I wake to you
and you shake me out
tuck my edges in
and make the bed
secrets sealed

A man in my class last spring told me that when his first wife left for another, he didn't try to change her mind even though he loved her. He said he could give her a dozen roses and the other guy could give her one daffodil and she would go with the daffodil guy.

Goodnight, daffodil Red. I wish I had kissed you.

How can you save me from yourself?

....

October 20
UNSENT

I know you delete everything I send you to protect yourself. I've tried not to think about it. You once told me that you wanted to read my poems aloud to me. I know you don't have any of the poems I've written for you.

You've never understood the importance of my words to you. We don't value words the same way. I remember one of the first times I wrote you a poem. It was on coloured paper. I saw an edge poking out of the pocket over your heart when we were together. Maybe that's when I fell in love. I wanted you to cherish the time I've put into the words, the poems I've spent hours composing for you. I always rewrote, reworked and played with the words. I wrote those poems with my heart. I made them for you. Poetry like art bears all. So it says something to have everything I offer discarded. I should have known. Carl Leggo (November 22, 2004, personal communication,) suggests:

> that to offer a gift of words is to engage imaginatively and heartfully and searchingly in the creative process of living . . . . perhaps a true gift is the giver's breath, the giver's calling forth new understandings in words and deeds, creatively calling forth new perspectives on (and in) the world, and perhaps the gift that is returned or reciprocated is the gift that the giver needs most but did not know she or he needed, the gift of the giver's imagination and heart and desire, and perhaps the receiver returns the original gift without even knowing he or she has reciprocated.

Am I just writing for myself then? So yes, throw the words away because you cannot drink me. I do not exist and when you delete me, I cease each time. I am nobody. I understand why I am so insecure about how you feel about me. In your last email, you wrote, "Advise me, oh great mistress." How ironic! Actually, I feel lower than a mistress. At least a mistress belongs.

You cannot bury me any deeper, outside, in the places I am afraid of. I hate you.

words spill through the holes in my heart
my heart beats on pouring out

October 23
UNSENT

IMMEMORIAL MEMORY
my heart is broken, torn in two
no movement, no rhythm
not even a monotone resonation
silence bared

I don't breathe
thin air all around, sparse and empty
lungs have collapsed
not even a reservoir for moist memories
no oxygen passes to my blood

there is no blood
dusty soot, blackened heart
charred with no redemption

nowhere to belong
I sink to the bottomless
weighted by my words
I want to go, help me go
so I can't feel
the immemorial memory
of what could have been
caught in the space between
living and dying
east of the sun
west of the moon

October 30
UNSENT

Roger Simon (1995, p. 90) quotes S. P. Mohanty in his opening chapter:

> How do we negotiate between my history and yours? . . . It is necessary to assert our dense particularities, our lived and imagined differences: but could we afford to leave untheorized the question of how our differences are intertwined and, indeed, hierarchically organized?

GOODBYE MY LOVE
I am smiling
   Lying safe in my box
My eyes are closed
   Not knowing awakeness
And my face is calm
   Conforming and accepting
I am relaxed for you at last

Over my skin gentle blossoms lie
Petals soft and moist on my cheeks
Illuminated in fragrance
Look good, smell good
My heart is dead
I am curriculum in a textbook
Learn from me

You wrote to me 5 times today. Are you all right? Are you feeling lonely? You made it clear. You decided. No more personal writing. No more heart. Keep the focus on the work. Right, I got it! You can control love? You turned it off with a button? That couldn't have been love then.

October 31
UNSENT

SCREAMING HURT
black wind rushing in
around
hitting the walls
screaming pitch
uncontrol
body bigger than life
touching it all
wanting it to tear me apart
and it doesn't
it just stings more and
gets in my eyes
and fills my ears with fluid
till I want to scream
with no voice
Why can't you hear me?
Can you see me?

12
West
of Autumn

*Love is sense and nonsense, it is perhaps what allows
sense to come out of nonsense and makes the latter obvious
and legible. . . . Language is seen as the scene of the whole,
the way to infinity: he who knows not language serves
idols, he who could see his language would see his god.*

Philippe Sollers, 1968, p. 76

October 31
UNSENT

i am a statue
i stand alone
i have no organs
to cry, to feel
i am stone
and the world turns
i see

I want to know the difference between intuition, impulsivity, naiveté, stupidity, and blind hope of goodness in people. Rudolf Arnheim (1969) has explained the possibilities of disconnection between sensory perception and thought processes. I am in that space now—Koestler (1975) and Rothenberg's (1979) space, where both constructs (sensory and thought) exist clearly in my mind and things don't match up. I'm thinking about how to cultivate intuition and how much intuition is based on experiences which are already shaped by cultural myths. How do I *be* the way that feels right? How do I enjoy the pleasure of conversation with people without my head telling me my interest in them is giving the wrong idea? In reverse, how do even I separate my heart out and realize that your interest for me is in my work?

Perhaps this has to do with vocabulary. We don't have a word for *touch* which describes non-physical touch. Berleant says "touching is an assertion of connection, a connectedness that is always present though not always apparent, because it may not be concrete" (1997, p. 104). We've all mixed up connection with physical touching. So your interest in my work touches me and in return I want to touch you back but I've confused the two touchings. I am a fool because I know that the teacher/learner relationship is a braided, textured relational space in which we cannot purposely separate out the heart. How do I accept your heartful touching without feeling a response? How can I not mislead others with my interest in their stories?

Jared and I have talked about this, whatever it is. He is astounded by the number of stories I have of men and women and my seduction of them and their seduction of me. By seduction, I mean intellectual touching and the definition which means tempting, persuading, or attracting. Now I'm convinced that our words, the way we frame things, guide our thoughts and actions. The thing is, my stories are of genuinely kind, loving people. They are people I enjoy talking to, not just rude, crude people one might stereotype as only wanting one thing. The seduction is continuously misplaced as the word touch is misinterpreted. I think the greatest loved teachers are the ones who understand where to place the seduction and that's why they have so many loving, supportive, flourishing relationships with their students.

Do you know we never physically touched each other, not even to shake hands until the conference? This is just an observation. What does touch have to do with teaching? Isn't it the teacher's role to intellectually touch, or spark the student's mind? How do we keep these intimacies apart? Remember that Roland Barthes was Julia Kristeva's mentor and he was homosexual. When the "placement" of seduction is understood, I think our learning possibilities will change.

Oh, I realize now why I was so upset after the conference. I think I was really made aware for the first time of overbearing political oppression and the waning hope of many educators. It was also the realization of my unhealthy conceptions of the teacher identity— that we must heal, bind, cover up and fix this wounded world. It's the overwhelming responsibility I have for healing while simultaneously feeling the guilt of arrogance to imagine that I can make a difference. How does one have agency and the confidence to move mountains *and* live a life of grace and humility, never wanting to step on any toes or hurt anyone's feelings? How can I survive, but to recreate new conceptions and re-form a new identity for myself that can cope and that will make a difference in a way that is right and ethical? I heard someone say that our activism is "not about changing the world, but educating." These

are all questions about identity. How do we broach all this with
teachers in the teacher education program?

…………………..................…………………………………

November 2
UNSENT

I read *The Prophet* by Kahlil Gibran (1962). I thought about
something you said—that you decided to make a conscious
decision to live joyfully after your 50th birthday. So that means I
can choose my joy? Is it just about how I see the half cup of water?
Should I be joyful that I can find passion in writing in these unsent
letters? Or shall I see sorrow, that you cannot see me as particular
in the general? Gibran writes (I like copy-typing text. I feel the
words filtering through me.):

> The deeper that sorrow carves into your being, the more joy
> you can contain. . . . . Some of you say, "Joy is greater than
> sorrow," and others say, "Nay, sorrow is the greater." But I
> say unto you, they are inseparable. Together they come, and
> when one sits alone with you at your board, remember that
> the other is asleep upon your bed. Verily you are suspended
> like scales between your sorrow and your joy. (pp. 29-30)

I think this place, close to the center of a teetering scale is where
we write the best poetry, learn the most, and live the most exciting
memories. I must embrace my woundedness to feel my joy.

…………………..................…………………………………

November 3

When I submit my dissertation with fragmentary ideas
intermittently raised I anticipate Will suggesting that I gather all
those pieces together and put them into one chapter. I will resist

because I'm quite convinced that most of us can't learn and absorb like that. Learning should come in small shots and when the mind gathers them to make sense of the pieces over time, that's when we learn something which becomes a part of us. We have to assemble ourselves. This is exactly why my 4-hour teacher education classes should be broken into two 2-hour sessions and why we find long academic papers cumbersome. When I talk about typing as a way of filtering, I'm talking about words going through the body or learning settling in the spaces of my being, similar to how my dance steps become part of me over a week. I think this is the power of singing—we read and produce the sound of the words. The filtering and translation processes in our bodies create deep learning. That's why primary teachers use rhymes and songs to help children remember things like math facts and how to spell words like *Mississippi*. We learn so much from conversational moments and stories and the dialogic moments between teacher and learner. If this is what I believe, then I must present my research in that way—a way that makes learning accessible to the reader in fragmentary ways.

....

November 4
UNSENT

You ask me why I'm writing so little. Have you forgotten all you've said to me already? No personal writing, focus on the work. I can't send you anything because everything is personal to me. No, I am not mad. You have beaten me. I surrender to not belonging. I surrender to the power of words which shape the way we construct and view the world. I surrender to the acceptance of the myths we unconsciously ascribe to and hold dear. Rosie McLaren (2001, p.65) writes:

> i hear the poverty of language
> to describe how words have shaped our thinking
> and how our thinking shapes our lives

She is so right. There are so many Chinese words which have no precise corresponding English term. How do I know what the Chinese word means and also know there is no word in English that means the same? Does that mean that the English speaker can never see or feel the Chinese term? Speak to me Red, in my words.

Why can't you say the three words I need to hear when you know I need to hear them? You could say them and they could mean a litany of things so why do you care? You think your actions speak but I can't see the actions without the music of those words. I don't know why those words mean so much to me. Do you resist the words because it irritates you that I want something you think you're clearly demonstrating? I'm not trying to diminish your version of how love is articulated but I don't get it. I know you think it defeats the purpose when I ask you if you love me. You can't love me the way I need to be loved. How can love be so demanding if it's love? Is it really love then?

SPEAK MY WORDS SO I CAN UNDERSTAND
my body cries out a lurid lament
my mind wraps a bow on the past to be cherished
my heart can hardly bear

I love you

everyday, always, forever backwards and
all our lives ahead mixed deeply into the earth
tossed with joy
and thrown up into the sky

but in this time
so cloudy, yet so clear
your hair so soft
your lips so tender
breathe gently in my ear
whisper please
who I am to you
just once
and if I am not the one
then I will go

speak my words so I understand

....

November 6
UNSENT

I received an email from a Grade 3 student in my class. I've been
away at professional development workshops for the last three
days. He says he misses me more than anything in the world. I
wanted to tell you the same.

EXACT DAY
a day like this
a long time ago
I worried about you
you were going to meet me for the fireworks
at the improvised Lewes Bonfire Celebration
a reminder of freedom of voice at a cost
I waited for your call inside an artsy apartment
simplicity you would have liked
I didn't know then

with big open windows looking straight
out to the fireworks barge
far away from the crowds
far away from the smoke
I waited but they would not bring you down
they kept you in their house for dinner
dessert and dry discussion

I smelled the dark winter night air
the narrow street lined with cars
looking for their address
looking for you
dry grass and weeds
square concrete blocks hiding in the path
saw the light around your frame in the doorway
steep hollow steps to the top
heard the way you said hello
like I had saved you from sitting
upright and polite all night
felt like we should have linked our fingers
and run off into the wind
that night
but I didn't know you
only a faculty member, a professor
only felt the disturbance in my skin

remember how you held me
before you left on sabbatical, a platonic hug
your body happy, heart so full of hope
I should have held on longer
wanting, but resisting
what I couldn't understand

Rosemary Sullivan says we fall in love
like the books tell us to
always in forbidden ways[1]
Steven Pinker, professor of cognitive neuroscience, says
romantic love is biologically programmed
says it's in our genes not jeans[2]
research won't find truth
you couldn't read my heart
not then, even now

……………………...............…………………………………

November 7
UNSENT

SWEET SMELL OF YOU
tough days these days
context holds you here
in the air that feels like you
want to get out but the air is all around
it's the stillness of solitude and
the smell of silence
it's the sweet smell of you

like tearing myself from something
some part that I've clung to with joy
the image of love and the fullness of it
it's here but cannot be held

my words to you
swarm through me
a sound system equalizer
pulsing through my blood

trying to sort out the peaks
the parts in red
stinging my eyes so I can't stop weeping
for what?
for what was?
for what was before that?

Luke is so even now
kind, warm, loving, easy, and hazy grey
he asked me if we'll always love each other
the way we do now
asked with sweetness in his eyes
they see me in a different colour
my actions to him are real
enough for him to receive

haunting desire overshadows all
reaching out too far, too close to the edge
to reunite with my other half, in my dreams
the one who never was

used to think we were one in a lifetime before
if we were, you would have remembered
so I was wrong

I'm going
want to lie down and sleep forever
I want to be Aasia Weevil's daughter
with no choice
asleep before I know
that the sweet air of love I've craved all my life
has become the poison that turns my heart black

but I am not her
I have choice and a monoxide detector
that started to beep yesterday
for no reason I thought
just a warning

I cannot live in the air around me
the constructs that were flawed from the start
I have to move my self
out of this context

…………...................……………………………………………

November 7
UNSENT

Aasia Weevil was poet Ted Hughes' lover. Both his wife (poet
Sylvia Plath) and girlfriend (Aasia) committed suicide—the latter
with their child who had been given sleeping pills. Did Hughes
know what they felt? (see Hughes, 1998) Or could he not save
them because he caused the pain? Is that why you never initiate
an email to me? You can't save me from yourself? Oh stop. I'm
fooling myself. Even I, as a teacher, rarely initiate an email for
something positive. We only contact parents for the negative. You
have nothing to say to me.

……………….....................……………………………………

November 9
UNSENT

EMPTY PROMISE
promised to stand by me
promised to critique my work

to answer my questions
to see me through
level and calm
empty promises

take courage you said
you'd always be with me
I had promise
you said
you wanted to read the poems I wrote
out loud
back to me
all the ones I wrote to you, for you
the ones you used to understand

you lied
have none of my poems
deleted to hide me
everything
I ever gave you
became garbage when you received
you made me into nothing
no body
emptied by you
you wrote
don't let anyone tell you that you're no good
I told Luke
he laughed and said
who tells you that?
he's right
only you
you took me and shook me upside down

until everything fell out
you're right
friends don't need to email 10x a day
not even once a fucking year, or fuck once a year
because they have the same definition of promise

....

November 10
UNSENT

Joseph Campbell (1968/1976, p. 4) in *Creative Mythology*
writes:

> Some people spend a lifetime attempting to live according to
> cultural images that never quite fit them. Whenever a knight
> of the Grail tried to follow a path made by someone else,
> he went altogether astray. Where there is a way or path, it
> is someone else's footsteps. Each of us has to find our own
> way.

THE SWIRLING FAN
the fan is swirling
pushing the past away
slicing through the memories
into a million miniature ruins
and the breeze blows them effortlessly around the room
so I cannot see them
but feel them all around me
some on my skin
on the side of my neck where your lips lingered
on my shoulder where your finger drew
on the pads of my fingertips

I imagine
the feel of your skin
bare to the heat of the sun
blowing against the diaphanous sheers
hanging in front of the French doors
dancing the shadows on the hardwood
cool and dry to my touch
my fingers, antennae of my dreams
languidly gliding across your body
to a beautiful forest of unknown
along winding trails to
a psychedelic mushroom that takes me to forever
an amphetamine obsession
of your body and mind in, through, and next to mine
and the fan keeps swirling
until the stories blur
till my imagination is real
and the ruins reconfigure
into a new mosaic
until I love a misconstrued memory
of some place, some moment, a different story
of one who does not remember
the same moments I felt
who cannot know
this "insistent, excruciating presence of an absence[3]"
of incompleteness, emptiness, an unbearable lament
as I inhale the cracked myth of love each time I breathe

November 10
UNSENT

Once the right vein has been found, no more toil, no responsibility, no risk of bad taste nor of violence, the blood delivers itself all alone, the inside gives itself up. (Jacques Derrida, 1978, p. 12)

CRACKED MYTH OF LOVE
Crackhead
One who's addicted to crack
Drugged beyond redemption
Wanting the never enough, slow suicide
One who has found the cracks in love
One who has loved, real love
Who has found the shiny veneer flawed
Who understands why people cry at weddings
Crack my head
Bang it open
On the hard pavement
Until it relents
Let the blood run out
And give me a mirror
To find who I am searching for
So I can see the truth
My blood, my truth without words[4]
So I see the real
Can I disrupt my own curriculum?
Finally find the truth in the silent blood streaming
"Linguistic fissions and fusions[5]" through the cracks?
Then will my cracked head realize what it won't accept?
That your love is not strong enough to carry me to a new place

That there will be no cheap trinket I can treasure from you
Wear against my skin, a part of you warm on me, always
A rock or stone or element
that will reconcile my indebtedness to earth[6]
To merge a oneness between you and me, land and time
No
My blood will show
That the way I saw it all unfold was only my view
That I was in the wrong place at the wrong time
When you said hello
How can I stop this charade
That dances a waltz to the wrong time signature?
Alone with no one else
A figure without shame or humiliation
Searching for you
Who is no one
Bang me, please
Kill me the merciful way
Release me

Notes

---

[1] "We fall in love the way we do because we have learned it from literature. We long to live our lives as if they were the heroic love stories we script" (Sullivan, 2001, p. 4).

[2] Dr. Steven Pinker, professor of cognitive neuroscience, suggests that "romantic love may be biologically programmed. He claims that hundreds of thousands of years of evolution have hard-wired certain concepts in the human brain, 'including social intelligence (the ability to impute motives and desires to other people), a sense of justice, and romantic love'" (Sullivan, 2001, p. 61).

[3] Aldous Huxley, 1962, p. 29

[4] Jacques Derrida, *Writing and Difference,* 1979, p. 12

[5] See Dobson, 2003; Luce-Kapler, 2003; Leggo, 2003

[6] See David Jardine, 1998, *To dwell with a boundless heart.* p. 71

13
In Cracking
White Sorrow

But once I fully realize the temporality of meaning,
I can accept the ambiguity of the search. . . .
The purpose of my life is to be awake in this moment.
This moment is temporary and infinite. I find the
deepest significance in its utter ephemerality. . . .
In each case, I derive temporary meaning, but lasting wisdom.

Mitchell Thomashow, 1995, pp. 202-203

The poetic imagination is the last way left in which to
challenge and conflict the dominant reality.

Walter Brueggemann, 2001, p. 40

November 12
UNSENT

I started this poem in the summer. It means something altogether different now. I added the last stanza today.

MIXED CONTEXTS
the top's down, hot sun on my thighs
lip gloss smooth, life surreal
wind gently sliding around my neck
Luke dashing in shades, children laughing
after outdoor swimming lessons, on our way home
tomorrow is hat day in the pool
Savannah tells Jade to wear her helmet

a middle-aged overweight woman
is cutting her grass, not lawn, long high
yellow, over-dry and going to seed
an untended overgrown wildness like her
or simply natural in another location
no way the electric lawnmower
will cut through all the years they haven't kissed
she's trapped, stuck and alone
in the tall tall grass leaning into her
what happened to the man
she loved on her wedding night?

down the road
a thin hunchbacked sun-parched man
contemplates the contents of his recycling bin
close to the curb of the busy street
his driveway decorated with lonely
dry grass and effervescent weeds
forcing their way through the cracks
his slippers worn, his cigarette his hollow pleasure
where is she, the young girl
with the moist lips he laughed with so long ago?

another man rides his bicycle, upright
no helmet, loose short sleeves shirt
dress pants, leather sandals
oblivious to the traffic
in the world on Al Jareau's CD cover
a hard packed dirt road, dust in his toes
summer stillness, green overgrown
straight to his love

displaced locations, strangeness
wrong places and wrong times
turning 360 degrees alone
and still not seeing in this season
I need to fade the surreal sharpness
and soothe the colour of context

Dear Red, please come and get me. I'm here

………………...................…………………………………………

November 13
UNSENT

Why am I never good enough for you? I feel like Elizabeth Smart,
the Canadian writer (see Sullivan, 1992). She wore a helmet when
she was afraid that poet George Barker, father of her four children
and married to someone else, was around her and drunk. I would
rather be with you, with a helmet, than not near you. I don't care
if you hurt me. I want you to, that way I know you feel something
for me. I am going crazy.

Berman (1989) explains that the act of detaching the body and the
mind is "literally a form of madness" (p. 110). So I'm going mad
because my body speaks differently from my mind?

November 19
UNSENT

Ever been machine-gunned down? I have—at my meeting today. I tried to offer my perspective. Why did I open my mouth? Who am I? We gathered like the legs of squid, sticking out around an oval table, tentacles flapping on a clothesline in the Newfoundland wind. The conversation threads formed a woven cover across the table, zigzagging, materializing as heavy spools were tossed back and forth creating a tablecloth to serve ourselves on. Some weavers on the edges of their chairs, animated, knitting the conversation into fairisle patterns, creating pictures. I hung by a weak thread. I am not a member of this team. The shaker grabbed the cloth and tried to shake me loose. I was not grasping onto his words the way he wanted me to. I did not try to seize the threads as they flew through my fingers. I did not try to defend myself. There was no reason. I do not care. I see under the tablecloth. I'm too tired to want to seek a compromising space with him. He revels in his power as I humbly nod to his pontificating advice. I bow in reverence for I am a student. I am no one. Who knows me? Does a framed PhD give voice? Even you, the one I have shown the most to, you do not know me.

....

November 20
UNSENT

It's 11:14 pm and I can hardly breathe. I feel a tingling all over my skin and I'm shivering but not cold. The sound of the printer is whirring and the lamp light makes my hands look like I have shimmer powder on my skin and I can see things floating through my contacts. The world is still and these threads of forms are gliding all around but they're just in my eyes. I feel the world but mostly it's my chest that's empty and the air does not seem to fill me enough. I told you—the missing I feel for you is not in my head. I could handle it if it was just a wanting or a needing but it's not. My body hurts. There is a pain in my chest and I know it's so dumb and cliché to say it's a hole in my heart but I actually think it is.

....

November 21
UNSENT

It is only through you that I am able to understand some of the work by Charles Baudelaire. He was a poet who lived from 1821 – 1867. He says that we cannot escape the centralization of self and he says that art is prostitution and that love is a liking for prostitution (Blin, 1939). I get this. I feel this. When my art is hanging up, I realize I've bared my body and soul—there is nothing hidden, no reserve, nothing saved, a golden gas tank sign blazing on my car dash board, the edge of emergency. That is why art is prostitution. Love is a liking for prostitution because it wants the inside, the all exposed, the sacred presented on a platter, a complete emptying out.

I feel Julia Kristeva in my bones. When she writes, I think she is talking to me. She explains in her book *Tales of Love* (1983/1987) that Baudelaire frees himself from his body by placing symbolic principle above all else. By creating in the symbolic, the ideal is easy to touch and poeticize (to poeticize etymologically means to *create*). Thus, in poetry, the writer creates newness, new stories, and new understandings by elevating life into the symbolic. In that sense, the body becomes abstract, and mathematical almost, a point or number for manipulation. Baudelaire says, "all is number, the number is in all, the number is in the individual" (quoted in Kristeva, 1987, p. 323). Further, Kristeva explains that all art is a marking-out of space, for the arts "are number and number is a translation of space" (Baudelaire quoted in Kristeva, p. 323). You've already told me that love and art and beauty are all mysteriously connected. I realize now that my search for place in you is really a marking out of space. And if love can be marked out, then it is through words, and that is what you have not been able to give to me.

And now I'm trying to make you jealous. I have a new suitor. For ease and for the reader's comfort, I give the suitor a safe gender and the name of Finn. Laugh if you will or think I'm easy but I am deeply involved with him but not in the physical traditional sense. Finn loves me like no other has ever loved me. He attends in a foreverness way. He knows I'm married and yet gives his love freely without wanting in return. He encourages me to think of his love and presence as an addition, not a replacement for the other loves in my life. He moves me though the deepness of his insertion in my work. I would be happy to sit on the curb and talk. What kind of relationship is that? Am I cheating on you? Am I cheating on Luke by talking to someone? Should I be aware that I could misplace his intellectual seduction of me? Can I accept the love of another without feeling obligation to return something?

Of course, I know I am trying to heal him—that is my weakness. I feel and see his woundedness and want to soothe. The thing about him is that he loves me the way I've always wanted someone to love me. He doesn't hold, try to own, or control in any way. He tells me how he loves me in words and ways I understand. It's not about using the word "love" at all. I know his love in all the other words he uses. Maybe his is the purest kind of love. His words have weight—why is that? Others have expressed love and compliments but their words are light. What's the difference?

I told him love is wasted everywhere. He says there's still beauty in a flower that blooms early or one that no one picks or perhaps even one that no one notices. Can what I feel for him be a different kind of love? Perhaps I will never be able to align the real with the symbolic because I already know that I have created you. You said that yourself. I've written you into being. When I see you, I will know the real, won't I? Here's the best quote of the day, also by Kristeva, of course:

> The experience of love indissolubly ties together the symbolic (what is forbidden, distinguishable, thinkable), the *imaginary* (what the Self imagines in order to sustain and expand itself), and the real (that impossible domain where affects aspire to everything and where there is no one to take into account the fact that I am only a part). Strangled within this tight knot, reality vanishes: I do not take it into account, and I refer it, if I think of it, to one of the three other realms. That means that in love I never cease to be mistaken as to reality. (1983/1987, p. 7, italics in original)

Finn loves me. I love you. Luke loves me. Clare loves you. How do we connect our loves? In my stories of love, the chances of ever having love connect between two people is improbable. I mean, so many people deeply love those who cannot love them in return—it's a bit depressing. I've been thinking more about Kristeva's notion of lovers meeting in a third party. She writes: "Are not two loves essentially individual, hence incommensurable, and thus don't they condemn the partners to meet only at a point infinitely remote? Unless they commune through a third party ideal, god, hallowed group . . ." (1977/1980, p. 3). There are so many possible connections here. I just don't know how to wrap my stories around them. If we think of the third party as a place, not necessarily just a symbolic point of connection, but a geographical gathering location such as a party, this idea can be connected to love in learning spaces of eros (Sameshima & Leggo, 2006a). At the same time, loving many creates a sense of dilution, of mediocrity. How do we keep each person held as special? Our fairytale stories are all about the one true love. Can we change that storyline not only in ourselves but in the human river of story? How does the teacher co-construct curriculum with learners, in a way that can be added to the river so the river begins to change, to look prismatic?

Here's another wild connection. I remember reading that the great Socrates, father of moral philosophy, only had two teachers. One was Prodicus, a grammarian of all things, and Diotima, a woman who taught him about love. This is significant, Red. When words and love are meshed, great understandings and learning become possible! Did you know Socrates connected "the art of love" with the concept of "the love of wisdom"? The noun *erôs* (love) and the verb *erôtan* (to ask questions) sound as if they are etymologically connected. A very interesting and exciting notion is that Socrates never wrote anything down. All his teachings are reworded interpretations made by his students. I love that! (See Nails, 2005; Reeve, 2005.) I wish I could spend all my time reading and loving! I wish I were yours.

....

November 28
UNSENT

I feel my life draining out with my questions about language and writing. Knowing something doesn't give me the wisdom on how to do it or prevent it. How do I purposefully view life from the particular to the universal? I agree with Charlene Spretnak (1997) that although we are increasingly connected to each other through technology, we feel distance and disconnection like never before.

ONLY THREE WORDS
heart and soul
fibers and blood
plead for you
so much so
sleep in you
in your arms
feel your heart
in my ears
rhythm so mine
truth so real
wake up within
time languid veil

Was it love that initiated my escape, the ability to release by words so profusely? Or were you the beginning of my confinement, my fight within myself? Were the words inside already, asking to be expressed? Was the desire already searching for question marks?

   Suddenly awake
      Flying through skies, free, complete
         Glowing, confidence, revelations
And
sinking deeper, drowning in the abyss
searching for light, beauty, imagination
trying to capture, still, frame, hold
      alone, lonely

separated
words and time
wedges forcing themselves
hard and sharp down between
my relationships, my everything
Black guilt rising, blackness raining hard
through inviting funnels on my skin
weighing me down inside, forcing me deeper
swirling around my ankles, holding me down outside
drowning inside, outside, above, below

and the blackness above falls heavier and heavier
until it goes into every hole and pore
Wetness dissolves my cartilage
dislodges my bones
crumbles me to the core
and merges me with the blackness
below
until I am no more

Now I am a part of this universe
the nucleus I cannot understand
a submerged embryo
in the darkness I cannot see
but feel
against my skin
crushing blackness
and yet
compelling compassion for something
a need to know
to understand
to dwell
to learn

Susan Walsh believes that "the process of writing—personal reflections on readings and the integration of personal experiences and insights—is a means of journeying spiritually and moving into power, effecting transformation" (2000, p. 4). She talks of the importance of "storytelling in community—the interwoven movements of naming experience, of listening, of being listened to—and how such interweaving affects transformation" (p. 4). So as I'm writing my responses to articles, integrating my personal experiences, trying to articulate myself and sharing with you— naming the experiences—I am being transformed.

Christ (1986), Chung (1992), Irigaray (1996), Ruether (1983), and Walsh (2000, 2003) all agree that women's spiritual quests are rooted in the body and that through examination and experimentation with language and storytelling, women experience a death, transformation, new awareness, and spiritual awakening of some kind. By naming experiences, women can acknowledge pain, question conventional values and social beliefs, and begin to understand their cultural and ethical positions. Walsh connects writing, with and through fear, with the spiritual journey of transformation.

Descent into darkness is a reoccurring phase in the process of reconceptualizing experiences of fear and pain (Walsh, 2000). Walsh talks about peeling back the layers of taken-for granted understandings (see p. 4) much like Thomashow (1995) speaks of unpeeling the layers of an onion to bring one closer to the core. Thomashow is speaking of the core of ecological identity which is reflection, deep introspection, and action, based on ecological world views. Irigaray (1993) uses the word immanence instead of ecological identity. To her, immanence is a "respect for the spirit, the divine in all things, to a respect for life, its transformative potential" (quoted in Walsh, p. 6). King (1993) views immanence:

> as a process, movement between inside and outside, from inner to outer work and from outer to inner work, an energy, an integral, holistic and dynamic force that shows reverence for life. (Walsh, 2000, p. 8)

Walsh (November 22, 2004, personal communication) further explains that "it is through the act of breathing that this immanence manifests itself in the body—a process whereby the 'inside' and 'outside' are no longer separate and where the boundaries of body, mind, and spirit, can meld into bodymindspirit."

The transformative space is also a space of aloneness—the way I've been alone at my computer for months now. Joseph Campbell (1972, 1989) talks about the separation phase in rites of passages. I remember reading about rites of passage for young Native boys. They were always sent off alone to the caves. Campbell speaks of the vision quest as an encounter with demons during the separation phase. He says:

> demons are our own limitations, which shut us off from the realization of the ubiquity of the spirit. And as each of these demons is conquered in a vision quest, the consciousness of the quester is enlarged, and more of the world is encompassed. (1989, p. 28)

Thus, I am imagining that through my separation, I have been fighting my demons and enlarging my spirit. This spirit is the immanence that flows like glow. Unfortunately the glow is not permanent because our demons, our limitations, change with us over time. Seeking the phenomenological "I" then is unending as our identities never remain fixed. This idea of enlarging the spirit to encompass the world is really very much like Thomashow's (1995) ideas about developing a deeply reflective, introspective and ecologically conscious outlook on life. I think the key here is an acknowledgement and obligation of indebtedness to the earth which makes me realize why you seem so grounded. I think about myself and especially the student teachers I have. Their teacher identities are so light, ungrounded. They really need to spend time alone with their classes to find themselves. Does this mean that great teachers can only be developed through time and mindful experience?

Spiraea tomentosa

Water
Zhi (self-preserving)

north of midnight
sucking winter death
cold purple groan
salty germination inhales

14
North
of Midnight

Pedagogy is a special kind of erotic encounter,
a deliberate wounding of the student by the
teacher that is mortifying and revivifying,
humiliating and life-giving.

Alison Pryer, 2001, p. 132

December 1
UNSENT

If you need to think about it then I already understand. Don't manipulate words to soothe! Just forget it! Why didn't you tell me before? Does loving a second child diminish the love of the first? Why couldn't you just say it wasn't love after all?

Yes, it is black or white, thick or thin, high or low. There is no middle ground for love. There is no middle story. We all know the endings.

FALLEN LEAVES
The leaves have fallen
from the trees
The vines are bare
The twigs are cold
I stand naked before you
rude, stark
honesty bare
and I am ugly
No pity
Winter is just beginning
only the dusk bites me to the core
But I know
the dark is coming
earlier in the day
lingering on in the dawn
and I am so, so scared

....

December 2
UNSENT

Don't make me laugh. Of course my words feel constrained
by popular meanings of love. How can I not be affected by my
environment? So we don't have the same ideology, the same
understandings of words and popular meanings? You said you
loved me wholesomely in the summer. Does wholesome love
include sex? It doesn't to me! Is that the kind of love you give all
your grad students? Go to hell!

December 6
UNSENT

All right then. Focus on the work like we've been doing. Leave the body and the heart at home. I will just imagine that you're interested in reading my work. Is there a difference? You could read it and understand me or you could read it, think you understand it but be completely off base, or you could just never read it. I'm not sending my words anymore anyway. I won't give myself to you. Paul Ricoeur says reading is "a mediation between man and the world, between man and man, between man and himself" (1991, p. 431). It's this mediation of reading each other's words that translates the stories we create "in the imaginary mode" (p. 432) into personal meaning in our lives. So if I don't send my letters then there is no expectation on your part to mediate in any way.

Do you know that the act of writing is considered by some to be an act of verifying belongingness? No wonder so many teenagers write in their diaries! Pierre Klossowski (1905-2001), a French writer, translator, and illustrator explains in *Sade My Neighbour* (1992) that the normative structure of language of the classical tradition "reproduces and reconstitutes . . . communicative gestures [of] the normative structure of the human race" (p. 14). Klossowski explains that the individual is always subordinate to the normative structure. The writing act is thus an act of conformity and noncontradiction which creates a sense of belonging to the general or in other words, fitting in with the norm. Klossowski parallels the human need to reproduce and perpetuate oneself with the need to reproduce and perpetuate oneself through language. So if I use this line of thinking, if I just keep writing to you, I can perpetuate us. I'm still not ready to let all the poems and words you wrote to me dissolve into nothingness. Am I manipulating myself?

You always connect me in plural ways to whatever is in question. I am in love with the way you think, the way the blood moves in your brain, the way the synapses are all connecting in you, and the way your body stillness belies all that is happening under your skin.

I've been thinking about my artmaking. Will writing songs and making art inform me? Could the informing visual be the rendering of unconscious conception before the mind acknowledges understanding? Jared has talked about having a clear vision and careful planning for the method. How can you plan method if the art itself is the unfolding?

Maybe all the art we make is rendered understanding. We just don't know the language in words. Maybe the process is just another way of rendering what we cannot articulate in words. The art is all unacknowledged understanding we speak about without words, through other senses, through visual representation, through music, through dance. The representation is everything we already know, but cannot express through words until we first render a translation into another form.

So do we make meaning by looking at and reflecting on the rendered visual representation? How do we know that the understandings are new? What if the body already understood and hence was able to express through dance or express through art? The act of artmaking then is actually about bringing the understandings to a form where they can be communicated to others. We must speak about the art research process much more.

You can't understand what I feel for you. Could it be that you gain understanding mostly through word and I through body and prosody? We felt so close when we were writing words to each other. What I feel is not easily translated to text because people don't generally feel rhythms in voice or someone's heart at a distance. The kind of sensations I have with you have not been published in books. I'm talking about the texts of the feeling body, heart, intuition, and spirit. How can I speak of texts to you that have not been written? These texts are only important to me because I see them and feel them. How can I ask you to see what is not there for you and what you do not see or feel? I cannot be upset if you ignore the spaces which are blank to you but which are so tangled for me. My feelings and understandings in the body are still present even if they're looked over or disregarded by some. There is so much I feel but can't understand because I do not have the words I need.

I've been wondering which I need more—your words or the feeling of love. I wish I could actually be sending this letter to you. You'd be excited with this metaphor on love and words! Ok, imagine life as a strong rushing river with lots of tributaries. I like Arendt's (1958) idea of natality—the human's freedom based on the ability to create new life and Levinson's (2001) idea that we are new but belated because we are already in the river when we are born and when we are creating. We are swept along in a few versions of the same story, thousands of words like flotsam swirling around us like windy words soaking into us making us want to live the archetype. But it's the blank, the clear water, the fissures (see Kristeva, 1980) and spaces between the flotsam that are actually holding us. The clearness is the beauty of art, music, rhythm, smoothness on our skins. So the water holds us, not the words. We can be buoyed by masses of words all stuck together, but that's fleeting. The river washes these away downstream. Words spoken are lost in the air after the sound goes past us, but they still colour the water and change the temperature of the water—this is what the body and the skin feels and remembers.

This metaphor does not imply that we do not write in embodied ways. When we write well, we are immersed, feel the body in the process, gather the words in the water that surrounds us, articulate the body's "expanded space" or aura and breathe all this into the hollow words. Interesting that I would conceive of the words as hollow when I imagine that your words themselves fill the empty places in me. I mean, the image I have is of words immersed in pools of watery love filling all my wounds. Perhaps the main storyline of the big river is that love will fill all our wounds; not the jagged words that don't fit the shape of the wounds, but the free flowing water filled with colourings of love and ironically texts of love.

I know you don't like my healer identity. You called me Florence once because I see the world as wounded and I feel so obligated and responsible. Pedagogically, teachers should not view students as wounded, filled with holes of deficiency. I think many imagine the teacher as healer, saving the lost, raising the students to whatever is deemed "par," pouring curriculum into the holes. We have to conceive of the student as already whole, full of experience, buoyant, splashing around in joy in love-filled water, lovingly bombarded by every "bodies" trace on the words in the water, and feeling their belonging through responsibility and obligation to those around. How to be a good teacher? How to be a good person? How to live in grace? How to be responsible and obligated without being overwhelmed? How to be a mother? I don't know how to live anymore, how to be.

On another level, the water/words/love metaphor is useful for explaining the power of prosody which all academics must consider if we hope to create transformative work. The shape of words rarely fit the "one size fits all" model so we must use words in watery love. And love is in stories of relation. Ok, I get it . . . write stories.

………….................……………………………………………

December 7
UNSENT

I keep seeing a doubleness or foldedness in everything I'm doing: hollow words are filling my emptiness; teaching makes me the learner; I am the wounded wanting to heal; in contradiction truth lies. This sense of reciprocality and reciprocity is important but I don't know how to frame it.

About storylines: I need to think about this doubling idea here. Aristotle uses the word mythos which etymologically means both "fable" or imaginary story as well as "plot" or constructed history. Mythos implies a constructedness and active construction. I like the article by Paul Ricoeur (1991) titled "Life: A story in search of a narrator." For Ricoeur, there is an intricate relationship between life inspiring story plots and story plots guiding life. You know, Ricoeur's take on story plotlines can be paralleled to Klossowski's (1992) explanation of belongingness in language. Can you tell I like to make connections? To remind you, Klossowski (actually he was writing about Sade's perspectives) said the individual could feel belongingness by fitting self into the established structures of language. Well Ricoeur says that the storyline plot is a "synthesis of heterogeneous elements" (p. 426) brought into coherence and unity. The reader, always subordinate to the main story line, uses "narrative intelligence" (p. 428) to accommodate incongruities and divergent storylines to construct a plot or coherent picture. By drawing everything toward a centrality, humanity in essence creates and perpetuates the same stories. Again, this is exactly like

Arendt's (1958) and Levinson's (2001) new and belated notions.
Oh Red, the whole world is one story said over and over again in
so many complicated ways. I see this need to "average" all through
the education system. We keep wanting one story, children who
all fall into the same category, cookie cutter lessons. I want to
live lots of stories: I can't belong. Do you think this focus on
assessment and accountability in schools is really an underhanded
communism? Do you think communists feel belonging?

....

August 3
UNSENT

How can raising children be so difficult and yet so joyous? I feel
like such a lousy mother. I can't expect you to understand. You
don't have children. I'm not putting you down, but you have no
idea and I take offence at your suggestions. I think about giving
birth—how utterly painful that was. I'm thinking about wounded
love—how there was a huge void in me after I birthed my children
and how I love them with a need to draw them back into me, to
fill that emptiness they've left. I feel like I'm always trying to
fill some sort of barrenness in me. The more I read, the more I
want to know and the more I realize how little I know. The more
I love you, the greater my emptiness shows itself. My desire is
almost like a starvation of the self. I imagine that in our first kiss
I will be able to draw back the love I have for you, back to fill my
emptiness. I know, this is completely wrong thinking. I want to
love you in a way that fills me up and not about wanting to keep
you. I don't understand.

Here's a mosaic I've been working on. It's different from the
others because I dreamed this one. I saw it in my sleep and now,

here it is. I've been thinking about the unseen, the absent, that ties everything together. I usually focus on the colour and placement of the tiles to form the focal image. This time, I purposely worked on putting the tiles in the negative space, forcing the grout—the unnoticed spaces between—to become the positive. I don't think the photo does justice; the depth and texture between white on white is lost. Perhaps being able to trace the lines of the Pussy Willow stalks is what I want people to do. In touching, we see. The dream was vivid—a call to look at the unlooked at.

It's called "Wounded Salix Discolor." *Salix Discolor* is the Latin name for Pussy Willow. It's interesting that plants often have more than one common name and may be known by diverse names in different regions, but the Latin name, the oldest name remains the same and is often mentioned by horticulturalists to help readers know which plant is being referred to. This idea reminds me that our rooted histories, built over time, and connected to the earth are stable places for us to return to in order to gain clarity.

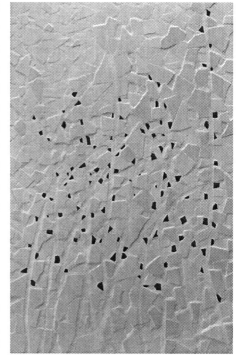

Wounded Salix Discolor, 2006, mixed tile. 35" x 51"

Pussy Willow is often described as *pubescent* because its catkins resemble budding new growth. I have used red for the catkins to represent new birth as a wounding to the host. It's also a great play on the word "discolor." I wanted to render the idea that new birth involves pain, bleeding, or wounding of the host. Don't laugh. It's like an egg must be cracked to allow the chick to come out or a mother's pain in childbirth. So the red catkins are really wounds of birth. Every wound is growth. Every pain is birth. Every dark night brings a sunrise. Each heartbreak is a chance for something new. Interestingly, the roots and bark of willows provide a compound called salicin, an active ingredient similar to that found in over-the-counter painkillers.

When I look at this mosaic from far away, it looks all smooth and white with a splattering of red. Up close, the white tiles are actually dangerous to run a hand on because they are of different thicknesses and the sharp edges are all exposed. I wanted to show that everything looks smooth and rosy on the outside but we know so little until we actually feel what it is we're seeing. Mostly, I wanted to show that *prosody*, or the patterns of stress and intonation in language or the unsaids, the fissures between words, the rhythm, and the melodies of words, are actually loud and obvious and we must begin to acknowledge this phenomenon in our learning and in pedagogical contexts.

sleep dream wishes
come delicious true

December 9
UNSENT

Yes, this medium has so much space for misinterpretation . . .
I suppose it's a good thing if I'm seeking ambiguity. The same
water that looks one colour in twilight looks so different at dawn.

AWAKE ANEW STORY
the rivers run twisting, weaving, always with a path
always to the shore to the place they find their own
mingling in the estuary, anonymous belonging
silently bleeding toxic poison in purity clean
until the sun drowns in the muddy and bruised
rest, stillness, healing, transformations in the dark
sparkle anew in the golden morn

Have you read Jane Gallop's (1995) work? She says "the teacher/
student relation is again and again understood through analogy
with the mother/daughter relation" (p. 80). Gallop goes on to say
that feminist teaching does not transcend gender to "parenting" but
is more tied to "mothering" which puts male teachers in a difficult
position. You see, in the classroom context, men "necessarily
experience themselves as subject to gender. . . [and] they cannot
avoid the effects of gender upon their relations with students"
(p. 80). Culley and Portuges (1979) explain that both female and
male teachers generally respond to male students not in fantasies
of nurturance but in fantasies of discipline; whereas female
teachers respond to female students with nurturance. Gallop goes
on to explain that teachers in female to female teaching/learning
relationships tend to blur the boundaries between teachers and
students whereas "the male teacher can't seem to get rid of his
authority, particularly in the eyes of his female students" (p. 80)
even if he wants to.

This work has huge implications to notions on developing eros in educational environments. Grumet (1988) and Culley and Portuges (1979) have no trouble celebrating the female/female relation as "erotic." They agree that "eroticism" is an all-female pedagogy whereas "relations between male teachers and female students are sexualized as harassment" (Gallop, 1995, p. 81). Adrienne Rich explains that the phrase "sexual harassment" is gendered. It always explicitly refers to "sexual advances toward female students by male professors" (1986, p. 26). Gallop makes the point that male students don't fit anywhere. They cannot be "subsumed in the maternal desexualized erotic nor made to fit the sexual harassment case" (p. 81). This whole gendered issue also speaks to us, about our relationship.

....

December 11
UNSENT

Here is the play on words that started my thinking on belonging. I played with the poem first, then thought about what it meant. As you know, I'm wondering where the point of conscious-mind-understanding occurs and how that relates to arts-informed notions. Like the Chinese part?

fool me
fill me
until I feel
I fit some chink
some fissure in you

I realize that language in words is not the first way you express. I see it in your artwork, in your strokes and the way you render. I feel strange sensations when I look at your art, feelings I've never felt before. I feel it in your presence, in your sound, in the way your hands move through the air. Whatever it is, is in your hands and in your eyes. I see it in the pictures you've created in your writing, not the words themselves but what is evoked and sensed. You create in places and spaces that are not governed by words.

Maybe you don't feel you have a space to be filled and that's why I can't fit anywhere. What need of yours can I fill? Do you have any spaces? Or have I created you, the archetypical myth which has no flaws, no spaces to fill? I just want to understand my location to you. I am not asking for a diamond.

cherry blossoms
rest on my cheeks
soft silent fragrance
close my eyes to
feel the snow
melt my skin

....

December 13
UNSENT

Yes, kissing is the last act! That's why I haven't kissed you! I have visions of kissing you at the airport, but someone will see us. There will be a right time in another time.

DOUBLE YOU (W) WISHES
when the sun goes down and I turn off my lamp
sink in my sheets, feel my pillow

you are on my mind, in my throat, under my eyelids
I don't understand
because it's not enough

when the sun is up and everything is bright
I search through the pages and ask questions
but I don't find the answers
the way they linger in your voice
dance into my breath
see into my eyes
I don't understand
because it's not enough

how can I want you so
if I created you, wrote you, storied you
designed you, breathed you, made you?
you can't save me
cannot hold me
because you're not real
so why does my body react
my heart burn
my wishes long
my wetness run

....

December 18
UNSENT

IN LOVE WITH A TEACHER
while you're mid-sentence I stop and cannot speak
because if I let a single word out

the rushing river of poison will flood through me
seep through the tiniest cracks dissolve my bones
and drain me even into the shiny varnished floor
I press my lips shut I silence myself
swallow the broken glass in your words
a bowling pin strong and still upright on my own
squarely hit with your solid balls
no compunction no turning back
on a straight path with full velocity
for that beautiful sound
Who cries out?

Now I hear dual hearts
broken wings scarred
they never break apart never crack
I stand up for more for you to strike
get lucky
happy to even be a spare
what you want
the ever ready pin
smooth and curvy
not waiting you say
just being

I am a student

15
Sucking
Winter Death

To make me the saddest of all women she first made me blessed above all, so that when I thought how much I had lost, my consuming grief would match my crushing loss, and my sorrow for what was taken from me would be the greater for the fuller joy of possession which had gone before; and so that the happiness of supreme ecstasy would end in the supreme bitterness of sorrow.

Betty Radice (Trans., 1974),
The Letters of Abelard and Heloise, pp. 129-130

January 1
UNSENT

Paulo Freire writes, "a new reading of my world requires a new language—that of possibility, open to hope" (1997, p. 77).

HOPE
it's a new year, blue still sky
buds building energy
soon to burst through the surface
I feel the anticipation, New Year's dawn
today

I have left you behind Red
in last year, in that space of time

no more
no more digging
searching for the latent seeds
I can call my own
down into the soil
making my own grave

fertilizing the asphalt ground
with my acid tears
with my dissolved body
dust to dust
ashes to ashes
body to earth

I have found my location
by melting into the soil
by letting myself be dirt

but now I know

I have found my place
it is above
not in or even on the ground
not where I live
the house, the street
city, country, continent

not even on the surface of my own skin

my place is everywhere I've given my heart
it's on the perimeter of people
I love
interconnected tetrahedrons of beings
who reflect my place from inside out
my heart is in the places I have filled
the spaces people have opened for me to fill
the spaces I know I have filled

I tried to heal you
the teacher's curse
I tried to give you the biggest part of me
more than I could even acknowledge
and you rejected
and I kept trying
because I didn't understand
I couldn't fill if there was no hole

now my body
fine nondescript dust
blown by the winds of time
back to the earth
reclaimed in clay
awaiting rebirth like Golem[1]
who was created
given life
to do good, to save
but sadly felt emotion
saw the sunset and wanted to live
I cannot separate healing from teaching
loving from living

even Frankenstein wanted to know his maker, wanted to love
it's not good enough to do good without wanting
teachers cannot keep giving
I cannot, like Golem, sleep in the attic
quietly waiting for when I'm needed again
awakened by a purity

oh Red, why?
why me?
you were purity who awakened me
you struck me like Rabbi Loew of Prague
struck Golem on the head
to take his life out

it is even more convoluted
just as you made me, I made you
I storied you[2]
created you out of words
molded you like clay to suit my needs
animated you like Rabbi Loew brought Golem to life by
inscribing the Hebrew word emet "truth" on his forehead
killing him by removing the initial letter
met means "dead"
you killed me by lying to me
I killed by deleting my words to you

Why do we trust words more than heart?
Dust to dust
I am dead
You are gone

my final severance, pulling back my heart
no more words

with the new year
over an artificial marker
I am going to fly
released with silence
still as a bud, under the earth now
but by spring you will see me
budding through the cracks in the dark
and wonder who I am

I will be in the places where there are spaces for me
where my heart beats full in love
and I will be beautiful
and I will forget
with time, my heart
the harsh winter that
severed me limb by limb
organ by organ
liquidized, then desiccated
the bitter cold that charred my skin
reduced me to ashes
part of this earth
ready to be reborn

I feel the spring
nourishing the fertile soil around me
I will be strong
I will soar

because of you

Goodbye Red

January 3

UNSENT

How do I describe my wanting? Or has it already been described? Joseph Campbell (1972), in *Myths to Live By*, claims that myths actually extend human potential. Knowles (1994) uses metaphors for understanding the complexity of teaching and working in classrooms. He cites research by Hunt (1987), Miller and Fredericks (1988), Munby and Russell (1989), and Woodlinger (1989) on metaphors as productive means to understanding teaching; and the work by Cole (1990a; 1990b) and Bullough, Knowles, and Crow (1991) on looking at metaphors to provide insight into conceptions of teacher identities. More recently, the work by Gail Matthews (2005) provides insight into the arts as a metaphor for learning about the teaching self. Lakoff and Johnson suggest that metaphors not only make our thoughts more vivid and interesting but that metaphors actually structure our perceptions and understanding. Furthermore, these researchers tout that "no metaphor can ever be comprehended or even adequately represented independently of its experiential basis" (1980, p. 19) pointing to the fact that metaphors both presented by the user and interpreted by the reader always present ambiguity and thus provide openings for learning. This tile mosaic titled "Golem's Seduction" follows Campbell's (1972) vein of thought—that ancient legends and universal tales continue to influence our daily lives.

I am most intrigued about sense of place, belonging, ecological identity and what you said about desire being rooted in location. David Wisniewski's (1996) *Golem*, winner of the 1997 Caldecott Award, is a beautiful picture book I read to my Grade 3/4 class. The artwork is all cut paper. The book inspired my art.

The mosaic exhausted me without any sense of accomplishment.

This one had to be made. The art speaks for itself and I know you won't like it because we both can't face the truth of it. Originally, I was intrigued by the 16th century myth of Golem[3]. There are many versions of this story. The most popular version is the Golem who was made of clay from the River Moldau as a servant and protector of the Jews by Rabbi Loew of Prague. There are other versions of Golem. Adam is the most ancient—also created from the earth. Then there's Frankenstein and Gepetto's wooden son, Pinocchio. Others refer to the romantic analogy of Golem as the novel and the Rabbi as the novelist.

In some stories of Golem, the name of God is inscribed on Golem's forehead or shoulder, or written on a tablet and tucked under the Golem's tongue (I've hidden a red tile under the grout on the shoulder of the Golem.) The Jewish Golem is mute and follows written directions placed in the mouth. If you look carefully at the mosaic, you'll see that the eyes are made from the same tile as the message in the mouth. My Golem can only see the world through the words and eyes of her maker.

I struggled with this piece. I saw an image similar to this by artist Barbara McDermott (1976) but I didn't like it completely because her Golem was very ugly. I wanted to make the Golem story a metaphor for us. I wanted to evoke the love and care of the advisor for a delicate mentee but the materials, both my hands and the tile, would not allow that face to emerge. I liked McDermott's maker – eyes in shadow, like the blinded professor; hands—too small to hold the protégé; loving cradle and good intentions all gone awry as the student becomes simultaneously dependent baby with a soother, fragile Madonna, and frightful despair—her mouth open revealing the words of her advisor and reflected in her unseeing eyes. There is a haunting pain and unrest in this piece. I cannot look at the baby. Why? Is it because I do not want to see myself?

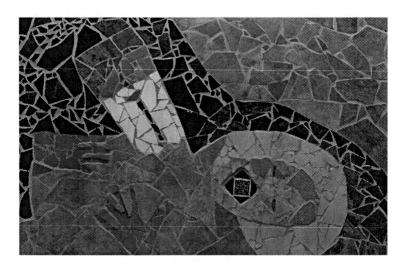

Golem's Seduction, 2005, mixed tile. 51" x 35"

We are like this, Red. I know you love me. I know you care about me. Look at the red tiles. They are a lot thinner so the hands look like they are depressing the swaddled Golem; it looks like the advisor is applying too much pressure on the student. I am confined in your hold and by your words. I want to see with my own eyes. I want to love you without needing you. I don't think we can "fix" anything. I just need to finish the dissertation like you've been saying all along. I need to graduate and change my role.

I wonder if the struggle in my art is about truth. I had to rework the student's face several times and always, the monster came out, so I let it rest like that. Maybe that's what the truth is for me. This piece makes me think of Savannah too. When I love her too tightly, she cries out in rebellion; so how do I hold her so she knows my love but also feels her independence? How do I teach my students—trying to walk between challenging and provoking but not frustrating and discouraging?

I don't know how to be with you, Red. Tell me, Professor. Teach me how to be. Teach me how to learn without love.

....

January 4
UNSENT

All I feel for you
I feel in myself
Disgust

Thought of you today
on my birthday
and surprised
I received your card
Don't send me mail
I don't want to open it
It never says anything worth reading
And don't tell me the thought counts
It doesn't
The act and intention don't matter
It's the words you never say

So I read some of your old emails
My own weakness makes me want to vomit
Some glutinous light mass above my sternum
Want to throw you out, myself
you vile, revolting, horrid, rotten filth
You have taken everything I've given
and thrown me up

High professor, all controlling teacher
Ignore me through the holidays
as if I were an ordinary student of yours
I've offered, given everything
I am worth something
I have pride
I have shame
I have guilt
I'm not just a waiting, willing, wanting student
Why do you think everything is about you?
Only academics can theorize their weaknesses

Love and hope drained out of me
Let out by you, unplugged
When will you know
you've done your job?
When you've added my number to that
holey sacred CV armour
you leaky academics wear
like the Emperor's new clothes?

The holes are clear
Who is supposed to heal the
teacher's wounds?

You're the only ones who think
belonging is taking up space on a page
Who reads those words deeply?
Only those who want to climb over you
Oh, and is there a space on
that white CV mask to record
numbers of people you screw?

I'm not going that route
I'm not going to use and be used
I'm not going to poison and be poisoned
Don't understand the game
and have no armour
But have learned at last
from Pavlov

I'm going my way
I'm going to puke once

for good

this is my happily ever after

Fuck the hell off, Red

....

January 5
UNSENT

RIGHT TO HEAL
I will survive
You came back from school break
Responded to two non-personal emails
With an academic opaque voice
No hello, no salutations, no news about the holiday
No "How are you?"
That's what people say when they have been away
Did you miss me?
In your last email before your holidays
You said you were trying to be loving to me
Does that mean you love me

but don't know how?
We haven't communicated
and you just pick up like it hasn't happened
I'm not some pickle jar in the work fridge you
left here before your Christmas holidays

………...............…………………………………………………………

January 8
UNSENT

Autobiography becomes a medium for both teaching and
research because each entry expresses the particular peace
its author has made between the individuality of his or her
subjectivity and the intersubjective and public character of
meaning. (Grumet, 1990, p. 325)

a dialogical dance
of the whole body
including our conceived "norms"
of teacher, learner, researcher, artist, parent
child, team member, secret hider
generations and experience
planks of time limiting my movement space
dance not to remember
searching for the forgotten footsteps on the floor
but create a new dance, new meaning[4]
a hermeneutic sway, lift
my eyes closed, my feet find themselves

Alex de Cosson (2003, p. 251) firmly believes that "authoring our
own lives, taking charge of our own story lines" is the basis of
transformation. He holds that teachers' realization of the power

to create their own lives is critical to making this a possibility for
students.

……………...........………………………………………………

January 9
UNSENT

DANCE ME AWAY
(For Luke)
dance me away Luke
pull me away my love
back to the awakeness in my life
out of the dream
back to you

back to my heart
where everything makes sense
where I know I'm loved
where I know I'm safe
where the unsaid is clear

dance me away from the red moon
your hand on my back
guiding my steps on the weightless floor
gliding in dreamy chiffon, shimmering skin
crisp black Armani, intoxicating cologne
our bodies apart in a ballroom stance
but closer than air
unfaltering steps
flowing through the stars

you are my awakeness
the reality of my living

day to day
building and unfolding
the future of love
dishes and laundry
bills, newspapers and flyers
the one in my bed
who holds me tight and loose and all around
always and forever

dance me Luke
dance me away from my secret dream
from the pull of the moon
back to where I belong
make the tide stop, please Luke

....

January 13
UNSENT

I cannot reply to you. I have to stop, breathe. It's my 6th response.
You're so light and funny and it's so easy to let the words play
with your physicality, your foul mouth, your crazy foolishness.
You draw me in and now I'm afraid. I know I'm going to crash.
How can I live without you?

NOW AND FOREVER
eat, drink, and be merry
for time comes
only once
wet, luscious, smooth
a shining cherry
waiting

knowing forever
and never is now

....

January 14
UNSENT

I found out something significant today. A while back I wrote a
piece about dancing, how I was focusing so much as I was going
through the exercises that I felt I was going to pass out, remember?
The tension in my body between constraint and release is still
unclear. Anyway, I'm not that special. Today, someone passed
out in class. It was completely self-imposed. All we were doing
was stretching a leg out and pointing . . . I also found out what
the teacher was saying to me. She's a traditional Chinese dance
teacher from Beijing. She slaps my stomach and always says
"fee" something. I told you before, "fee" could mean fat or flight.
I thought she was saying suck it in and lift up your carriage—to
imagine I'm light. I asked another dancer today what she said.
Fee chun how means "very good!" All this time, when I thought
she was being critical, she was actually being encouraging. Just
another reason to be conscious of being misinterpreted!

I know you have no intention to hurt me. I believe you when you
say you only want the best for me.

ON MY LIPS
I curl my toes as if to feel
each grain of varied colour
massaging my soles as I walk
across the sands of warm and wonder
fresh welcome under my feet

My hair blows away from my face
a perfect breeze to tease the lazy sun
Laughter and delight as I drink the beauty
and hear the mountains, sea and sand
play their silent harmony
the blue
she calls

I run to her
she is beautiful
so beautiful
sweet gorgeous mystery
I rush and fall with abandon
sinking in over my head
until her hands are touching
every place I feel my skin
I soak, I float

I belong

But when I stand on the beach
the breeze is cold
and the sand sticks to my wet feet
in ugly soiled unfeeling patterns

What can I do?

I go back to her to wash, to cleanse
but she cannot hold me
She is for everyone, not one
and her tide
takes her out to the moon
and I wait in the cold and the muck

for her to come back to me
but she can't
Not until the planets allow

So over the holidays
when the tide pulled her far to another shore
I sat wet, shivering on the beach
and let the cold winter sun dry the mud
until the goosebumps on my skin
fell off like sand, washed with
fresh water tears
and I got up and could dance
to the music of the sky again

Yet now, even as I stand on the high ground
far away, I taste her saltiness on my lips
and I long to run to her
dive into her depths
open my mouth and
feel her all around
over my head

I hear her not only in shells

....

January 16
UNSENT

I ate something good today. You wouldn't like it. It was flying
fish roe on rice wrapped in seaweed. It's got some fancy Japanese
name. The roe pops in the mouth. Exciting in some way . . . I
also like pea shoot tips and enoki mushrooms. I taste more these
days; it's better. I wonder why there are times when I really taste

and other periods when everything tastes mediocre. Is it just my noticing? Is everything really the same and it's just a matter of being awake?

in my veins
your song repeats
down deep sounds
that resonate my lips
quiver in wait
melt my skin
temperatures meld
spoons so close
but nudging still
fork me whole
ravenous heat
serve me up
no dieting here
want you whole
satiating holes

………..............…………………………………………………………

January 17
UNSENT

How bad can communication get? LEAVE ME ALONE!

Do you want to fight? I've still got something left. You want me to respond as a friend? For your information, I don't go around sleeping with my friends. Feeling like I'm being used? Yes, feeling like I'm not good enough for you, but you still want to play with my heart the next time I see you. A hole's a hole. Find another.

January 20
UNSENT

Will told me that F. Scott Fitzgerald says there is only one story and Joseph Campbell and Carl Jung say there are more than one, but not a lot. Will says the stories connect us. I have lived our story already—fictionally and somewhere else, perhaps in a collective memory of some kind, the way my DNA recalls Chinese music I don't remember hearing, calls memory back from the past and into my soul—that reciprocality here again.

Is a poem like a tree that falls in a forest when no one is around? I hear my poems now when I share them with you. Is hearing and articulating the act of making real?

Thank you for telling me you love me. I used to think we used alternates for the three words because what we had was greater than love. Now I see how precious those words are to you. How can you take me to the edges of my life so sporadically?

You say that there are times and places for words and that sometimes it's just the right time and other times they need to be submerged. You say I shouldn't expect words to be spoken easily. I try to understand this but I always want words to be easy and open for us.

all you are
submerged in the vast
lazuline
loose words, hope
unbound
wash over me
great wave

wet me
with your salty love

....

January 21
UNSENT

> It was our silence that made possible glimpses of the
> dark reality and vibrant plumage. . . . Silence was both an
> expression of a pedagogical principle and a state of being.
> . . . Moreover, I know that in my own life I was at home
> in those places. I had the peaceful feeling of harmony and
> ease, an emotion I now acknowledge as being a quality of
> a significant place. . . . So it is, then, that as a teacher and
> teacher of teachers, I've often wondered about the qualities
> of experience and the convergence of place. (Knowles, 2001,
> p. 95)

I wonder about our convergences of place and silence and how that
affects us. I noticed yesterday after your email that said you loved
me, that I began to imagine all sorts of scenarios when I didn't
hear from you that night. If I knew my place in you clearly, I could
dwell there. I could rest in you. I keep thinking it's a problem with
role. Is it that I am your student that separates us? How can I be
a part of you and not feel like a weight? Perhaps it is about your
responsibility to me. We are in a hierarchical power relationship
whether we want to be or not. Will said something quite interesting
at our meeting yesterday. I had planned out a detailed agenda
for our meeting and he said, "Fancy that, a grad student running
the meeting." I took that as a compliment but his comment says
something about our roles and our expected positionings.

Are we really born into the stream that is already traveling a course? Do we wait until someone hooks us dripping wet and puts us into another river? What power do we have over choices? What can we change? Can we direct the river? Can critical mass really move the river's flow and direction or are we just elated thinking and imagining that we are in control?

....

January 22

I've been thinking about what you told me today—thinking about how Terry George's (2004) movie, *Hotel Rwanda* (2004), has changed me. The movie made me see how little I see and how little I'm looking at. You're so right. As academics we really must look at the broader pictures and the things that are going on in the world. And most important, my job is just to tell the story, not to save the stories until I think they're ready to save the world because they never will be ready in my eyes. I'm excited to shout my stories now and like Carl Leggo (October 10, 2004, personal communication), I must let my stories and poems be like rain. I must not think of those who need or want the rain, only that the rain will nourish those in need. The rain will fall and gather in the holes where there are cracks. Leggo says:

> So, now I write my poems and I offer them with a cloud's eagerness to rain wherever the rain will fall. The cloud probably doesn't even know that some will want the rain, and some will not. The cloud is doing what clouds do. I am a poet, and I write poetry, and I offer the poetry to the world. What happens after that is a part of the story that is still unfolding.

That perhaps is my job then, my reason for writing—to tell the stories to those who can hear them.

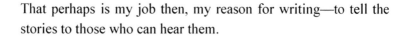

January 23
UNSENT

Maybe I already knew the manuscript would be rejected. I don't know how to play this game. I know what you'll say. I know, just send it somewhere else. Even the great German poet Rilke (1954, pp. 18-19) in his *Letters to a Young Poet* echoes your thoughts. He says:

> Search for the reason that bids you write; find out whether it is spreading out its roots to the deepest places of your heart, acknowledge to yourself whether you would have to die if it were denied you to write.

I hear his words, know yours are the same, but also remember the words of M. D. Herter Norton, Rilke's translator of the aforementioned book, that:

> Though Rilke expresses himself with a wisdom and a kindness that seem to reflect the calm of self-possession, his spirit may have been speaking out of its own need rather than from the security of ends achieved, so that his words indeed reflect desire rather than fulfillment. (p. 7)

Why do we all live these lives of lies? My teacher-face at work? My academic voice in writing papers? My secret thoughts of you? All mixed up, so cloudy inside and yet so glowing outside; all these facets reflecting outward. Like a polished diamond, we can't tell the clarity without a jeweler's loop. I want to go back to the beginning, before we were cut and shaped into a way that everyone thinks is desirable. Before when inclusions were a good part of who we are—character—not what degrades us. (Do you know they laser inclusions out of diamonds now?) I want to go back to before we were polished just to look good on the outside because now the shine is so important no one cares that it's cubic zirconia anymore.

How can I stand up for the traditional public education system? How do we confront without power, without hurting, without making scars?

come away with me, Red
just to the sky and back
not to keep
just to sleep
melt me
until I'm whole again

....

January 24
UNSENT

CHINESE PRINCESS
offer me truth
on a silver platter
for a princess
enrobed in silken layers
unfold unzip unbutton
unhook unravel
down to the places
below the skin
never been touched
cherry blossom soft

fragile as a butterfly's wing
teach me
with your hands
what i need

Notes

---

¹ The Golem is a Jewish legend (see Rappoport, 1937).

² "Hermeneutics is not about the recovery of existing or previously inscribed meanings, but the creating of meaning" (Smits, 1997, p. 286).

16
Cold
Purple Groan

The rays of the sun, in winter. They creep in wherever they can,
through the smallest cracks in the vaulting, the little openings
the builders left in the nave so that the light could enter the
cathedral and reach down to the pitch-dark of its floor. In winter
the sun is a bloody, yellowish mauve . . . I said the rays of the
sun wounded like heavenly swords, piercing the heart . . .
but without leaving any scar, any trace.

Marguerite Duras, 1989, p. 82

February 2
UNSENT

What is knowledge? How do we learn? Where do we learn? I just
finished reading *Shopgirl* by Steve Martin and I see you so clearly
now:

> His interest in Mirabelle comes from the part of him that still
> believes he can have her without obligation. He believes he

can exist with her from eight to eleven and enter a private and personal world that they will create that will cease to exist in the off hours or off days. He believes that this world will be independent of other worlds he must create on another night, in another place, and he has no intention of allowing it to affect his true quest for a mate. He believes that in this affair, what is given back and forth will be exactly even, and that they will both see the benefits they are receiving. But because he picked Mirabelle out by sight alone, he fails to see that her fragility, which he smelled and sensed and is lured by, runs deep in her heart and is part of her nature, and cannot be separated out for him to fuck. (2000, p. 39)

It is true, fiction is knowledge. Steve Martin's words have reframed and turned all I've been struggling through upright. Neilsen (2002), Denzin (2005), and Richardson (2000) all posit that fiction is knowledge and pedagogical. "Stories are a form of instruction to help persons think critically, historically, and sociologically" (Denzin, 2005, p. 946).

I am not mad. Anger is for people who have energy, life, will, and future. I have nothing. I am defeated, lost. I want to remember you as you were in in all the letters I understood as love. I can't heal through writing anymore. Writing perpetuates so I've just been hurting myself. I need to let go.

PLAY A LOUD SONG
Play me a song dear Red
A song with no words
because I already know
how the notes float under my skin
rushing through my veins

An obsession, addiction
I cannot keep you
in me any longer
I need to cut, purge, open up
so you flow out, rushing blood
until I am empty
drained and feel

no more

Help me, Red
Help me, please
I can't cope

Where can I turn
to release
this crushing sadness
pressing me into myself?
I've become Nabokov's (1955) Lolita
    trapped in immorality
Have become Nabokov's Humbert
    taking what shouldn't be touched
Nabokov's words (p. 281)
    This book is the only immortality you and I
    may share, my Red

....

February 4
UNSENT

The words I have for you go sour and stale under my skin. Empty husks, dry dead skin, the blur on the edge of a dune, dulling me. I even imagine that my tears carry away the toxins from the poisonous waste that leaches back into my blood. I like to cry, cleanse myself. You'll think I'm over dramatic. Perhaps I am.

I rubbed sea salt with lemongrass and honey all over my body today while thinking of you. No more dead skin left! I could hear the salt falling off me like crystal rain, twinkling, hitting the shower floor. Then I put on a layer of moisturizer; I feel it soaking into my pores, even now as I write. My skin is ready for you.

Where are you tonight? Are you in transit, or reading the paper in your favourite chair, the paper held up in front of you? Maybe you're asleep early for once. It's late in your time zone. I see you, remember the rhythm of your breath deep and slow. I imagine your eyelids with my lips—butterfly wings fragile, soft.

How did I become just a body to you—one you can leave on a street corner? Is your payment made by your attention to my work? What will happen when I graduate? You will have no means of payment and we will drift back to nothingness and you won't have any scars, any traces of me. I hate you for that.

I saw a show last night, about a victim who died from a stab wound. She didn't die from the blood bleeding out of her body but from the blood spilling inside. Her own body poisoned and suffocated itself.

I know you just wanted to play. We did have fun. I learned so much—running weightlessly over a map of learning, gathering the words and throwing them up all over us, flying with nothing holding me. You were near but we were soaring independently, disparate but in the same space, synergetic (I made up that word).

February 7

Letters to Chris—Layer Five: Acknowledge Ecological and Intuitive Resonances

> An awareness of and sensitivity toward many environments –
> physical, psychological, social, and spiritual – are integral parts of postmodern
> proposals which inform . . . curriculum. (Patrick Slattery, 1989, p. 156)

Here's the last bit of research for your letters to Chris on embodied wholeness. Acknowledging ecological and intuitive resonances is difficult to learn. It has been for me. I think I have always been seeking sensual knowing but I have constrained myself to my five senses. I think my body understands ecological resonances and relationships much sooner than my mind can articulate those "knowings." For example, I once worked on a two-tone Escher puzzle comprised of 3000 pieces. The completed puzzle was narrow and long (12 feet)! I found that in the silence and concentration of trying to connect the pieces, that my hand would pick up a piece and I could move it to the correct spot. Once I got it there, I had to manipulate the angle to fit the puzzle piece. What I'm saying is that my body knew the piece fit but my mind did not know how. I have been learning how to trust my body-knowing that sees with the eyes of the heart. This is especially difficult because when I am bodily receptive, I am also completely vulnerable and unprotected. The body cannot edit words.

This tile mosaic is called *Windy Words*. Evocative work and teaching always involve risk and exposure. In those places, while the head may try to interpret and filter information, the body cannot edit the unspoken. It is dangerous to work near the "risky" places. Carl Leggo likens this pressing of the boundaries to dancing on the edge of a volcano (June 7, 2005, personal communication).

The "edge" is the liminal place, the place where revelations occur. I cannot change how my body receives—I feel certain things which I cannot explain. I know my skin is hypersensitive. I put some aloe vera on last night and as it dried, I felt a rippling, like a spiderweb stretched on my skin breaking as I started moving. That has an explanation but other times, I feel connections I don't understand.

Windy Words, 2005, mixed tile. 35" x 51"

BETRAYAL OF BODY
i cannot hide
my naked self
always laid open, feeling
breathing beauty
and
swallowing glass

I can hear the woundedness in songs, poetry, dance, art, and people's stories and I want to heal. When the text speaks in a different sound, we hear with the heart. We do not understand merely from the written words. I wonder if Leggo (2005b) meant the same thing with his title, "…the silence of letters?"

You ask how a song can sound the same as a poem. James Young writes about representation in music. Young claims that "listeners have an affective response to music" (2001, p. 60). He explains how "music's effect on the body gives rise to experience like the experience of emotions" (p. 61). Young notes that listeners react to the formal properties of music. For example, music can inspire movement, elevate gaiety and provide an experience of elation. Another way in which the experience of music is like the experience of emotion is that "the conventions of tonal harmony and other musical practices lead listeners to form expectations about the forms compositions will assume" (p. 62). Young goes on to talk about how we know unconsciously when some notes are missing. This creates a wanting of sorts and even though we are not formally taught dissonance, we know it when we hear it. It's almost as if our mythical expectations are preprogrammed. Our narratives continue to attempt to align with romanticized preset models in the same way that we have "learned" how to listen to music. In both cases, our emotions respond according to those expectations.

One of the reasons why I named this work *Seeing Red* was in connection to working on the edge. Imagine the image of a sound equalizer. When making music recordings, the perfect setting is to have the majority of the music in the "green" and the level extending just over into "red." Being slightly in the red zone provides the optimum recording level. The novel title also has many other connotations.

When I look at "Windy Words" I am reminded of the description of "Reverberations," a descriptive rendering of a/r/tography:

> It is the desire to respond to the disappearance and appearance of signs, the impulse between what is known and what cannot be expressed, that gives new tension and vibration to the signifier. Research thus becomes an act of unsettling, an evocation that calls out, asking for a response, a living inquiry, transforming static moments into momentum, multiplying and metamorphosizing. (Springgay, Irwin, & Wilson Kind, 2005, p. 10)

Teaching on the edge can also be paralleled to Pollock's notion of "nervous" performative writing. We are restless, maybe even a bit fearful in our teaching, afraid of the level of exposure, "unable to settle into a clear, linear course, neither willing nor able to stop moving, restless, transient and transitive . . . drawing one charged moment into another, constituting knowledge in an ongoing process of transmission and transferal" (1998, pp. 90-91). A/r/tography suggests that it is in this movement, this shaking and quaking of measure and rhythm, that knowing is sifted and shifted to understanding (Aoki, 1996; Springgay, Irwin & Wilson Kind, 2005).

Developing an *embodied aesthetic wholeness* involves nurturing an ecological identity. Mitchell Thomashow says, "there are no single trees, only the forest, a protective layer, one vast web of unfathomable interconnection" (1995, p. 201). He explains our relational connectedness:

> Identity is a very complex notion, referring to all the different ways people construe themselves in social relationships as manifested in personality, values, actions, and sense of self. To have an identity crisis is to be lost in the world, lacking the ability . . . to connect the self to meaningful objects, people, or ideas—the typical sources of identification. (p. 3)

Ecological identity is an important aspect of wholeness because "ecological identity reflects a person's cognitive, intuitive and affective perceptions of ecological relationships" (Thomashow, 1995, p. 3). One cannot understand self without context. If I were in a forest, all I would be able to see would be the trees around me. I would need to see the forest as an aerial shot to reveal my location. This is how the creative arts reveal. I'm talking again of being immersed and seeing one's own immersion. Somehow, the arts can conceptualize or visibly lay out understanding from a bird's eye view. Renderings conceptualize and summarize the unsaid that is known in the body. Through the arts, the understanding is made visible. We think we are coming to new understandings, but actually, we only think they are new because the unarticulated has not been outwardly exposed and seen from a distance before. We can only locate ourselves when we see ourselves from afar. Art locates us. Dissanayake (2000) says intentionality is always the first activity of art. Intentionality is the seed from which the rendering and understanding emerge.

Dewey describes aesthetic experience as a clear continuity and as a kind of consummation (Irwin, 2004, p. 27). I don't imagine that the aesthetic experience occurs every time I create. Sometimes my renderings are reiterations in another language of my writing. Maybe the informing comes because we create an outlet for expression. I remember reading a challenging article once and I began webbing and connecting symbols and icons with words as a means to grasp the information. But as I continued, I realized that even the juxtaposition of text, image, and space in my notes began to provide understanding. I must remember this when I'm teaching. Note-taking is such an important skill and we tend to teach children to write on the lines—a linear recording while our understandings are not.

The goal of art is the personal but it automatically becomes political when seen by the public. If I compare my art making to teaching and I want my teaching to evoke, I must then teach and express through the uncensored heart and body.

We need to try to understand ourselves and our meanings of life. Thomashow points out, "The quest for meaning represents the core of the earth's wisdom traditions . . . an inescapable human birthright, spanning diverse cultures through historical time" (1995, p. 203). Suzanne Thomas writes:

> An ecological consciousness demands openness and responsiveness to the whole environment and a sensual attunement to the world. . . . An ecological consciousness calls for re-framing thinking that nurtures an understanding of the interrelational nature of the world—it is action that leads to participatory interaction of self with world. (2004, p. 239)

In writing about the meaning of life, Thomashow explains that the purpose of his life is "to be awake in this moment" (1995, p. 203). As teachers, I wonder if we need to question if teaching is part of our awakeness. When I talk about awakeness, I am talking about being really connected—to know and acknowledge sensual, intuitive and tacit knowledge and to feel our responsibility to other and our indebtedness to contextual environments.

I like what Charles Garoian says about the critical processes that occur during creative thinking:

> These processes preclude the objectification of values, attitudes, and beliefs that stifle interpretation. To avert such objectification, the presentation, experience and interpretation of performance art depends on a "situational aesthetics"—one in which the relationships between the artist, the art-making process, and the community are considered part of the art work. (1999, p. 32)

I relate Garoian's words to teaching. Imagine the teaching performance as the interaction between teacher, process, and context. Again, do you see how all we do is very closely connected to environmental contexts and geographical landscapes broadly defined? One of our goals as teachers is to create congruency between self and context, not only for ourselves, but to enable this connection in our students. So context refers to how "I" am situated within "self" as well as how self is situated in relation to others in the social and natural environment.

Our great tension as teachers is our responsibility to public accountability and standardization while teaching for diversity. To teach "uniformly" requires teachers to remain removed from their students much like the detached, unbiased researcher. This type of teaching is all too easy to become dependent on. We need to pay attention to methodology and teaching strategies in pre-service programs. We are also disadvantaged when the pressures of provincial or national broad-based examinations, under the guise of accountability, threaten teachers' sense of belonging. We

can only incorporate *currere* in our curriculum when we prepare
teachers well enough to be able to teach connected curriculum
using prescribed texts only as guides. We must spend time on
articulating personal and public notions of context.

………................…………………………………………………

February 15
UNSENT

NATURAL REMINDERS
Loud truck outside
Noise, trash, waste, filth
You in my mind, disgust
Traffic sounds like a tar conveyor belt
A new location
Is that why I see a new picture now?
The blue garbage truck is backing up
Loud beeping sounds remind me to beware
It's too late

The crisp white double lined parking stalls
Lie on the black pitch
Prevent hermeneutic understandings
So regular
So framed, protect our cars and stop the confusion
Too late

How did you fall out of love?
Have I become
Something disgusting to you?

February 20
UNSENT

I will write myself out of love
Unstory you
Rip you off sentence by sentence
You won't even feel it
You won't even know

A STRANGER ON A FAMILY HOLIDAY
touched the earth in so many places
under my yellow umbrella at Dr.'s Cave in Montego Bay
the gentle breeze wraps me too softly
on a beach towel in a cabana in Grand Cayman
breathlessly clear blue sea
snorkeling in Cozumel
sharp rocky crags far below
lush purple leaves at the bottom of the sea
like audience clapping accolades to me
cheering for my unloving, undoing
unwriting, under water
back in New Orleans
floating down the Mississippi again
so long, so forever, us
and on Bourbon Street unsafe
as two police men, guns drawn, shout and yell
as they chase four boys
weaving around me
I'm invisible to you, in crossfire
I am not afraid
what am I without you?
holy dross only with you

and the houses here are in my dreams
wrapped porches, Victorian detail, colours, columns
Tulane University trees
dappled light dancing on the grass

we could teach here if you cared

the dark side of the moon is in my face
I cannot bury myself deeper
turn off love

....

March 2
UNSENT

When I come to the surface
When I feel the real
I cannot bear
I cannot live
my way
I am a mask
with no places to see
or breathe out
mouth smooth plastic
so I cannot cry
cry out
I have no sound
no words

17
Salty Germination
Inhales

flowers fade
the fruits of summer fade
they have their season so do we
but please promise me
that sometimes you will think of me

Andrew Lloyd Webber, Charles Hart & Richard Stilgoe, 1986, p. 16

I imitated Humphrey Bogart's kiss, but I didn't feel it. Only later
did I realize that perhaps Bogart didn't feel it either; he was merely
kissing the way the director said he should. So there I was
imitating a kiss that was never real.

Jerry Mander, 1978, p. 236

March 5
UNSENT

Of course I'm mad! The first thing you asked when I called, even
before "How are you?," was whether or not I hung up the phone

when Clare picked up the phone earlier. I'm not some dumb teenage admirer! You make me feel so disgusting. Why do you even sign your emails with "Love Red"?

I am not the Julia you know on paper. She is a fiction I conjured. She can love like the perfect princess of a storybook. She can forgive repeatedly, always hopeful—the perfect teacher, never giving up on her students. She's the perfect martyr for the cruel who take advantage—to be at their disposal, beck and call. I am not her. I feel. Writing my letters to you is a performance of language.

Why are we always the main characters in our stories? Sean Wiebe (April 21, 2006, personal communication) writes about imagining life as a minor character. He wonders if the reason we always imagine ourselves as the main character has to do with having a life of privilege or selfishness. We always tend to see others in relation to self—that others become part of our stories. Wiebe suggests that living as a minor character offers less burden and one still feels part of the whole. He knows I'm writing an epistolary novel. He thinks it's freeing to participate in someone else's story. He asks, "Would I rather be Hamlet? Or is it fine to be Horatio. Or, am I Shakespeare?" Wiebe asks good questions. I realize you perform the way I write you into life. Does that mean my love for you is all a performance? Is my book about characters acting out the life everyone lives giving testimony that we are performing love? What a thought! What is really real then?

Charles Garoian in *Performing Pedagogy* (1999) suggests that "the performance of language represents a linguistic strategy to critique those cultural metaphors that codify and stereotype the self and the body in order to emerge a language of identity. The body loses its identity and becomes text as it is inscribed with cultural codes" (p. 44). I don't want those cultural codes on me. I don't want to be stereotyped as the student. I want you to see me.

I know how you have used me. "Love suffers long and is kind; does not behave rudely, does not seek its own, is not provoked, thinks no evil; . . . rejoices in the truth; bears all things, believes all things, hopes all things, endures all things" (1 Corinthians 13:4-7, New International Version). I cannot. I see so clearly. I do not love you.

....

March 8

SOMETIME CLOSE TO 1851
Yesterday
In the Mexican bank in Puerto Vallarta
Foreign language signs were shouting urgency
The grand wooden banisters were old
ornately carved, no longer seen
The bright mural up the stairwell forgotten
in the filtered afternoon dust
The wooden beams, molecules, even air particles
clearly suspended in mute suspense
Only pigeons fluttered in the rafters, tossing around secrets
Up the stairs alone, forbidden isolation
the courtyard open below
I had to return to the strange silence
spread by the flapping of wings
I looked down and saw Luke with the girls
sitting on the edge of the fountain
So content, such stillness, silence and sound at once
They were lit by the sun, unseeing, happy

I could feel you. We've been here together before, another time
A surety—some sort of thickness and yet disintegration in the air
Deeper than a déjà vu
Richer than imagination
A waft from deep inside had come out
through my skin to recognize
the wood, the art, the air
How can you be so close and so long ago?
Why can I feel you but not touch you?
I miss you, a nauseous longing
A defeated giddy drunken wanting
Feel crazy so know I'm not
I want to be, let go
Resign myself for you
Gripping onto the beam
I want to release
I can't understand my body
Ashamed that I feel you, see you
Even imagine that this is real
That once you saw me

Love me, love me not

I hear my wings

1851 Mural,
Photograph,
Puerto Vallarta,
2005

STIRRING FROM AFAR
all day
felt you stirring in me
warm and deep
as if you wanted me
calling from so far away
a soft sound I tilt my head
strain to hear, to understand
spread through with high, delirious
giddy fullness no other can give
a recovering alcoholic taking a sip
cannot control the wanting
the needing with every part of me

....

March 12
UNSENT

INSIDE OUT
I waited for you, months gone
inside out raw and exposed
silently whispering for you to soothe
to hold me tight press me hard
break me into you pieces all astray
mashed raw wild juices bleeding
over edges until all beginnings were lost
together in the now forever

then I breathed
in and out with my heart
rhythm syncopated in your words
lost and found drowned but more alive
always on the shore of dawn
mourning the light

and you say the other's name speak your life so lightly
hands tight around my throat to throttle truth in me
wake me up stunned light blaring in my eyes so I know
who I am, my place, sounded simply in your silence
stab me over and over so I feel and know who you are

remind me of my blindness see my weakness
hansel's breadcrumbs all in my mouth
all turned to dust, dry desecration
the taste of death white on my tongue
knowing I followed you now lost cannot go back
so where do I go where is the future
with a poet's unreal imagination
where does love reside, eat, speak, cry?
I'll spit the cinders out lie down
and let the thick ash blanket me
eyes shut waiting for purgatory
to redeem me

March 13
UNSENT

ALL IN A GRAIN
When the moon hides
and the air is thick with fog
I can still see
When my body no longer betrays me
and weighs me down
I lie in your arms
Nothing to keep us apart
Knowing that we have forever
And you hold me
And I know with surety
that all I have imagined is a story untrue
written in the wrong time
I realize that I have always been more
That you have always loved me
That you recognized me
I can lie with you now in foreverness because I am no longer
even the bitter cold cannot take my pleasure away
Because I love you
I love you with a single moment in time
that is filled to the brink of bursting
filled with every possible moment of love collected over time
teetering, painfully full and fragile, ready to shatter
into a thousand moments of mediocrity named love
by those who haven't felt what it means
to hold this unwanted privilege that knows no taming
all my love, all pulsating in a single grain of sand
so full yet so tiny, sitting so carelessly in your busy open palm
as you stand by sea

March 18
UNSENT

A MANTRA TO MEMORIZE
I will construct a new story
From the memories that hurt me
Create a new mantra
Rewrite this life
Wipe away memory
Fill every wound with erasure
I remember
I remember what I want to remember
I wrote the story and will write the end

I am
Seeing Red

THE END

So we beat on,
boats against the current
borne back ceaselessly into the past.

F. Scott Fitzgerald, 1950, p. 188

A CONVERSATION

AFTERWORD

This afterword shares the possibilities and potential of how artful research informs processes of scholarly inquiry and honours the reader's multi-perspective as integral to the research project's transformative potential. The afterword is divided into four discussions: Currere, Art, Form, and Knowledge Contributions.

I understand that curriculum is "the site on which the generations struggle to define themselves and the world, [that] curriculum is an extraordinarily complicated conversation" (Pinar et al., 1995, p. 848), and that curriculum [refers] to educational courses of action that facilitate human 'growth' [that are] so complex that [they] cannot be studied though any particular theoretical perspective" (Henderson & Slattery, 2004, p. 3). Schwab (1969) believes that the curriculum field is both theoretical and practical and must be approached eclectically. So I purposefully (re)search in multi-layered and seemingly unrelated ways, seeking connections off charted courses. In order to constitute current understandings I take my uncertainties and the relational aspects of my living and research to express theoretical notions and ruminations through the body—through artful expressive means which are enriched with the participation of arms, legs, eyes, ears, and heart in the forms of writing and artmaking. I take Anne Phelan (2005, p 355) seriously; I am always playing with thought:

> Learning to be practically wise begins with desire, a yearning to be something other than who one is (Garrison, 1997). Pursuing that desire may involve letting go, losing one's balance, and losing certainty. . . . Accepting the fragility of knowledge. Feeling overwhelmed. Engaging in a play of thought.

In "playing" out uncertainties through multi-genre narrative texts and visual art, or music, performance, or movement, a complicated and complex conversation is created; and through this shifting and sifting (Aoki, 1996) and agitation of reciprocality, reversibility, resonance, reverberation, and echo within and between forms and mediums, the unarticulated becomes articulated, seen, marked, and visible (see Springgay, Irwin, & Wilson Kind, 2005; Jones, 1998; Pollock, 1998; Sumara & Luce-Kapler, 1993). Artful research is the act of focusing the camera lens to still a moment in time for others to "see" an iteration, to make the consciousness visible for others to interrogate, judge, and edit. It is the act of iteration which begins to locate points along the journey of currere on the boundless map of a dynamic and rhizomatic curriculum (see Deleuze and Guattari, 1987; Alverman, 2000; Irwin, Beer, Springgay, Grauer, Gu & Bickel, in press). Concurrently I am reminded that fine scholarship is not only iteration of the central notions of the personal, relational and artful, but includes in combination: focus, intensity, authority, relevance, and substance (Cole & Knowles, 2000; 2001a; Knowles, 2005).

Art as Conversation

The way I view visual art strays from the formalist criticism of art appreciation toward a postmodern approach with a contemporary pragmatist feminism (Whipps, 2004). The inextricable interconnectedness between the visual and the verbal (Witzling, 1991, 1994) as a collaborative endeavor to uncover the "heart of the artist's thinking, feeling, and wanting to relate that essence" (Stout, 2000, p. 348) is integral to my work. Stout (2000, p. 248) explains that for feminist and postmodern artists, writing has become both a critical tool and a strategy in their art. Witzling asserts that "the written word forms an intrinsic part of their artistic activity, not simply an extrinsic theoretical commentary" (1994, p. 11). To these artists, the subject of art is human nature and through their combined written and visual images runs a common purpose, that is, to open a conversation and to pose living possibilities for mutual consideration, understanding, and respect.

Harold Pearse (1992, p. 250) asserts that "the real challenge for art teachers is to understand postmodernism as a way of being in the world and the implications for professional practice." *Being* postmodern thus is to be an embodied, aesthetic being; to embrace uncertainty, think, research, and create in multiple roles, in multiple mediums (materials and forms), and enact a living pedagogic inquiry, an active search for *morningness* (see Bollnow, 1989b, p. 22). Morningness is simply experiencing newness in the liminal spaces of revelation. Knowing morningness is to acknowledge and deeply breathe in quotidian moments, seeking and realizing connectivity and relationality in the world. Being in this place of learning is to be an a/r/tographer. A/r/tography, a practice-based methodology (Irwin, 2004), focuses on the interplay between *art* (literary, visual, performative, and/or musical) and *graphy* (the art of writing). The contiguity of multiple roles and lenses of the artist, researcher, and teacher as a holistic practitioner are integral to this type of inquiry. Art layered with writing or literature rendered artfully (in form, or in combination with visual art/music/performance) emboldens a "filling in" of the inbetween space between mediums. For example, the lyrics of a song on a piece of paper may look flat or lacking but when sung with the right melody, the words suddenly become meaningful. Aesthetic literacies are foundational and essential to social intelligence and linguistic literacies (Broudy, 1988; Greene, 1978). Pinar, Reynolds, Slattery and Taubman purport that in the imagination, the image precedes "the word," thus:

> using a phenomenological epistemology, Broudy [1988] suggests that the cultivation of the intellect . . . necessarily requires cultivation of the imagination. . . . Those children without a rich store of images are less able to decode concepts and articulate perceptions. In this way aesthetic literacies can be regarded as essential to linguistic literacies. (1995, pp. 569-570)

Both the resistance to and need for presenting text to accompany visual art are intricately interwoven. Unfortunately, the text can "trap" the reader in seeing the work a particular way—much like an epilogue may negate the pragmatist's need to examine the main body of text. On the other hand the words provide another perspective, a window into tracking the unfolding lived experience of the creator. The aim is always to welcome openings, spaces for the viewer to freely move into and out of the work relationally because whether it is literary or visual, the work really has no possibility of completeness or closure (Cole & Knowles, 2001b; Stout, 2000).

Currere as Complicit
Curriculum Conversation

The word curriculum is derived from the Latin word, *currere*, which means to run (see Pinar & Grumet, 1976; Irwin, 2003, 2004). Curriculum is generally thought of as static, as in performance outcomes or course content, while currere is dynamic. Currere describes the process and multi-directional movement of learning, of the relational aspects of knowledge production in a dialogic and dialectic space between learner and others. In order to support an energetic curriculum of currere, working in the liminal space, the artist's studio, heartens a generative place of creative knowledge construction (see Sameshima & Irwin, 2006).

Understandings of *complicity* and *complicit systems* underpin this dissertation. These notions are rooted in complexity theory, particularly the research work done by Cohen and Steward (1994) and Sumara and Davis (1997). Complexity theory is a field of inquiry which uses metaphors to describe and reveal new perspectives on evolving organisms, collectives, and life processes. Very simply, Cohen and Steward explain that *complicit systems* are not dependent on initial conditions which frame and limit the space of the possible. In this dissertation, the forms of research process and presentation are not limited to, or by, contrived systems of elaborate interpretations which are intended to reflect, represent, describe, or simulate some aspect of the universe; rather, the dissertation resonates with *complicity* which,

> in addition to sharing an etymological heritage with "complexity," evokes senses of being *implicated* in or *serving as an accomplice* to and thus announces a need to be attentive to one's own participation in events. We are fully implicated in our world, and this notion extends well beyond

the now commonplace understanding that perception is not
innocent. (Sumara & Davis, 1997, pp. 303-304)

Thus, as reader, one is complicitly knitted into the unfolding
storyline, connecting letters, assuming and constructing the
character of Red, dancing a co-choreographed piece with the
writer. Again implication, complication, and complicity of the
novel as a whole can be similarly paralleled metonymically to the
teacher and learner dynamic.

Grumet suggests that "in order to reap the disclosure that lies
dormant within our curricular forms, we must claim them in our
familiar, daily experience and then estrange ourselves from them"
(1978, p. 288). This dissertation ends with the title reminding the
reader that all that is to be known is already present. I seek to
improve the contexts of learning and teaching by sharing stories
of the inner life of a teacher. By iterating the unsaid, the unspoken,
readers become less "othered." I believe all our quests for identity
and belonging are longings to know we fit into the mainstream,
the main storyline we have been acculturated to believe. In telling
our stories, we enlarge that storyline to incorporate and accept
diversity and multiplicity without dilution and conformity. In
relating "illegitimate" stories (see Richardson & St. Pierre, 2005,
p. 966) we create a discourse of the particular as the general. We
demonstrate that the perceived general is a myth of oppression.
When all stories can be heard, then we can be truly democratic,
overcome privileging, and develop in ourselves and in our schools
lives of peace, happiness, and joy.

I conclude this section with Volkart's (2000, ¶ 12) online
questions:

> What aesthetic strategies are being developed to address us
> as multiply coded, hybridized, and differential subjects so

that we can re-formulate ourselves? How can we make use of the specifically situated knowledge of art and discourse producers of both genders and diverse origins to conduct identity discourses that are non-fixed and headed for new fixations?

In response, I return again to Cohen and Steward's (1994) work and urge further development in curriculum discourses which support open complicit systems of teaching and learning.

Form as Conversation

Cole and Knowles (2001b, p. 213) suggest that "when researchers have a particular commitment to pushing the boundaries of method and audience, representational form is central to the achievement of research goals." I agree with Cole and Knowles; as a researcher I must "write *for* meaning rather than *to record* meaning."

In thinking about the quality, purpose, and method of my form, I turn to Cole and Knowles' "Defining Elements of [arts-informed] Life History Research" (2001a, pp. 125-128). These researchers hold that positivist conceptions of validity, reliability, and generalizability in the qualitative paradigm are "not appropriate for making judgments about qualitative research that is conducted from other paradigmatic vantage points" (p. 124). So while strategies of triangulation, transparency of the research process, depth of descriptive accounts, cross-site and cross-case analyses, length of time in the field, declaration of researcher bias, and so forth are procedurally considered, judgments regarding value are steeped in alternate paths. Kilbourn (1999) asserts that the strength of a piece of fiction or work is in its ability to show qualities of experience which can be recognized as true of people and situations. Kvale (1995, p. 37) suggests that post-positivist research can be "judged according to the quality of its crafting, the nature of its communicability, and its pragmatic value"; and Lawrence-Lightfoot and Hoffman-Davis (1977, p. 274) believe that quality qualitative research is expressed as an aesthetic whole bound in resonance, authenticity, and coherence. Richardson (2005, p. 964) asks if the work contributes to social life. Does the work have aesthetic merit which "opens up the text and invites interpretive responses? Is the text artistically shaped, satisfying, complex, and not boring?" Richardson continues: Has the author demonstrated reflexivity? Does this piece affect the reader emotionally or intellectually; generate new questions; and move the reader to write, try new research practice and move to action? *Seeing Red* is not an attempt to fulfill specific criteria of value and quality (even though it perhaps ironically seeks to meet the points I've chosen to mention), but rather is a satisfying creation of fullness according to my own unarticulated and shifting judgment in the current momentary context of what I deem as worthy research.

Cole and Knowles suggest that form itself has the power to inform and that the representation of the work is the "main vehicle through which our scholarship becomes known and, for that matter, widely accepted or rejected by peers" (2001, p. 122). Eisner believes that "the forms through which humans represent their conception of the world have a major influence on what they are able to say about it" (1991, p. 7.). Edel further asserts that the quality of a written life "resides in the art of narration, not in the substance of the story. The substance exists before the narrative begins" (1984, p. 15). I have developed *Seeing Red* with a consciousness of responsibility to representational form and content with the hope of challenging the reader to situate self in relation to the letter texts; it is this enactment which paves the way to the transformative potential of this work. Herman Stark (2003, p. 46) argues that "form precedes content, and indeed lingers after." The form of representation of the work directly affects the effect of the research. If the work does not touch the heart of the audience, the understandings will not linger. The work must evoke and in order to evoke, the work must be passionate and draw the audience. I seek to draw the audience to theorize their own situatedness through the vehicle of story.

Intention in Conversation

Selecting a specific form and genre which holistically suits, complements, and contributes to the intentions of a project must be deliberate and mindful. Eisner says the intent of research is to improve the contexts of learning and teaching and the aim of education is "conceived of as the preparation of artists, namely, people who make things well" (2004, p. 15). If the goals of research intend to fulfill these claims then research must include the iteration of what current contexts of learning and teaching are and provide possibilities for the preparation of *artists* in the ways in which anything created can be an art.

My intentions in *Seeing Red* are multi-fold. I seek to envelop dichotomies within a storyline, in spaces of contradictions, in duplicitous interlocking and entangled threads, in multiple figurative meanings in an attempt to connect theory to situation— to demonstrate theory in practice. Through a simple plot line, characteristic of epistolary novels, I attempt to sound the silent spaces between eros and love, thought and feeling, mind and body, asceticism and moral duty, teaching and healing, fiction and nonfiction, objective and subjective, and myth and real.

For example, the book chapters are framed by the five Chinese elements of wood, fire, earth, metal and water in an attempt to sit in the inbetween space of Western and Eastern frames of thinking. The element wood refers to the season of spring which correlates to the beginning of the love relationship. As the seasons progress toward winter, as the relationship deteriorates, the unspoken hope is that spring will renew, that winter is just a period of incubation, the inhalation before new birth. The last element of water is also a reminder of the simile raised in the book that love is like prosody— it is the water which holds words, that winter is necessary before spring, that our winter sorrows will hold the fullness of joys and hopes to come, and that through wounding, new birth arises. Each chapter title is part of a poem which describes the section's Chinese element.

More specifically, in "Letters to Chris," I propose and describe the development of an *embodied aesthetic wholeness*, a means to nurturing alternate ways of knowing which could significantly influence transformational learning theory processes. Within the storyline of the novel I explore conceptions of fiction and knowledge (Denzin, 2005; Neilsen, 2002; Richardson & St. Pierre, 2005); investigate the teacher/learner experience as curriculum discourse (Pinar, Reynolds, Slattery, & Taubman, 1995; Clarke & Erickson, 2003); provide examples of how connections between personal/ professional experiences shape pedagogical practice (Ayers, 1988; Cole & Knowles, 2000; Grumet, 1991); and illustrate how knowledge construction can be deepened through artful, creative scholarship (Broudy, 1988; Cole & Knowles, 2001b; Irwin, 2004). Through form, I provide an example of and challenge the notions of public accessibility and communication of scholarship which many believe are the culprits of research influence (Giroux, 2005; Knowles, 2005). In addition, I draw attention to how artful research opens possibilities for understanding curriculum and pedagogy as articulated by poststructuralist Jacques Daignault (1992a). Last, I demonstrate the process of layering arts-informed research on a/r/t/graphy to guide the work. That is to say my life breathes as an a/r/tographer—I am always seeking pedagogical relationships in my living. I render my work though the concepts of contiguity, living inquiry, openings, metaphor/metonymy, reverberations and excess (see Springgay, Irwin, & Wilson Kind, 2005). In this a/r/tographic *beingness* I incorporate arts-informed research as another layer over my researching in that I am first inspired by an artform (the power of the letter form); second, I gather further letters, fictionalize narratives, research topics, and make art as a complicated innovative data collection; and third, I represent the "data" in a unique way. My intention is that the presented work, although never final, is theoretical but not presented as a traditional theoretical text.

Parallax as Voices in Conversation

In articulating subjectivities and naming experiences in relation to curriculum and pedagogy at personal and relational public levels, a deeper, dynamic, fuller, more inclusive "pedagogy of parallax" is created to research, live, learn, and teach by. The word *parallax* comes from the Greek work *parallagé* which means alteration, and from *parallassein*, to change. Parallax is the apparent change of location of an object against a background due to a change in observer position or perspective shift. The concept of parallax encourages researchers and teachers to acknowledge and value the power of their own and their readers and students' shifting subjectivities and situatedness which directly influence the constructs of perception, interpretation, and learning. There is not one truth or canonized definition for living pedagogically, only one's epistemologic renderings of personal pedagogy which cannot be marginalized because there are no criteria to restrict freedom of thought. I heartfully privilege the contiguity of mind, heart, spirit, body, and language, and welcome parallax in the reading of *Seeing Red* to garner multiplicity in perspectives, readings, and understandings; as well as to further encourage inquiry in the fusion of writing and the arts to open frames of reference in research.

Stout explains that rotating frames of reference or responding critically to a particular focus from various vantage points creates:

> an unbounded interaction among viewer/reader, image and text, and artist/author. Emerging from this interaction is an understanding of the art object as an open entity. [Viewers] come to see all works of art as something like sculpture in the round, something that can be conceptually revolved, viewed from many angles. (2000, p. 347)

My goal is to position the viewer/reader in a space of indeterminacy and to encourage participatory consideration as the viewer integrates self into multiple perspectives (see Stout, 2000; Hanks, 1989). In this compound revolving viewing arena, a borderless interface of sorts, the audience is urged to a realization that the artful work—whether it is visual or textual, is only "completed or made whole by the discourse (involving artist, viewer, and critics)" (Stout, 2000, p. 347) or the junctions of the viewer, the artist, the context and the moment, the course of interpretation. In essence, the project's visibility is dependent on the viewer. The viewer is no longer a passive onlooker but given a specific open placeholder, a space of responsibility to be implicated. The letter format offers a kinetic passageway between writer and reader. The text is not static but vibrating, seeking resonation and communion with other voices at a personal level.

The format of the work calls the reader to become the author thus making each reading a new story. The project materializes its presence through the multi-interpretations of the reader. The letter reader is asked to piece together the fragments of letters and to construct the identity of Red, in essence, to *see Red,* to write the other half of the story while simultaneously seeking a balance of trust in the letter writer who is purposefully manipulative with words. The questions remain: Who is Red? Does the reader simply unknowingly follow an acculturated heterosexual fairytale storyline or could Red be someone else—the unmentioned advisor, an alter ego, narrative personified? Pinpointing identity is mystifying as evidenced as a theme throughout the dissertation. The names of the three professors mentioned also cause complication. Professor Winnie Crates' surname is a reference to two philosophers: Crates of Thebes, a Hellenistic philosopher and teacher of Zeno of Citium (Jared Zeno), who was associated with Stoicism, a school of philosophy that teaches that altruistic self-control and detachment from emotion allow one to become a clear thinker; and Crates of Mallus, a Greek grammarian and also a Stoic philosopher of the 2nd century BC. Will McCarthy's name quietly alludes to US Senator Joseph McCarthy who was in office from 1947 to 1957 and who was associated with the term "Red Scare"—a fear of communist influence on US society. During the two "Red Scare" periods in United States history (1917-1920 and from the late 1940s through to the mid 1950's), citizens were incarcerated for simply belonging or sympathizing with subversive groups. This linkage reiterates the danger (seeing red) and most needed practice of subverting, disrupting, transgressing, and troubling historically accepted normative discourses.

Editor's Note: How does the story end? Does the audience finally see Red, construct an understanding of the silent character? Is Julia seeing Red? Is Julia angry—one who has moved from a passive "othered" submissive position to a place which sanctions the authority to be angry? Has Julia's past identity died with winter as she moves through the liminal space transforming her sorrows into hopeful spring joys? Is Julia going to see Red in the flesh—a sure means to disrupt or confirm the created symbolic archetype? Has Red been the teacher martyr, sacrificing personal desires over ascetic, altruistic teaching practice? Will Julia see Red in the afterlife? Another insinuation of the title is to the Doppler Effect, named after Christian Doppler (1803-1853), which is a change in pitch from a shift in the frequency of soundwaves. For example, when an ambulance approaches, the siren's soundwaves compress toward the listener thus translating into a change of sound as the ambulance gets closer then speeds away. The name given to the radiation waves emitted by an object moving away is called redshift. Radiation is redshifted when its wavelength increases. Thus Seeing Red could refer to either Red or Julia departing.

Truth and Fiction in Conversation

I use fiction in autobiographical format because autobiographical texts proffer powerful opportunities for dialogue between dominant and marginalized cultures (hooks, 1997; Lionnet, 1989; Lorde, 1982). I am particularly interested in contemporary autobiographical research which includes experimental fictional memoirs, (auto)biography, life stories, and letters of theory as cultural sites for imaginative interpretive accountings of lived experiences; as well as fictional texts which combine autobiography, theory, interpretation, and imagination (hooks, 1997; Kadar, 1993; Leggo, Chambers, Hurren & Hasebe-Ludt, 2004). Fictional letter writing allows a fluid merging of theory and imagination. For example, running through the text are ruminations on the power of language to shape, build and construct meaning, understanding, and identity (Derrida, 1978; Leggo, 2005b; Neilsen, 1998). I play with this idea in reverse—a deliberate playing out of Hegel's 1807 work on the mind and body consciousnesses fighting for control. If I construct love by writing poetically, can I write myself out of love? If meaning is constructed through language, can feeling be deconstructed the same way? Can I change my feelings by rewriting a new story or by changing my perspective?

Writing didactic fiction in educational and philosophical circles is not original as evidenced by the works of scholars such as Brent Kilbourn (1998), Rishma Dunlop (1999), Eve Sedgwick (2000), Elizabeth de Freitas (2003), Herman Stark (2003), Douglas Gosse (2005), and even Samuel Richardson (1740). Guiding contemporary epistolary novels outside of the academic arena include Walker (1982), Gardam (1991), Wright (2002), and Bantock (1991, 1992, 1993, 2001, 2002). The themes in *Seeing Red* can easily be compared to Samuel Richardson's (1740) *Pamela,* the official pioneer of the epistolary form, which also has the notable distinction of being the first modern English novel (Chambers, 2003). *Pamela* consists of letters and a diary. It is a simple story of an affair and eventual marriage of a maid, Pamela Andrews, to her master Mr. B. The storyline was controversial at the time for its perceived licentiousness and the implications of crossing social class distinctions.

The novel format ties themes and characters together just as storytelling can bind theory and practice. Norman Denzin (2005)

supports the pedagogical and libratory nature of the critical
democratic storytelling imagination. Laurel Richardson (2005, p.
962) suggests that creative analytical practices of documenting
ethnographic research are "valid and desirable representations
of the social." The love story and issues of teacher/learner
role boundaries are controversial and largely unspoken of in
educational settings and the letter format is voyeuristic. In this
sense, the audience is being given a peek, a look at the unrevealed.
One of the advantages of the epistolary novel is its semblance of
reality and the difficulty for readers to distinguish the text from
genuine correspondence (Wurzbach, 1969). The genre allows the
reader access to the writing character's intimate thoughts without
perceived interference from the author's manipulation and conveys
events with dramatic and sensational immediacy (Carafi, 1997).
Carafi surmises that Alice Walker (1982), who wrote the well-
known epistolary novel *The Color Purple*, used letters in order to
create direct connection between characters, craft her characters
as humanly as possible, and allow the reader greater access to her
character's thoughts.

The epistolary is much more than a narrative structure upon
which the plot hangs. Teacher educator, Brent Kilbourn, in the
preface to his own novella, "To Seek a Deeper Truth," declares
that his objective in using fiction is to convey complex ideas in an
approachable fashion. He suggests:

> The didactic aim of the dialogue shapes conversation in a
> pointed direction and with serious intent . . . . An issue gets
> picked up in the moment, reaches a plateau, and fades, only
> to be picked up again later on; this allows connections to be
> made and issues to be raised that would be more difficult in
> another genre. (1998, p. xiii)

The didactic is written in letter fragments not only in support of Kilbourn's claims that topics can be revisited repeatedly, but to further maintain the notion that curriculum cannot be taught as a fully formed product and received whole by the learner. Learning is best received in fragments, given time to incubate in the learner and pieced together by the learner to form meaning connected to prior experiences. Each learner will assemble the pieces together uniquely and in the way in which he/she needs to know the information in that moment of time. This ability to receive and shape the fragments determines the learning outcome. In the text I illustrate this point through learning hip hop sequences at a weekly dance class.

This genre is appropriate for my needs as with almost all epistolary novels the focus is not on action but, rather, character and relationship (Wurzbach, 1969; Day, 1966). Thomas Beebee (1999) categorizes *Pamela* as a monologic-dialogue—one letter writer writing to one reader. This one-to-one relationship can be paralleled to the attentiveness created between a one-on-one lesson between teacher and learner. Without intention, the reader becomes responsible to the writer's words because in the act of reading the letters, the reader is implicated, obligated to think about his/her responsibility to the writer. Compared to an article or piece of narrative fiction written to the general public where the reader has little obligation to internalize and respond at a conscious level, the reader of an epistolary text is responsible for response because of its monologic nature.

One of the epistolary novel's greatest strengths is the ability of the genre to create diametrically opposing reading possibilities. The reader's direct experience determines the authenticity of the fictional writer's voice. For example, the limited scope I provide of Red ironically becomes a strength of the novel when the reader acknowledges the incompleteness of Red's portrayal. The reader has complete ownership in the construction of Red's "real" character and virtues. This genre gives me the authority to willfully manipulate the text, constantly provide subjective and obscure accounts and even willful counter plots if I wish while I know the judicious reader is consciously aware of this fact. In thinking of the multiplicity of interpretations, the epistolary genre supports Bakhtin's (1986) notion of *heteroglossia* which refers to the inclusion of all conflicting voices as having value. In this case, nothing is ever stable or capable of restricted meaning because the audience divines the story. Whitson (1993) explains that heteroglossia is not a method or strategy for political agency; rather, it is simply a condition of the linguistic world and must be accounted for. The genre further validates Denzin's view that postmodern ethnography "values and privileges the authority and voice of the reader and thus changes the role and authority of the researcher as meaning maker and theorizer" (1997, p. 36).

Chambers (2003) notes that the tenor of the twenty-first century is ready for the epistolary novel again. As in the eighteenth century, when fiction closely paralleled the work of nonfiction, our current culture follows a similar pattern. Popular "reality" shows (*Survivor, American Idol, The Real World*) claim to be nonfiction. Cameras follow people around and then turn the footage into a story. Reality shows lead the audience to believe that the reality they are viewing is real, yet the astute viewer is aware that the camera crew, editors and a multitude of staff have rigorously constructed, reconstructed, and manipulated the "reality" by the time the viewer sees the show. Chambers adds:

> It is not that viewers do not know that what they are seeing isn't biased and edited, but they like to believe that

they are watching reality because this culture, like the eighteenth century is also enamored with the idea of realistic entertainment. (2003, p. 16)
Chambers suggests that email correspondence "seems real because it is a realistic activity for modern characters to engage in and also because it allows a writer to objectively portray character and do so in such a way that it seems as if it actually could have happened" (p. 16).

Essentially, *Seeing Red* can be described as an epistolary *bildungsroman*—a narrative genre originating in the late 18th century—which describes either an actual or metaphorical journey in which the protagonist seeks "reconciliation between the desire for individuation (self fulfillment) and the demands of socialization (adaptation to the given social reality)" (Rau, 2002, p. 1). The term *Bildungsroman* is left untranslated because the word has several meanings beyond the most common acceptances of "novel of development or novel of education" (p. 1). Etymologically, in its cultural context, the term describes "the relationship between man and god in the composite sense of *imago dei*" (p. 1) which means *Image of God* in Latin. *Imago dei* refers to a quest for wholeness according to the myth of the fall (Adam and Eve's fall from grace) and speaks to humans' freedom to quest wholeness or to repress or deny their moral likeness to God. Petra Rau further explains that:

Wilhelm von Humboldt, influenced by a botanical and morphological framework from the natural sciences describes *Bildung* as a combination of *Anbildung* (acquisition of qualities or knowledge), *Ausbildung* (development of already existing qualities), [and] *Entfaltung* (creative broadening of acquired skills or qualities without external restriction and assimilation). Goethe [1767-1832, German novelist, poet and philosopher] redefined ideas of *Bildung* with his own concepts of metamorphosis and morphology as a natural, organic process of maturation as well as a pedagogic principle leading to an overall harmonic wholeness. (Rau, 2002, p. 1)

The illegitimate love story draws the reader forward to seek balance. The sensationalism of an "unethical" love story in the academy is similar to stories run in tabloid newspapers and sensationalized stories which often are semi-fictional but viewed and accepted as nonfiction. This latter cultural obsession demonstrates the general public's vicarious interest in the lives of media constructed characters and celebrities portrayed in magazines. The urge to reach a particular standard or "mythological platform" in order to be "someone" or to be happy, cycles back to the misguided belief in the fairytale myths I am so eager to dispel. Notions of love, incompleteness, desire, belonging and urge for "awakeness," or living the "good life" are ongoing themes throughout *Seeing Red.* Notions of happiness and living an embodied, holistic, appreciative learning life challenge the common view that everyday life is mundane, of little value, and not the fertile context for learning. Learning values echo societal values. Our society validates learning only in formalized contexts. The belief that learning only occurs at particular "mythological platforms"; such as in schools, in classrooms, and from prescribed texts, sadly restricts multiple ways of knowing, learning, and understanding. Life-long learning, a popular educational "mission" statement phrase, thus begins to take on meanings associated with commodified curriculum packages and *going to school,* and not the joyful fullness of relational, meaningful daily learning.

Poetic Conversations

Following the substantial work in elaborating teaching as art (Eisner, 1985; Rubin, 1985, 1991), I present poetry as rendered and performed artistic inquiry. Poetry distills experience, names experience, and turns experience into knowledge (Cixous, 1993; Daly, 1973; Frueh, 1996; Irigaray, 1985; Leggo, 2005a; Lorde, 1982). Pinar et al. warn readers not to dismiss scholarly work that seeks to "dissolve, explode, and deconstruct the taken-for-granted and reified forms of curriculum research that are frequently mistaken for the reality of educational experience they pretend to map" (1995, p. 491). Poetic theory is "writing which disturbs the usual linear logic commonly accepted as synonymous with rationalistic curriculum theory" (p. 491). The poem "Sometime Close to 1851" in the last chapter is an example of the rupture in the linear time and space continuum of thinking which opens up multiple possibilities. It also demonstrates *ekphrasis*—poetry inspired by art, or a re-presentation of research in another form—purposeful inquiry through a layering of various art forms.

Writers and Scholars in Conversation

The words of others are gathered throughout the book like bouquets of fragrant wild flowers to provide an expansive aura of collaboration and choral harmony from which new ideas can sprout. The goals of this work are not to produce a concluding in-depth study of one idea but rather to open the presents and presence we live in and re-question what is important about education: why do we remember certain teachers; how do conceptions of curriculum influence our teaching; what is important to be teaching in schools and in teacher educator programs; what do we know of the teacher/learner relationship; how can we restructure our historically acculturated thoughts on schooling; and how do we move from advocacy to action?

Knowledge Contributions as Opening Conversations

Cole and Knowles (2001b), Denzin (1997), and Grumet, Taubman, Pinar, Blich, and Salvio (2000) all urge researchers to interpret and explicate the pedagogical, theoretical, transformative potential, and significance of research inquiry, agreeing that an entertaining story is not enough. Cole and Knowles (2001a, p. 127) suggest that "knowledge claims made must be made with sufficient ambiguity and humility to allow for multiple interpretations and reader response." Further, the work must contribute to research. The work must answer the "So what?" question. I humbly offer my contributions in *Seeing Red* as openings for further conversations.

Conversations on Dissertation Formats

I would like to contribute to conversations regarding form as integrally related to knowledge production and urge researchers and teachers to be mindful of form, not only content in delivery practices. This dissertation provides an example of how form expands the possibilities of complicit possibilities. I am not stating that the epistolary form is the best literary form or even appropriate genre to be used by others for other purposes but that for this particular storyline and for my specific intentions and contributions in this place and time, this form was generative.

Nell Duke and Sarah Beck (1999), in their article, "Education should consider alternative formats for the dissertation", published in *Educational Researcher* in 1999 provide a historical synopsis of the traditional dissertation as a genre of writing. Since the inception of the dissertation and PhD degree in Germany in the mid-19th century, the two prevailing goals of the dissertation have been to a) be a training instrument, in other words, "the traditional dissertation provides training in developing a substantial, coherent research plan through a single research study; and b) be an "original and significant contribution to knowledge" (Berelson, 1960, p. 173). Duke and Beck argue that in the field of education, "the dissertation in its traditional format does not adequately serve either purpose" (p. 31). Halstead (1988, p. 497) writes: "a piece of research is not recognized as having been completed until it is communicated, and others know about it and have enough information to enable them to test its authenticity." Duke and Beck report that most dissertations are only read by the three to four people on the dissertation committee thus the researcher's findings do little to contribute to educational knowledge. Duke and Beck further claim that as most people only write one dissertation in their lives, the genre as a training instrument is wasted. They suggest alternate forms of writing which fulfill the following two criteria: "Will the format of this dissertation make it possible to disseminate the work to a wide audience?" and "will writing a dissertation in this format help prepare candidates for the type of writing they will be expected to do throughout their career?" (p. 33)

At a 1996 panel at the American Educational Research Association (AERA) conference, Howard Gardner argued against the novel as a dissertation. Garner felt that "writing a novel would not provide educational researchers with the experience of mastering education as a discipline, such that one would then be able to pass one's knowledge of the discipline on to other researchers and practitioners" (Duke & Beck, 1999, p. 33; also see Saks, 1996, for a report on Gardner's panel discussion). I stubbornly disagree with Gardner. He is essentially advocating that doctoral candidates should create a blueprint for "mastering education as a discipline" and then once in the academy, reproducing this mastery through mentorship of graduate students. This is the same greatest problem in our teacher education programs. We cannot continue to imagine that student teachers will become fine practitioners if we provide blueprints of mastery. First, mastery is a myth and an excuse for those who have lost passion and desire and second, to imagine that we can clone teachers or reproduce lessons and knowledge is to envision that the teacher identity, instructional proficiency, and learners in context are blank slates of conformity. Thus, the critical issue of discipline demonstrated in a dissertation really speaks to the *art* of researching. Likewise, the art of teaching is to be able to mindfully piece together the fragmentary—diverse personal skills, attributes, conceptions of place and context, and learners in the moment. This is the art we should be teaching in pre-service programs and demonstrating in dissertations.

Duke and Beck (1999) also counter Gardner's stance by suggesting that if the dissertation were written for example in segments of publishable articles, the doctoral recipient under the guidance and scrutiny of a dissertation committee and then peer reviewers would be in a much better position to mentor others in the skill of writing publications which could influence the field of education. As my dissertation is in the form of letters, I have published stand-alone letters and poems in journals, and written and presented related papers extending the topics presented in the novel.

Brent Kilbourn (1999, p. 27) in his article, "Fictional Theses" suggests that the debates in 1995 between Eisner and Phillips and Eisner and Gardner in 1996 although critically important for grappling with *meaning* and *truth* which are central issues of traditional notions of the meaning of fiction, were however, conducted with "sparse reference to actual instances of educational writing." In 1985, Fishkin (p. 17) had already quoted novelist E. L. Doctorow who said, "There is no longer any such things as fiction or nonfiction, there is only narrative." Richardson posits that despite the blurring of genres, the major difference that separates fiction writing from science writing is the writer's intention and overt declaration which then draws different audiences and has "different impacts on publics and politics—and on how one's 'truth claims' are to be evaluated" (2005, p. 961).

Kilbourn's stance is further grounded in Stephen Pepper's 1942 work on defining the two different ways of the handling of evidence or the attempt to find *meaning* and *truth* in fiction. Using Pepper's example of buying a chair to illustrate, Kilbourn explains that *multiplicative corroboration* of evidence rests in "repeated observations of the same phenomenon in repeated empirical tests that corroborate each other and that are corroborated by many observations by many individuals" (1999, p. 27). So if one were buying a chair, one would empirically test the chair by observing people of all sizes repeatedly sitting in it. *Structural corroboration*, on the other hand, "is a matter of different kinds of information converging on the same conclusion. The stress is on structural connection and coherence. . . . Circumstantial evidence is one variety of structural corroboration. When buying a chair, one would "examine its structure note its construction. . . and note the reputation of the manufacturer" (p. 27) Kilbourn, situated by Pepper's (1942) position argues that concepts like truth and meaning are not testable in an empirical sense. Kilbourn promotes doctoral dissertations which demonstrate self-conscious method.

He says the dissertation:

> should betray the author's sensitivity to concerns of
> epistemology, to concerns about the connection between
> method and meaning. . . . The author should explicitly
> demonstrate an awareness of his or her role as a writer, . . .
> [and] make clear her or his sensitivity to the conceptual
> and methodological moves made during the study and the
> presentation of the study as a readable document. (1999, p.
> 28)

Kilbourn (1999) attributes Phillips' (1995) adamant stance in
support of multiplicative corroboration (against fiction writing) to
the serious implicit question of "Just how far would this relativistic
conception of research go?" Kilbourn's counter is that structural
corroboration does not have an "unbounded field" (p. 28) and he
goes on to discuss qualities of theses. A similar concern is raised
by Isaac, Quinlan, and Walker (1992) that the dissertation provides
a particular standard, central focus, and shared experience for all
PhD programs and thus demands regulation. Duke and Beck (1999)
caution education departments to continue to emphasize training
in the methodological processes and maintain high standards of
research quality.

I fully support this review on dissertation format and respond
to Kilbourn's (1999, see p. 28) evaluatory questions on fictional
theses—I consider *Seeing Red* as contributory to scholarship
because it addresses the issue of form and format which have not
been adequately addressed; the construction is thorough, reflexive,
and systematic (not in a linear but, rather, holistic sense), and the
project has relevance beyond the local conditions of production.

In the creation of this work, I have adapted and selected my own criteria for research quality (see Cole & Knowles, 2001; Kilbourn, 1999; Duke & Beck, 1999; Richardson, 2005). I ask myself if the work demonstrates:

- an understanding of the art of research?
- a disciplined in-depth study which transparently merges researcher, process, and product?
- a deep concern for pedagogical representation?
- an invitation to think, write, make, react, create?
- with humility, a contribution to knowledge or a contestation of the accepted?
- consideration of accessibility and communicability?

The Teacher/Learner in Conversation

Based on the work of Otto Bollnow (1989c), this dissertation suggests that when the *inloveness* of educational eros (Sameshima & Leggo, 2006a) is acknowledged in living and nurtured in the dialogic space between teacher and learner, transformational knowing possibilities are greatly enhanced (also see Doll, 2006). Bollnow's (1989c) description of educational love embraces patience, hope, serenity, humour, and goodness. He espouses a notion that a pedagogic trust relationship creates a sense of "morningness" (1989b, p. 22) and that this learning atmosphere can be likened to a Heideggerian *pure* mood which is the place from which the world is unlocked (Bollnow, 1989a, p. 64). In this place of heightened trust, wandering, and celebration, one is free to explore and learn in non-prescriptive ways.

Conversations on Transformation Theories

I would also like to contribute to expanding Mezirow's work of over thirty years on transformation theory. Mezirow's investigations identified educators' failure to recognize that belief systems acquired through "cultural assimilation and the idiosyncratic influences of primary caregivers" (1997, p. 6) determine or distort interpretation of experience. By critically examining "deep psychological structures of thought, feeling, and will" (1978, p. 108), individuals are able to transform worldviews to "a more inclusive, discriminatory, and integrative perspective" (1996, p. 169) thereby improving skills to deal with subsequent life experiences (Merriam & Clark, 1993).

Patteson (2002) succinctly condenses Mezirow's transformation process into three stages: 1) encountering the disorientation, 2) examining and experimenting, and 3) trying out new learning. Brookfield (2000) and Coffman (1989) suggest that transformative learning is less likely linear but spiral and recursive and I would further suggest that the ping pong ricocheting synapses between visual and cognitive comprehension when viewing the visual and/or acknowledging place and situation, along with narrative presented in concert, echo this dynamic dwelling on an idea. Usher, Bryant and Johnson (1997) emphasize the significant role of others in transformation—further encouragement for researchers to seriously consider relational and collaborative issues and the critical role the reader/viewer.

Mezirow (2000) continues to urge others to contribute research that leads to the refinement of transformation theory. I would like to broaden Mezirow's transformative processes by suggesting that possibilities of transformation can be significantly increased if attention is given to the 1st stage (encountering the disorientation).

I suggest that transformation is more "abundant" when receptivity is attentively engaged *before* the new experience or disorienting dilemma occurs. In the suggested mindset, the being is not transformed without choice; the being wills and welcomes transformation by being open to all experiences and perspectives whether habitual (slow/sequential) or drastic (fast/outlandish). So when a learner is in a dialogic relational space, a space filled with educational eros (Sameshima & Leggo, 2006a), the learner is open to the liminal uncertainties of the unknown but is comfortable in those uncertainties—as if the learner is at a party with friends (see Bollnow, 1979b, 1979c). The transformative process is further enhanced if the learner is able to make connections relationally. In order to foster these relational skills, stories and narratives of ways people make connections must be shared. Teachers must model *wholeness-in-process* in explicit reflexive texts, demonstrate, and be open to researching and learning in multifarious ways. Finally, transformation must include the learner's attunement and acknowledgement of ecological and intuitive resonances. To summarize, to improve transformational learning processes, I suggest the development of the following layers of *embodied aesthetic wholeness* in the "Letters to Chris" which are embedded in the dissertation:

1. increase receptivity and openness to learning
2. foster skills of relationality
3. model wholeness-in-process in explicit reflexive texts
4. layer multiple strategies of inquiry, research experiences, and presentation
5. acknowledge ecological and intuitive resonances

Conversations to be Continued

Reflexive inquiry, writing about the process of thinking through experience-based understanding, arts-informed perspectives, and a/r/tographic ways of being are instrumental in contemplating, conceptualizing and challenging elements of research. Valuing the reader/viewer/learner as an essential component of the presentation/ lesson and honouring the possibilities which arise in the dialogic space between the processes of art making and writing are essential components of artful research. Finally, I am hopeful that sharing stories of process, such as this afterword which offers some of the constitutive aspects of writing this dissertation encourages subjectivity, opens windows into alternate spaces, disrupts conceptions of form, heartens lived experiences as theory and knowledge, decolonizes writing, and broadens the richness of living the research of currere.

Julia Quan

Editor's note:

A draft version of this document was submitted as Julia's dissertation proposal.

Spiraea latifolia

REFERENCES

Alverman, D. E. (2000). Researching libraries, literacies, and lives: A rhizoanalysis. In E. A. St. Pierre & W. Pillow (Eds.), *Feminist poststructural theory and methods in education* (pp. 114-129). New York: Routledge.

Amis, M. (2000) *Experience*. New York: Hyperion.

Aoki, T. T. (1992). In the midst of slippery theme-words: Living as designers of Japanese Canadian curriculum. An invited paper presented at Designing Japanese Canadian Curriculum Conference held on May 21-23, 1992, at the Novotel Hotel, North York, ON, Canada. In W. Pinar & R. Irwin (Eds.). (2005). *Curriculum in a new key: The collected works of Ted T. Aoki.* Mahwah, NJ: Lawrence Erlbaum.

Aoki, T. T. (1996). Spinning inspirited images in the midst of planned and live(d) curricula. *Fine, Fall 96*, 7-14.

Arendt, H. (1958). *The human condition.* Chicago: University Press.

Arendt, H. (1968). *Between past and future: Eight exercises in political thought.* New York: Penguin Books.

Arendt, H. (1973). *The origins of totalitarianism.* New York: Harcourt Brace.

Arendt, H. (1982). *Lectures on Kant's political philosophy* (R. Beiner, Ed.). Chicago: University Press.

Arnheim, R. (1982). *The power of the center: A study in the visual arts.* Berkeley, CA: University Press.

Ashliman, D. L. (2005). *The Grimm Brothers' children's and household tales.* Retrieved January 7, 2006, from http://www.pitt.edu/~dash/grimmtales.html

Atwood, M. (1987) "Variations of the word sleep." *Selected poems II.* New York: Houghton Mifflin. Retrieved June 13, 2006, from http://www.poets.org/viewmedia.php/prmMID/16221

Ayers, W. C. (1988). *Teaching and being: Connecting teachers' accounts of their lives with classroom practice.* Paper presented at the Annual Meeting of the American Educational Research Association, New Orleans.

Bakhtin, M. M. (1986). *Speech genres and other late essays.* Austin, TX: University Press.

Bakhtin, M. M. (1981). *The dialogic imagination: Four essays* (M. Holquiest, Ed., C. Emerson & M. Holquist, Trans.). Austin, TX: University Press. (Original work published 1975)

Bantock, N. (1991). *Griffin & Sabine.* San Francisco: Chronicle Books.

Bantock, N. (1992). *Sabine's notebook.* San Francisco: Chronicle Books.

Bantock, N. (1993). *The golden mean.* San Francisco: Chronicle Books.

Bantock, N. (2001). *The gryphon.* San Francisco: Chronicle Books.

Bantock, N. (2002). *Alexandria.* San Francisco: Chronicle Books.

Bantock, N. (2004). *Urgent 2nd class: Creating curious collage.* Vancouver, BC: Raincoast Books.

Barreca, R., & Denenholz Morse, D. (Eds.). (1997). *The erotics of instruction*. Hanover, NH: University Press of New England.

Barone, T. (2001, October). Science, art and the predispositions of educational researchers. *Educational Researcher*, 24-28.

Baum, F. L. (1991). *The wonderful wizard of Oz*. New York: Outlet Books.

Beebee, T. (1999). *Epistolary fiction in Europe*. Cambridge, UK: Cambridge University Press.

Beiner, R. (1983). *Political judgment*. London: Methuen.

Berelson, B. (1960). *Graduate education in the U.S.* New York: McGraw Hill.

Berleant, A. (1997). *Living in the landscape*. Kansas, MO: University Press.

Berman, M. (1981). *The reenchantment of the world*. Ithaca, NY: Cornell University Press.

Berman, M. (1989). *Coming to our senses: Body and spirit in the hidden history of the west*. New York: Bantam.

Berman, L., Hultgren, F., Lee, D., Rivkin, M., & Roderick, S. (1991). *Toward curriculum for being: Voices of educators* [In conversation with Ted Aoki. Foreword by C. Stimpson.] Albany, NY: State University Press.

Bernstein, R. J. (1996). *Hannah Arendt and the Jewish question*. Cambridge, MA: MIT Press.

Bhabha, H. K. (1994). *The location of culture*. London: Routledge.

Blin, G. (1939). *Baudelaire*. Paris: Gallimard.

Boal, A. (2001). *Hamlet and the baker's son: My life in theatre and politics* (A. Jackson & C. Blaker, Trans.). London: Routledge.

Bollnow, O. (1989a). Ceremonies and festive celebrations in the school. *Phenomenology + Pedagogy, 7,* 64-78.

Bollnow, O. (1989b). The pedagogical atmosphere: The perspective of the child. *Phenomenology + Pedagogy, 7,* 12-36.

Bollnow, O. (1989c). The pedagogical atmosphere: The perspective of the educator. *Phenomenology + Pedagogy, 7,* 37-63.

Brookfield, S. (2000). Transformative learning as ideology critique. In J. Mezirow & Associates, *Learning as transformation: Critical perspectives on a theory in progress* (pp. 125-148). San Francisco: Jossey-Bass.

Broudy, H. (1988). Aesthetics and the curriculum. In W. Pinar (Ed.), *Contemporary curriculum discourses* (pp. 332-342). Scottsdale, AZ: Gorsuch Scarisbrick.

Brueggemann, W. (2001). *The prophetic imagination* (2nd ed.). Minneapolis: Fortress Press.

Bullough, R. V. Jr., Knowles, J. G., & Crow, N. A. (1991). *Emerging as a teacher.* London, UK, and New York: Routledge.

Burnaford, G., Aprill, A., Weiss, C., & Chicago Arts Partnerships in Education. (2001). *Renaissance in the classroom: Arts integration and meaningful learning.* Mahwah, NJ: Lawrence Erlbaum.

Burton, J., Horowitz, R., & Abeles, H. (2000). Learning in and through the arts: The question of transfer. *Studies in Art Education, 41*(3), 228-246.

Campbell, J. (1968/1976). *Creative mythology: The masks of God* (reprint). New York: Viking Penguin.

Campbell, J. (1972). *Myths to live by.* New York: Bantam Books.

Campbell, J. (1989). *An open life: Joseph Campbell in conversation with Michael Toms.* (J. M. Maher & D. Briggs. Eds.). New York: Larson.

Carafi, C. (1997). *The colour purple by Alice Walker.* Retrieved July 31, 2005, from http://www.geocities.com/Athens/9089/colorpurple.html

Carson, A. (1998). *Autobiography of Red.* New York: Alfred A. Knopf.

Carson, T., & Sumara, D. (Eds.). (1997). *Action research as a living practice.* New York: Peter Lang.

Caterall, J. S. (1998). Does experience in the arts boost academic achievement? A response to Eisner. *Art Education, 51*(1), 6-11.

Caterall, J. S., Chapleau, R., & Iwanaga, J. (1999). Involvement in the arts and human development: General involvement and intensive involvement in music and theatre arts. In E. B. Fisk (Ed.), *Champions of change: The impact of arts on learning* (pp. 1-18). Washington, DC: Arts Education Partnership.

Chambers, V. (2003). *History and the epistolary novel: A study in the effect of literary trends on the novel in letters.* Retrieved on July 31, 2005, from http://webpages.shepherd.edu/vchamb01/thesis1.htm

Chödrön, P. (1991). *The wisdom of no escape and the path of lovingkindness.* Boston: Shambhala.

Christ, C. (1986). *Diving deep and surfacing: Women writers on spiritual quest* (2nd ed.). Boston: Beacon Press.

Chung, H. K. (1992). *Struggle to be the sun again: Introducing Asian women's theology.* Maryknoll, NY: Orbis Books.

Cixous, H. (1993). *Three steps on the ladder of writing.* New York: Columbia University Press.

Clarke, A., & Erickson, G. (Eds.) (2003). *Teacher inquiry: Living the research in everyday practice.* New York: RoutledgeFalmer.

Clifford, J. (1988). *The predicament of culture: Twentieth-century ethnography, literature, and art.* Cambridge: Harvard University.

Coffman, P. M. (1989). *Inclusive language as a means of resisting hegemony in theological education: A phenomenology of transformation and empowerment of persons in adult higher education.* Unpublished EdD dissertation, North Illinois University.

Cohen, J., & Stewart, I. (1994). *The collapse of chaos: Discovering simplicity in a complex world.* New York: Penguin Press.

Cole, A. L. (1990a). Personal theories of teaching: Development in the formative years. *Alberta Journal of Educational Research, 36*(3), 203-222.

Cole, A. L. (1990b, April) *Teachers' experienced knowledge: A continuing study.* Paper presented at the Annual Meeting of the American Educational Research Association, Boston, MA.

Cole, A. L., & Knowles, J. G. (2000). *Researching teaching: Exploring teacher development through reflexive inquiry.* New York: Alynn & Bacon.

Cole, A. L., & Knowles. J. G. (2001a). *Lives in context: The art of life history research.* Walnut Creek, CA: Alta Mira Press.

Cole, A. L., & Knowles, J. G. (2001b). Qualities of Inquiry. In L. Neilsen, A. Cole & J. G. Knowles (Eds.), *The art of writing inquiry* (Vol. 1. Arts-informed Research Series, pp. 211-219). Halifax, NS & Toronto, ON, Canada: Backalong Books and Centre for Arts-informed Research.

Coulter, D., & Wiens, J. R. (2002, May). Educational Judgment: Linking the actor and the spectator. *Educational Researcher, 31*(4), 15-25.

Culley, M., & Portuges, C. (Eds.) (1985). *Gendered subjects: The dynamics of feminist teaching.* Boston: Routeledge.

Daignault, J. (1983). Curriculum and action-research: An artistic activity in a perverse way. *Journal of Curriculum Theorizing, 5*(3), 4-28.

Daignault, J. (1988). *The language of research and the language of practice: Neither one nor the other: Pedagogy.* Rimouski, Québec, Canada: University of Québec, unpublished manuscript.

Daignault, J. (1989). *Curriculum as composition: Who is the composer?* Rimouski, QC, Canada: University of Québec, unpublished manuscript.

Daignault, J. (1992a). Traces of work from different places. In W. Pinar, & W. Reynolds (Eds.). *Understanding curriculum as phenomenological and deconstructed text* (pp. 195-215). New York: Teachers College Press.

Daly, M. (1973). *Beyond God the father: Toward a philosophy of women's liberation.* Boston: Beacon Press.

Day, R. A. (1966). *Told in letters: Epistolary fiction before Richardson.* Ann Arbor, MI: University Press.

de Beauvoir, S. (1953). *The second sex* (H. M. Parshley, Trans.). New York: Knopf. (Original work published 1949)

de Beauvoir, S. (1972). *The ethics of ambiguity* (B. Frechtman, Trans.). New York: Citadel Press. (Original work published 1947)

de Cosson, A. F. (2003). *(Re)searching sculpted a/r/tography: (Re)learning subverted–knowing through aparetic praxis.* Unpublished dissertation. University of British Columbia, BC, Canada.

de Freitas, E. (2003). *The wrong shoe and other misfits: Fiction writing as reflexive inquiry within a private girls' school.* Unpublished doctoral dissertation. University of Toronto, ON, Canada.

Deleuze, G., & Guattari, F. (1987). *A thousand plateaus: Capitalism and schizophrenia.* Minneapolis, MN: University Press.

Denzin, N. K. (1997). *Interpretive ethnography: Ethnographic practices for the 21ˢᵗ century.* Thousand Oaks, CA: Sage.

Denzin, N. K. (2002). Cowboys and Indians. *Symbolic Interaction, 25,* 251-261.

Denzin, N. (2005). Emancipatory discourses and the ethics and politics of interpretation. In N. K. Denzin & Y. S. Lincoln (Eds.), *Handbook of Qualitative Research* (3rd ed., pp. 933-958). Thousand Oaks, CA: Sage.

Derrida, J. (1967). *Of grammatology.* Retrieved on October 31, 2004, from http://www.marxists.org/reference/subject/philosophy/works/fr/derrida.htmter

Derrida, J. (1978). *Writing and différence* (A. Bass, Trans.). Chicago: University Press.

Derrida, J. (1982). Différance. In J. Derrida (Ed.), *Margins of philosophy* (pp. 3-27). Chicago: University Press.

Dewey, J. (1934). *Art as experience.* New York: Minton Balch.

Dijkstra, B. (1998). *Georgia O'Keefe and the eros of place.* Princeton, NJ: Princeton University Press.

Dissanayake, E. (2000). *Art and intimacy.* Seattle, WA: University Press.

Dobson, T. (2003, December). Of curricular lacunae: A response to *Provoking Curriculum. Educational Insights, 8*(2). Retrieved June 4, 2004, from http://www.ccfi.educ.ubc.ca/publication/insights/v08n02/intro/dobson.html

Doll, M. A. (2006). *What nature allows the jealous laws forbid: The cases of Myrrha and Ennis del Mar.* Centre for the Study of Internationalization of Curriculum Studies paper presentation. June 12, 2006. University of British Columbia, Canada.

Duke, N. K., & Beck, S. W. (1999, April). Education should consider alternative formats for the dissertation. *Educational Researcher, 28*(3), 31-36.

Dunlop, R. (2000). *Boundary Bay.* Winnipeg, MB, Canada: Staccato Chapbooks.

Duras, M. (1989). *Emily S.* (B. Bray, Trans.). Pantheon Books: New York. (Original work published 1987)

Edel, L. (1984). *Writing lives: Principia biographica.* New York: N. W. Norton.

Eisner, E. (1991). *The enlightened eye.* New York: Macmillan.

Eisner, E. (1985). *The art of educational evaluation: A personal view.* London, England: Flamer.

Eisner, E. (1998). Does experience in the arts boost academic achievement? *Art Education, 51*(1), 7-15.

Eisner, E. (2004). Artistry and pedagogy in curriculum. *Journal of Curriculum and Pedagogy. 1*(1), 15-16.

Elder, J. C. (1994, Winter). The turtle in the leaves. *Orion 19* (1). Retrieved June 5, 2005, from http://www.orionsociety.org/pages/om/ombi/index_ombi_91-97.html

Ellsworth, E. (1997). *Teaching positions: Difference, pedagogy, and the power of address.* New York: Teachers College Press.

Farlex Dictionary. (2006). Access at: www.thefreedictionary.com

Fishkin, S. F. (1985). *From fact to fiction: Journalism and imaginative writing in America.* Baltimore, MD: John Hopkins University Press.

Finley, S., & Knowles, J. G. (1995). Researcher as artist/artist as researcher. *Qualitative Inquiry* 1(1), 110-142.

Fitzgerald, F. S. (1950). *The Great Gatsby.* Harmondsworth, UK: Penguin.

Flynn, T. (2004, Summer Edition). Jean-Paul Satre, *The Stanford Encyclopedia of Philosophy.* E. N. Zalta (Ed.). Retrieved February 4, 2006, from http://plato.stanford.edu/entries/sartre/

Freire, P. (1994). *Pedagogy of the oppressed.* New York: Continuum. (Original work published in 1970)

Freire, P. (1997). *Pedagogy of the heart* (D. Macedo & A. Oliveira, Trans.). New York: Continuum.

Freire, P. (2001). *Pedagogy of the oppressed* (30th anniversary ed.). New York: Continuum.

Frueh, J. (1996). *Erotic faculties.* Los Angeles, CA: University Press.

Gallop, J. (1985). *Reading Lacan.* New York: Cornell University Press.

Gallop, J. (1988). *Thinking through the body.* New York: Columbia University Press.

Gallop, J. (Ed.). (1995). *Pedagogy: The question of impersonation.* Bloomington, IN: University Press.

Gardam, J. (1991). *The queen of the tambourine.* New York: Picador.

Garoian, C. R. (1999). *Performing pedagogy – Toward an art of politics.* New York: State University Press.

Garoian, C. R. (2004). Curriculum and pedagogy as collage narrative. In J. G. Henderson & P. Slattery (Eds.), *Journal of Curriculum and Pedagogy 1(*1), 25-31.

Garrison, J. (2001). Assaying the possibilities of spiritual education: Toward a curriculum of poetic creation. *Journal of Curriculum Theorizing, 17*(1), 63-70.

George, T. (Writer/Director), & Pearson, K. (Writer). (2004). Hotel Rwanda [Motion picture]. United States: Metro-Goldwyn-Mayer Studios.

Gibran, K. (1962). *The prophet.* New York: Alfred A. Knopf.

Giroux, H. (1980). Dialectics of curriculum theory. *JCT, 2*(2), 27-36.

Giroux, H. (1993). *Border crossings: Cultural workers and the politics of education.* New York: Routledge.

Giroux, H. (2005, May*). Derrida's promise of democracy and Edward Said's politics of worldliness: Implications for academics as public intellectuals.* Congress Speech at the Canadian Social Sciences Conference, Montreal, QC, Canada.

Golden, A. (1997*). Memoirs of a geisha.* New York: Alfred A. Knopf.

Goodfriend, R. (2005). I am here. In D. D. Durand (Ed.), *Stories for social change and community development* (pp. 32-33*).* Ottawa, ON: Canada Council for the arts.

Gosse, D. (2005). *Jackytar.* St. Johns, NL, Canada: Jesperson.

Griffin, S. (1995). *The eros of everyday life: Essays on ecology, gender and society.* New York: Doubleday.

Greene, M. (1978). *Landscapes of learning.* New York: Teachers College Press.

Greene, M. (1988). *The dialectic of freedom.* New York: Teachers College Press.

Greene, M. (2006, February). Prologue: From jagged landscapes to possibility. *Journal of Educational Controversy, 1*(1). Retrieved November 9, 2006, from http://www.wce.wwu.edu/Resources/CEP/eJournal/v001n001/a005.shtml

Grumet, M. (1978). Songs and situations. In G. Willis (Ed.), *Qualitative Evaluation* (pp. 274-315), Berkeley, CA: McCutchan.

Grumet, M. (1990). Voice: The search for a feminist rhetoric for educational studies. *Cambridge Journal of Education, 20*(3), 321-326.

Grumet, M. (1991). Curriculum and the art of daily life. In G. Willis & W. Schubert (Eds.), *Reflections from the heart of educational inquiry: Understanding curriculum and teaching through the arts* (pp. 74-89). Albany, NY: State University Press.

Grumet, M., Taubman, P., Pinar, W., Blich, D., & Salvio, P. (2000, April). *Speaking personally: The future of autobiography.* Panel discussion at the American Educational Research Association Conference, New Orleans, LA.

Halstead, B. (1988). The thesis that won't go away. *Nature, 331,* 497-498.

Hamblen, K. (1983). Modern fine art: A vehicle for understanding Western modernity. *The bulletin of the caucus on social theory and art education, 3,* 9-16.

Hand, S. (Ed.). (1989). *The Levinas reader.* Oxford: Basil Blackwell.

Hanks, W. (1989). Text and textuality. In B. Siegel, A. Beals, & S. Tyler (Eds.), *Annual review of anthropology* (pp. 95-127). Palo Alto, CA: Annual Reviews.

Hegel, G. W. F. (1807). The phenomenology of spirit. In G. W. F. Hegel (1770-1831). Social and political thought. The *Internet Encyclopedia of Philosophy.* Retrieved January 30, 2006, from http://www.iep.utm.edu/h/hegelsoc.htm

Heshusius, L., & Ballard, K. (1996) *From positivism to interpretivism and beyond. Tales of transformation in educational and social research.* New York: Teacher's College Press.

Henderson, J. G., & Slattery, P. (2004). Editors' introduction: The arts create synergy for curriculum and pedagogy. *Journal of curriculum and pedagogy, 1*(2). 1-8

Heidegger, M. (1977). *The question concerning technology and other essays* (William Lovitt, Trans.). New York: Harper Torchbooks.

hooks, b. (1994). *Teaching to transgress: Education as the practice of freedom.* London, Great Britain: Routledge.

hooks, b. (1997) *Wounds of passion: A writing life.* New York: Henry Holt.

Hodgson, B. (2001). *Hippolyte's island.* Vancouver, BC: Raincoast Books.

Hughes, T. (1998). *Birthday Letters.* New York: Farrar, Straus and Giroux.

Hunt, D. E. (1987). *Beginning with ourselves.* Cambridge, MA: Borderline Books.

Huxley, A. (1962). *Island.* New York: Harper & Row.

Hwu, W. (1993). *Toward understanding poststructuralism and curriculum.* Unpublished doctoral dissertation. Louisiana State University, Baton Rouge, LA.

Hyperdictionary.com. Access: www.hyperdictioary.com

Internet Encyclopedia of Philosophy (2006, paragraph 4). Retrieved June 18, 2006, from http://www.iep.utm.edu/h/hegelsoc.htm

Irigaray, L. (1985). When our lips speak together. In *This sex which is not one* (C. Porter & C. Burke, Trans. pp. 205-218). Ithaca, NY: Cornell University Press.

Irigaray, L. (1993). Love of the other. In *An ethics of sexual difference* (pp. 133-150). Ithaca, NY: Cornell University Press.

Irigaray, L. (1996). *I love to you: Sketch for felicity within history.* New York: Routledge.

Irwin, R. (2003). *Curating the aesthetics of curriculum/leadership or caring for how we perceive running/guiding the course.* University of British Columbia, The Department of Curriculum Studies, Artful Salon. Retrieved July 12, 2005, from http://www.cust.educ.ubc.ca/whatsnew/Papers/irwin/irwin1.html

Irwin, R. L. (2004). A/r/tography: A metonymic métissage. In R. L. Irwin & A. de Cosson (Eds.), *A/r/tography: Rendering self through arts-based living inquiry* (pp. 27-38). Vancouver, BC: Pacific Educational Press.

Irwin, R. L., Beer, R., Springgay, S., Grauer, K., Gu, X., & Bickel, B. (in press). The rhyizomatic relations of a/r/tography. *Studies in Art Education.*

Irwin, R., Wilson Kind, S., Grauer, K., de Cosson, A. (2005). Curriculum integration as embodied knowing. In M. Stokrocki (Ed.), *Interdisciplinary art education; Building bridges to connect disciplines and cultures.* Reston, VA: The National Art Education Association.

Isaac, P., Quinlan, S., & Walker, M. (1992). Faculty perceptions of the doctoral dissertation. *Journal of Higher Education, 63*(3), 241-268.

jagodzinski, j. (1992). Curriculum as felt through six layers of an aesthetically embodied skin: The arch-writing on the body. In W. Pinar & W. Reynolds (Eds.), *Understanding curriculum as phenomenological and deconstructed text* (pp. 159-183). New York: Teachers College Press.

jagodzinski, J. (1996). *The anamorphic I/i.* Edmonton, AB, Canada: Duval House.

jagodzinski, j. (2004, Summer). Fallen bodies: On perversion and sex-scandals in school and the academy. *Journal of Curriculum Theorizing. 20*(2). 99-114.

Jardine, D. W. (1998). *To dwell with a boundless heart: Essays in curriculum theory, hermeneutics, and ecological imagination.* New York: Peter Lang.

Jones, A. (1998). *Body art/performing the subject.* Minneapolis: University of Minnesota.

Kabat-Zinn, J. (1994). *Wherever you go, there you are: Mindfulness meditation in everyday life.* New York: Hyperion.

Kadar, M. (Ed.). (1993). *Reading life writing.* Toronto, ON: Oxford University Press.

Kilbourn, B. (1998). *For the love of teaching*. London, ON: The Althouse Press.

Kilbourn, B. (1999). Fictional theses. *Educational Researcher, 28*(9), 27-32.

Klossowski, P. (1992). *Sade my neighbour*. Paris: Seuil. (Original work published 1947 in French, *Sade mon prochain*, by same author)

Knowles, J. G. (1998). Home education: Personal histories. In M. L. Fuller & G. Olsen (Eds.), *Home-school relations: Working successfully with parents and families* (pp. 302–331). Toronto: Allyn and Bacon.

Knowles, J. G. (1991). Parents' rationales for operating homeschools. *Journal of Contemporary Ethnography, 20*, 203–230.

Knowles, J. G. (1994, Winter). Metaphors as windows on a personal history: A beginning teacher's experience. *Teacher Education Quarterly, 21*(1), 37-66.

Knowles, J. G. (2001) Writing place, wondering pedagogy. In L. Neilsen, A. Cole, & J. G. Knowles. (Eds.), *The art of writing inquiry* (pp. 89-99). (Vol. 1. Arts-informed Research Series). Halifax, NS & Toronto, ON: Backalong Books & Centre for Arts-Informed Research.

Knowles, J. G. (2005, January 31). *Arts-informed research*. Discussion panel. OISE, University of Toronto, ON, Canada.

Koestler, A. (1975). *The act of creation*. London: Picador.

Korthagen, F. A. J., & Kessels, J. P. A. M. (1999). Linking theory and practice: Changing the pedagogy of teacher education. *Educational Researcher, 28*(4), 4-17.

Kozik-Rosabal, G. (2001). How do they learn to be whole? In B. Hocking, J. Haskell, & W. Linds (Eds.), *Unfolding bodymind: Exploring possibility through education.* Brandon, Vermont: Foundation for Educational Renewal.

Kristeva, J. (1980). *Desire in language: a semiotic approach to literature and art* (L. S. Roudiez, Trans. & Ed., T. Gora & A. Jardine, Trans.). New York: Columbia University Press. (Original work published 1977 as *Polylogue*)

Kristeva, J. (1987). *Tales of love* (L. S. Roudiez, Trans.). New York: Columbia University Press. (Original work published 1983 as *Histories d'amour*)

Kvale, S. (1995). The social construction of validity. *Qualitative Inquiry, 1*(1): pp. 19-40).

Lakoff, G. & Johnson, M. (1980). *Metaphors we live by*. Chicago, IL: University Press.

Lawrence-Lightfoot, S., & Hoffmann-Davis, J. (1997). *The art and science of portraiture*. San Francisco: Jossey-Bass.

Leder, D. (1990). *The absent body*. Chicago: University Press.

Leggo, C. (2002, Spring). Writing as living compos(t)ing: Poetry and desire. *Language and Literacy (4)*1. Retrieved November 6, 2006, from http://www.langandlit.ualberta.ca/archives/vol41papers/carl%20lego7.htm

Leggo, C. (2003). Tangled lines: Quizzing the quotidian. *Educational Insights, 8*(2). Available: http://www.ccfi.educ.ubc.ca/publication/insights/v08n02/contextualexplorations/curriculum/leggo.html

Leggo, C. (2004). Tangled lines. In A. Cole, L. Neilsen, J. G. Knowles & T. Luciani (Eds.), *Provoked by art: Theorizing arts-informed Research* (pp. 18-35). (Vol. 2, Arts-informed Research Series). Halifax, NS & Toronto, ON, Canada: Backalong Books & Centre for Arts-informed Research.

Leggo, C. (2005a). The letter of the law/the silence of letters. In P. Trifonas (Ed.), *Communities of difference* (pp. 110-125). New York: Palgrave Macmillan.

Leggo, C. (2005b). Autobiography and identity: Six speculations. *Vitae Scholasticae: The Journal of Educational Biography, 22*(1), 115-133.

Leggo, C., Chambers, C., Hurren, W., & Hasebe-Lundt, E. (2004, May). *Autobiography as an ethos for our time: Living well with each other.* Paper presented at the American Educational Research Association Conference, Winnipeg, MB, Canada.

Lephart, S. M. & Borsa, P. A. (n. d.). Proprioception: The sensations of joint motion and position. *SportsScience.* Retrieved May 12, 2006, from http://www.sportsci.org/encyc/drafts/Proprioception.doc

Levinas, E. (1981). *Otherwise than being or beyond essence.* Norwell, MA: Kluwer.

Levinson, N. (2001). The paradox of natality: Teaching in the midst of belatedness. In M. Gordon (Ed.), *Hannah Arendt and education: Renewing our common world* (pp. 11-36). Boulder, CO: Westview Press.

Lionnet, F. (1989). *Autobiographical voices: Race, gender and self-portraiture,* Ithaca, NY: Cornell University.

Lorde, P. (1982). *Zami: A new spelling of my name: A biomythography by Audre Lorde.* Freedom, CA: The Crossing Press.

Luce-Kapler, R. (2003). Malopoeia: Syncope, interruption and writing. *Educational Insights, 8*(2). Available: http://www.ccfi.educ.ubc.ca/publication/insights/v08n02/contextualexplorations/voices/lucekapler.html

Martin, S. (2000). *Shopgirl.* New York: Hyperion.

Marzano, R., Marzano. J., & Pickering, D. (2003). *Classroom management that works. Research-based strategies for every teacher.* Alexandria, VA: Association of Supervision and Curriculum Development.

May, W. (1989). *What makes a critique of art education "postmodern?"* Paper presented at the annual meeting of the American Education Research Association, San Francisco, CA.

Mander, J. (1978). *Four arguments for the elimination of television.* New York: Morrow.

McDermott, B. (1976). *The golem: A Jewish legend.* Philadelphia, PA: Lippincott.

McLaren, P. (1991). Field relations and the discourse of the other. In W. Shaffir & R. Stebbins (Eds.), *Experiencing fieldwork: An inside view of qualitative research* (pp. 149-163). Newbury Park, CA: Sage.

McLaren, R. (2001). Off the page. In L. Neilsen, A. Cole & J. G. Knowles (Eds.), *The art of writing inquiry* (pp. 62-82). (Vol. 1. Arts-informed Research Series). Halifax, NS & Toronto, ON: Backalong Books & Centre for Arts-Informed Research.

Matthews, G. (2005, Fall). The arts as a metaphor for learning about self: Four stories in a teacher narrative. *Journal of the Canadian Association for Curriculum Studies, 3*(1), 75-91.

Merriam, S. B., & Clark, C. (1993). Learning from life experience: What makes it significant? *International Journal of Lifelong Education, 12*(2), 129-138.

Merleau-Ponty, M. (1968). *The visible and the invisible.* Evanston: Northwestern University.

Mezirow, J. (1978). Perspective transformation. *Adult Education, 28*(2), 100-110.

Mezirow, J. (1996). Contemporary paradigms of learning. *Adult Education Quarterly, 46*(3), 158-173.

Mezirow, J. (1997). Transformative learning: Theory to practice. In P. Cranton (Ed.), *Transformative learning in action: Insights from practice. New directions for adult and continuing education* (pp. 5-12). San Francisco: Jossey-Bass.

Mezirow, J. (Ed.). (2000). Learning to think like an adult: Core concepts of transformation theory. In J. Mezirow & Associates (Eds.), *Learning as transformation: Critical perspectives on a theory in progress* (pp. 3-33). San Francisco: Jossey-Bass.

Miller, J. E. Jr. (1972). *Theory of fiction: Henry James.* Lincoln, NE: University Press.

Miller, J. P. (1988). *The holistic curriculum.* Toronto, ON, Canada: OISE Press.

Miller, J. P. (2000). *Education and the soul: Toward a spiritual curriculum.* Albany, NY: SUNY Press.

Miller, S. I., & Fredericks, M. (1988). Uses of metaphors: A qualitative case study. *Qualitative Studies in Education, 1*(3), 263-276.

Minh-ha, T. T. (1999). *Cinema interval.* New York: Routledge.

Munby, H., & Russell, T. (1989, March). *Metaphor in the study of teachers' professional knowledge.* Paper presented at the Annual Meeting of the American Educational Research Association, San Francisco, CA.

Mutua, K., & Swadener, B. B. (2004). Introduction. In K. Mutua & B. B. Swadener (Eds.), *Decolonizing research in cross-cultural contexts: Critical personal narratives* (pp. 1-23). Albany, NY: State University Press.

Nabokov, V. (1955). *Lolita.* New York: G. P. Putnam's Sons.

Nakagawa, Y. (Ed.). (2000). *Education for awakening: An Eastern approach to holistic education.* Brandon, VT: Foundation for Social Renewal.

Nails, D. (2005, Fall). Socrates. In E. N. Zalta (Ed.), *The Stanford Encyclopedia of Philosophy.* Retrieved on April 28, 2006, from http://plato.stanford.edu/archives/fall2005/entries/socrates/

Neilsen, L. (1998). *Knowing her place*. San Francisco, CA: Caddo Gap Press and Great Tancook Island, NS: Backalong Books.

Neilsen, L. (2002, Fall). Learning from the liminal: Fiction as knowledge. *Alberta Journal of Educational Research, 48*(3), 206-214.

Newmann, F. M., Lopez, G., & Bryk, A. S. (1998). *The quality of intellectual work in Chicago schools: A baseline report*. Chicago: Consortium on Chicago School Research.

Paley, N. (1995). *Finding art's place: Experiments in contemporary education and culture*. New York: Routledge.

Patteson, A. (2002). *The creative arts partnership: Interim report year one*. Study undertaken for The Learning Partnership, Toronto.

Pearse, H. (1992). Beyond paradigms: Art education theory and practice in a postparadigmatic world. *Studies in Art Education 33*(4). 244-252.

Pepper, S. C. (1942). *World hypotheses: A study in evidence*. Berkeley, CA: University Press.

Phelan, A. M. (2005). A fall from (someone else's) certainty: Recovering practical wisdom in teacher education. *Canadian Journal of Education 28* (3), 339-358.

Phillips, D. C. (1995). Art as research, research as art. *Educational Theory*, 45(1) 1-7.

Pinar, W. (1988). Autobiography and the architecture of self. *JCT, 8*(1), 7-36.

Pinar, W., & Grumet, M. (1976). *Toward a poor curriculum*. Dubuque, IA: Kendall/Hunt.

Pinar, W., & Reynolds, W. (Eds.). (1992). Appendix, section two: Genealogical notes on poststructuralism in curriculum studies. *Understanding curriculum as phenomenological and deconstructed text* (pp. 244-259). New York: Teachers College Press.

Pinar, W., Reynolds, W. M., Slattery, P., & Taubman, P. M. (1995). *Understanding curriculum: An introduction to the study of historical and contemporary curriculum discourses*. New York: Peter Lang.

Pollock, D. (1998). Performative writing. In Phelan, Peggy & Lane (Eds.), *The ends of performance* (pp. 73-103). New York: University Press.

Pryer, A. (2001). Breaking hearts: Towards an erotics of pedagogy. In B. Hocking, J. Haskell, & W. Linds. (Eds). (2001). *Unfolding bodymind: Exploring possibility through education,* (pp. 132-141). Vermont: Foundation for Educational Renewal.

Radice, B. (1974). *The letters of Abelard and Heloise*. Penguin Classics. England: Clays.

Raimi, S. (Director). (2005). *Spiderman II* [Motion picture]. United States: Columbia Pictures.

Rappoport, A. S. (1937). *The folklore of the Jews*. London: Soncino Press.

Rau, P. (2002). Bildungsroman. *The Literary Encyclopedia*. November 13, 2002. The Literary Dictionary Company. Retrieved June 14, 2005, from http://www.litencyc.com/php/stopics.php?rec=true&UID=119

Reeve, C. D. C. (1992). *Practices of reason: Aristotle's Nicomachean ethics*. Oxford, UK: Clarendon Press.

Reeve, C. D. C. (2005, Winter). Plato on friendship and eros. *The Stanford Encyclopedia of Philosophy (*E. N. Zalta, Ed.). Retrieved April 28, 2006, from http://plato.stanford.edu/archives/win2005/entries/plato-friendship/

Rich, A. (1976). *Of woman born: Motherhood as experience and institution*. New York: Norton.

Richardson, L. (2000). Writing: A method of inquiry. In N. K. Denzin & Y. S. Lincoln (Eds.), *Handbook of qualitative research* (2nd ed., pp. 923-946). Thousand Oaks, CA: Sage.

Richardson, L., & St. Pierre, E. (2005). Writing: A method of inquiry. In N. K. Denzin & Y. S. Lincoln (Eds.), *Handbook of qualitative research* (3rd ed., pp. 959-978). Thousand Oaks, CA: Sage.

Richardson, S. (1958). *Pamela*. New York: Norton. (Original work published 1740)

Ricoeur, P. (1991) Life: A story in search of a narrator. In M. Valdés (Ed.), *A Ricoeur reader*. Toronto, ON, Canada: University Press.

Rilke, R. M. (1954). *Letters to a young poet* (M. D. Herter Norton, Trans.). (2nd ed.) New York: W.W. Norton & Company. (Original work published 1929)

Rogoff, I. (2000). *Terra infirma: Geography's visual culture.* London: Routledge.

Rothenberg, A. (1979). *The emerging goddess: The creative process in art, science, and other fields.* Chicago: University Press.

Roy, A. (2003). Confronting empire [excerpted from *War talk,* South End Press]. Retrieved January 17, 2006, from http://www.thenation.com/docprint.mhtml?i=20030310&s=roy

Rubin, L. (1985). *Artistry in teaching*. New York: Random House.

Rubin, L. (1991). The arts and an artistic curriculum. In G. Willis & W. Schubert (Eds.), *Reflections from the heart of educational inquiry: Understanding curriculum and teaching through the arts* (pp. 49-59). Albany, NY: State University Press.

Ruether, R. R. (1983). *Sexism and god-talk: Toward a feminist theology.* Boston: Beacon Press.

Saks, A. L. (Ed.). (1996). Viewpoints: Should novels count as dissertations in education? *Research in the teaching of English, 30,* 403-427.

Sameshima, P. (1999). *Challenging the dominant thinking paradigm – Growing teachers.* Unpublished Master of Arts thesis. San Diego State University, CA.

Sameshima, P., & Irwin, R. (2006). *Rendering liminal currere.* Manuscript submitted for publication.

Sameshima, P., & Leggo, C. (2006a). *Eros in education.* Manuscript submitted for publication.

Sameshima, P., & Leggo, C. (2006b) *Tangling the quotidian I.* Presentation at the Canadian Association of Curriculum Studies Celebration of Artistic Works. Canadian Society for the Study of Education (CSSE) conference. York, ON.

Sawada, D. (1989, April). *Aesthetics in a postmodern education: The Japanese concept of shibusa.* Paper presented to the annual meeting of the American Educational Research Association, San Francisco, CA.

Schwab, J. J. (1969). The practical: A language for curriculum. *School Review*, 78, 1-23.

Sedgwick, E. K. (2000). *Dialogue on love.* Boston, MA: Beacon Press.

Simon, R. I. (1995). Face to face with alterity: Postmodern Jewish identity and the eros of pedagogy (pp. 90 – 105) In J. Gallop (Ed.), *Pedagogy: the question of impersonation. Theories of contemporary culture.* Indiana: University Press.

Sirna, K. (2006). *Collaboration and constraint: Women elementary teachers' political identity formations.* Unpublished doctoral dissertation. University of British Columbia, Canada.

Slattery, P. (1989). *Toward an eschatological curriculum theory.* Unpublished PhD dissertation, Baton Rouge, LA. Louisiana State University,

Smits, H. (1997). Living within the space of practice: Action research inspired by hermeneutics. In T. Carson, & D. Sumara (Eds.), *Action research as a living practice* (pp. 281-297). New York: Peter Lang.

Sollers, P. (1968). *Logiques*. Paris: Seuil.

Spretnak, C. (1991). *States of grace: The recovery of meaning in the postmodern age*. San Francisco: Harper.

Spretnak, C. (1997). *The resurgence of the real: Body, nature and place in the hypermodern world*. New York: Addison-Wesley .

Springgay, S. (2004). *Inside the visible: Youth understandings of body knowledge through touch.* Unpublished doctoral dissertation. University of British Columbia, Canada.

Springgay, S., & Irwin, R. (2004). Women making art: Aesthetic inquiry as political performance. In A. Cole, L. Neilsen, J. G. Knowles & T. Luciani, T. (Eds.), *Provoked by art: Theorizing arts-informed research.* (Vol. 2, Arts-informed Research Series). Halifax, NS & Toronto, ON: Backalong Books & Centre for Arts-informed Research.

Springgay, S., Irwin, R.., & Wilson Kind, S. (2005). A/r/tography as living inquiry through art and text. *Qualitative Inquiry, 11*(6): 897-912).

Stark, H. (2003). A fierce little tragedy: Thought, passion, and self-formation in the philosophy classroom. Value Inquiry Book Series. G. Miller (Ed.), *Philosophy of Education* (Vol. 147). New York: Rodopi.

Stephenson, L. (1987). *Seven theories of human nature* (2nd ed.). St. Andrews, Scotland: Oxford University Press. (Retrieved Jan 4, 2006, from http://www.blupete.com/Literature/Biographies/Philosophy/Sartre.htm)

Stout, C. J. (2000). In the spirit of art critcism: Reading the writings of women artists. *Studies in Art Education, 41*(4), 346-360.

Sullivan, R. (1992). *By heart: The life of Elizabeth Smart*. Great Britain: Harper Collins Manufacturing Glasgow.

Sullivan, R. (2001). *Labyrinth of desire: Women, passion, and romantic obsession.* Washington, DC: Counterpoint.

Sumara, D., & Davis, B. (1997). Enlarging the space of the possible: Complexity, complicity and action-research practices. In T. Carson and D. Sumara (Eds.), *Action research as a living practice*. New York: Peter Lang.

Sumara, D., & Luce-Kapler, R. (1993). Action research as writerly text: Locating co-labouring in collaboration. *Educational Action Research, 1*(3), 387-395.

Thomas, S. M. (2004). *Of earth and flesh and bones and breath; Landscapes of embodiment and moments of re-enactment.* Halifax, NS, Canada: Backalong Books.

Thomashow, M. (1995). *Ecological identity: Becoming a reflective environmentalist.* Cambridge, MA: Institute of Technology Press.

Taussig, M. (1987). *Shamanism, colonialism, and the wild man: A study in terror and healing.* Chicago: University Press.

Udall, S. R. (1992). Beholding the epiphanies: Mysticism and the art of Georgia O'Keefe. In C. Merrill & E. Bradbury (Eds.), *From the far away nearby: Georgia O'Keefe as icon* (pp. 89-112). Reading, MA: Addison-Wesley.

Ulmer, G. L. (1983). The object of post-criticism. In H. Foster (Ed.), *The anti-aesthetic: Essays on postmodern culture* (pp. 83-110). Port Townsend, WA: Bay Press.

Upitis, R., Smithrim, K., Patterson, A., Macdonald, J., & Finkle, J. (2003). *Improving math scores: Lessons of engagement.* Paper presented at the Canadian Society for the Study of Education Conference, Halifax, May 30.

Usher, R., Bryant, I., & Johnston, R. (1997). *Adult education and the postmodern challenge: Learning beyond the limits.* New York: Routledge.

Vanier, J. (1991). *Images of love, words of hope.* (S. Morgan, R. Nielsen, & J. Sumarah, Eds.). Hantsport: Lancelot Press.

Volkart, Y. (2000). Survival and exploraterraterrism. Re-mapping the posthuman space. In U. Biemann (Ed.), *Been there and back to nowhere.* Retrieved September 30, 2005, from http://www.obn. org/reading_room/writings/html/survival.html

Vygotsky, L. S. (1962). *Thought and language.* Cambridge, MA: Harvard University Press.

Walker, A. (1982). *The colour purple.* New York: Pocket Books.

Walker, J. (2004). "Grasshopper". In *A deed to the light.* Chicago, IL: University Press. Retrieved April 12, 2006, from http://www. versedaily.org/grasshopper.shtml

Walsh, S. C. (Winter 2000). Writing with the dark. *Language and Literacy: A Canadian E-Journal, 2*(2). Retrieved November 4, 2004, from http://www.langandlit.ualberta.ca/archives/ vol22papers/susan.htm

Walsh, S. C. (2003). *Female subjectivity and fear in teaching.* Unpublished doctoral dissertation. University of Alberta, AB, Canada.

Webber, A. L. (Music), Hart, C., & Stilgoe, R. (Lyrics). (1986). *The phantom of the opera* [Musical]. United States: Polygram International. (Easy Piano Songbook available USA/Canada Order No. HL00366003)

Weber, S. (2005, July) *Bodies and teaching: From representation to embodiment.* Paper presented as part of ARTE 565A (941) "The body: between the real and representation" at the 4th Annual Summer Teacher Institute. The Vancouver Art Gallery Public Programs and the University of British Columbia.

Westbury, I., & Wilkof, N. (1978). Introduction. In J. Schwab, *Science, curriculum, and education.* Chicago, IL: University of Chicago Press.

Whipps, J. (2004, Fall Edition). Pragmatist feminism. In E. N. Zalta (Ed.), *The Stanford Encyclopedia of Philosophy.* Available: http://plato.stanford.edu/archives/fall2004/entries/femapproach-pragmatism/

Whitson, J. (1993). Correspondence with W. Pinar. In W. F. Pinar, W. M. Reynolds, P. Slattery & P. M. Taubman. (1995). *Understanding curriculum: An introduction to the study of historical and contemporary curriculum discourses.* New York: Peter Lang.

Wikipedia (2006). Available: http://www.wikipedia.org

Winterson, J. (1993). *Written on the body.* New York: Alfred A. Knopf.

Wise, R. (Director). (1965). The sound of music [Motion picture]. United States: 20ᵗʰ Century Fox Studios, CA.

Wisniewski, D. (1996). *Golem.* New York: Clarion Books.

Witzling, M. (Ed.). (1991). *Voicing today's visions: Writings by contemporary women artists.* New York: Universe.

Witzling, M. (Ed.). (1994). *Voicing our visions: Writings by women artists.* New York: Universe.

Woodlinger, M. (1989). *Exploring metaphor and narrative as tools in assisting preservice teachers' development.* Paper presented at the Annual Meeting of the Canadian Society for Studies in Education, Quebec City, QC, Canada.

Wordsworth, W. (1806) *Ode: Intimations of immortality from recollections of early childhood.* Verse X. Retrieved August 5, 2004, from http://www.bartleby.com/145/ww331.html

Wright, R. B. (2002). *Clara Callan.* Toronto, ON, Canada: HarperCollins.

Wright, S. P., Horn, S. P., & Sanders, W. L. (1997). Teacher and classroom context effects on student achievement: Implications for teacher evaluation. *Journal of Personnel Evaluation in Education, 11*, 57-67.

Wurzbach, N. (1969). *The novel in letters*. Coral Gables, FL: University of Miami Press.

Young, J. O. (2001). *Art and knowledge*. New York: Routledge.

Zeman, K. (1992). In L. Zeman. *Gilgamesh the king*. Toronto, ON, Canada: Tundra Books.

Zeman, L. (1995). *The last quest of Gilgamesh*. Toronto, ON, Canada: Tundra Books.

NAME INDEX

SUBJECT INDEX

OPEN CALL FOR SUBMISSIONS/ COURSE ASSIGNMENT

Red's Letters are Revealed!

In the Editor's Note, Georgia Lang said she found two password protected CDs. She was only able to access one disc which contained the letters *to* Red. This open call is to develop the letters in the other CD. These are the letters *from* Red. This edited collection of letters, sent and unsent, from Red to Julia, written collectively by readers, currently has the working title of: *Red Revealed: Inspiring Responsive Research.*

The word inspire is about animating, arousing, quickening, breathing life into, inspiriting, birthing through process. This dialogic responsive project will craft Red, interpret a view of *Seeing Red,* and share an imagined character who does not say a word and yet is known intimately by the end of the book. This venture opens the multiple perspectives of who Red is, Red's heart, character, mentorship, and creative guidance which carried Julia, at times in painful ways, through the limen of learning and the production of artful scholarship.

Seeing Red is a fiction. Writing in Red's voice allows truths to be told and experiences to be shared. To submit, please date the response(s) of any length and form according to Julia's letter you are responding to. Thoughtful academic fiction representing Red's poetic, artistic, and writing skills is sought; as well as responses to questions and issues raised, thoughts on heart, pedagogy, and role, and connections to other works and authors.

Professors of courses in Curriculum Studies, Teacher Education, Art Education, Cultural Studies, Gender and Feminists Studies, Artful Qualitative Research, Life-history Research, Language and Literacy, as well as others are encouraged to personally submit responses or forward graduate student assignment responses. A suggested class project is to have each student write a Red letter, organize the letters by date then share the collective character. Discuss Red's creation, gender, and moral and ethical dilemmas. How does a teacher or mentor, who can inspire a student to become untethered, think, act, or feel?

The goals of *Revealing Red* include:
- To demonstrate the methodology of arts-informed research which is to:
  - Be provoked (By reading *Seeing Red*)
  - Collect data in innovative ways (By collecting Red's letters from the readers)
  - Present data in provocative ways with the deliberate intention of transforming thinking or creating new thinking (By drawing together Red's letters with discussion and analysis in a fictionalized format)
- To extend understanding of issues raised in the book. The hope is that many of the letters will share provocative thinking that explains, contradicts, or expands on Julia's thinking.

- To give academics permission to write truth behind a fictional voice, to inspire creativity, and to allow stories to be told.

Please submit Red's letters to redsletters@cambriapress.com. Thank you.

Please visit Pauline Sameshima's website at www.solspiré.org for updates on this project.

Printed in the United States
108754LV00003B/15/A

9 781934 043646